THE ROAD TO HINDOSTAN

THE ROAD TO HINDOSTAN

STONE EUGENE CLARK

1

CHAPTER 1 – THE VISION

The wind bends toward fire.

The opulent study of the Whitmore Manor breathed around him. Wood groaned in protest as the wind pressed against the walls, slipping through unseen cracks, threading through the dimly lit room. The air smelled of candle wax and aged parchment, laced with the faint bitterness of ink. The scent had become part of him, settling into his clothes, his skin, his very breath.

At the heart of the room, beneath the flickering glow of candlelight, Elias Whitmore sat, his presence as formidable as the house that bore his name. He was a man carved from years of conviction and wealth, his frame still broad despite the slow erosion of time. A long, flowing white beard cascaded down his chest, the strands thick like a prophet of old, his hair swept back from his weathered face, untouched by the vanity of grooming. His skin, once smooth and proud as the Whitmore blood in his veins, now bore the fine lines of sleepless nights and whispered revelations.

His hands held a manuscript. His fingers traced the faded embossing on the leather-bound cover—Geheimnisbücher Moses. Beneath the original script, a newer inscription had been etched, almost imperceptible: *The City of the Divine.* The ink upon the pages should have stirred his soul, should have filled him with purpose. Yet tonight, the words were hollow things, relics of a past that no longer burned within him.

For months, he had waited. For months, he had listened. For months, there had been nothing.

The stillness clung to him, heavy as judgment, thick as the humid air of summer. The weight of silence was not new, yet tonight, it felt different—as if the very house held its breath, waiting alongside him.

A sigh pushed past his lips, slow and measured, yet his pulse thrummed beneath the surface.

Beyond the window, the last breath of daylight stretched thin across the horizon, smearing gold and crimson through the skeletal arms of the trees. The land outside was his. Not just by birthright, but by destiny.

Then, movement.

A shadow cut across the fading light.

Elias tensed.

A crow landed on the windowsill.

It did not flutter. Did not caw. It only watched.

Its black eyes swallowed the light, reflecting nothing back. Unblinking. Patient.

A slow shiver ghosted down his spine.

It was just a bird—wasn't it? A creature of flesh and instinct, drawn to the warmth of the manor, to the scent of burning wax. That was all. That had to be all.

And yet, still, it did not move.

His throat felt dry.

A sign? Or just a bird?

The crow tilted its head, slow and deliberate. The motion sent a ripple of unease through his chest.

A test. A warning. Or a beginning.

The night deepened, pulling the world into silence.

Inside the study, the candle burned lower, its flame flickering against the walls, stretching and shrinking as if caught in breath. The room had always felt secluded, but now, it felt severed—as though something unseen had taken notice and cut the study loose of the manor, pulling it into a realm of magic and shadow.

Elias knelt before the wooden table, his movements careful, deliberate.

Before him, the ritual lay arranged.

A brass scrying bowl, its surface tarnished with age, sat in the center of the table, filled with still water, so smooth it might have been glass.

A seer stone, pale and polished, its surface cool beneath his fingertips. He had held it a thousand times, but tonight, it felt different—like a living thing, pulsing faintly in the candlelight.

And the book—a manuscript. A relic of hands long gone, its pages thick, its ink faded but never forgotten.

Elias placed his palms together. Breathed in. Let his mind empty.

His voice was a whisper. "Let the unseen be revealed."

Outside, the wind howled against the shutters, a restless thing. The walls creaked, as though the manor itself braced against something unseen.

The candle flickered.

The flame leaned, not as if swayed by wind, but as if pulled toward something.

Elias opened his eyes.

The air in the room had changed. He could feel it pressing against his skin, a weightless presence, unseen but undeniable.

He reached for the seer stone. His fingers hesitated just before touching it, his breath shallow. The stone seemed colder now. Or perhaps his own body had grown feverish.

Lifting it, he held it over the bowl. The water beneath remained motionless, waiting.

Show me the place I must go.

Nothing.

Show me the people I must gather.

A pause. A long, aching stillness.

Then a single ripple.

The water trembled.

Elias did not move, did not breathe.

The ripple widened.

The water darkened.

And something began to take shape.

At first, there was only mist.

It swirled and shifted within the water's surface, moving like breath across glass. Elias's grip on the seer stone tightened, his pulse hammering against his ribs. He leaned forward, barely breathing, as the mist formed.

A landscape emerged, its edges blurred, shifting like a dream on the cusp of waking.

Rolling hills, golden beneath a sun too radiant to behold. A river winding through untouched land, its waters silver and alive.

And then, rising from the earth, placed rather than built—a city.

Towers of gleaming white stone. A grand central temple. Halls with vaulted ceilings, adorned with banners that unfurled in a wind that carried voices, not of men, but of something greater.

The name was given to him. Not spoken. Not written. But placed in his mind with an authority beyond question.

Empyrean.

His breath caught.

The vision deepened.

A city waiting to be claimed. A place of sanctuary, of promise.

And then, the change.

The sky dimmed.

The river darkened, thickened, until it ran red.

Figures appeared at the city's edge, cloaked in shadow. Watching. Waiting.

Empyrean was meant to be whole, but it would not remain so.

A voice, deep and distant, ancient, echoed through the vision, shaking the very foundation of the world beneath his feet.

"A kingdom shall rise, but it shall be divided. And only the faithful shall endure."

The figures in the dark did not move. They only waited.

For what? For when?

The water in the scrying bowl trembled, then shattered.

The world returned in pieces.

The manuscript had changed. The page he had left open was not the same.

His breath faltered.

The ink stood bold despite its age.

"A kingdom shall rise, and its people shall be gathered, yet it shall be divided, and only the faithful shall endure."

His hands trembled.

Empyrean will be.

And in the stillness of the house, beyond the flickering candlelight, a shadow passed through the hall unnoticed.

Solomon stood in the doorway of the study, watching his father.

* * *

The lodge was already breathing.

By sunset the following day, they gathered—called not by letters, but by intuition, by rhythm, by something older than war.

Beneath the courthouse in Front Royal, through a false wall in the cellar, the room waited: dim, earthen, lined with old casks and dust-veiled ledgers. The air was thick with the scent of wax and damp wood.

Abraham Mercer entered first, square jewel of office glinting at his chest, and took his seat in the East. Abraham was a mountain of a man—broad-shouldered, thick-necked, and rotund from decades of excess. His waistcoat strained slightly over the girth of his belly, the fabric etched with the faint sheen of sweat from the late spring heat. He carried his weight with a kind of stubborn authority, as though daring anyone to challenge the life that had built it.

His face was ruddy and full, framed by a well-kept beard now streaked with ash from the cigar that smoldered perpetually between his fingers. The smoke clung to him like incense—sweet, pungent, and constant—saturating his coat, his breath, and the very air around him. Years of smoking had left his eyes a touch watery, his voice gravel-edged and slow, like a shovel dragged across dry earth.

There was power in him still, but it moved through thick limbs and wheezing breath, a force dulled by indulgence and the slow erosion of the flesh. To see Abraham was to see a man who once could have charged a hill—but now preferred to sit atop it, smoking, waiting, issuing orders.

Elias Whitmore waited silently in the West, seated in the Senior Warden's chair, the hem of his coat barely touching the eye-insignia on the floorboards. His son Solomon stood near the door, Junior Deacon by posture and position, steady as a post. Hiram lingered in the South, his face unreadable, occupying the Junior Warden's chair.

Several other men—slaveholding Confederates, faces shadowed by candlelight—sat in the periphery, each in dark coats and silence.

Solomon stepped forward with flint and taper, lighting the three candles arranged in a triangle around the central altar. Once they were lit, he stepped back to the door and stood with arms clasped.

Abraham rose.

"One by one," he said, voice low. "Step forward and prove your fidelity."

Each man approached him in turn.

"What is the chief Care of a Fellow Knight?" Abraham asked.

"To see that his lodge is tyled," the brother responded.

"What is your business?"

"To serve the Master, receive instructions, and see the brethren rightly engaged."

A grip exchanged. Words given. Nod of affirmation. The man returned to his seat.

Each was examined. Each passed.

When all were seated again, Abraham approached the altar. He opened the Bible laid at its center, the flamelight catching the edge of the gold-leafed page. He removed his hat and spoke clearly:

"This Lodge is now open, in the Name of God and holy St. John, forbidding all cursing and swearing, whispering, and all profane discourse whatsoever, under no less penalty than what the Majority shall think proper."

He struck the gavel three times.

Silence settled over the room.

"We are assembled at the edge of fracture," Abraham said. "Front Royal has fallen. Jackson presses north, but the Union is not beaten. They will come back. And when they do, they will bring more than rifles. They will bring a new order."

He looked slowly around the room.

"They left Strasburg like ghosts—no shots, no fires. Just dust where the boots used to be. I expect it won't stay quiet long, but it won't be the same when it wakes. Makes you wonder if they were called away, or if they saw what was coming."

One of the seated men shifted in his chair.

"We held dances two weeks ago," the man said softly. "Candles in the orchard. My wife sang 'Bonnie Blue Flag.' And now..." He trailed off.

Elias, seated in the West, spoke without rising.

"Now you light the candles and wait for fire."

A pause.

"There is reason to believe," Abraham continued, "that this lodge has already been compromised."

He turned toward the South.

"Hiram."

The room turned with him.

"You've been silent. Watching. Carrying a satchel with ciphered pages. Red String code. Mentions this lodge. Names Elias."

Hiram didn't move.

Solomon stepped forward, at his father's signal, and drew a length of cord from beneath the lectern. Two of the seated brothers stood to flank Hiram.

He didn't resist.

They bound his hands—not cruelly, but with finality.

"I should have spoken sooner," Abraham said. "But I needed to be sure."

Elias's voice echoed across the room, calm and unshaken.

"He will not be harmed. I will take responsibility for him."

Abraham gave a small nod.

"What will you do with him?" asked one of the brothers.

Elias rose, eyes catching the Western flame.

"I will offer him a path. And if he walks it, he walks with us."

He paused, gaze fixed on Hiram.

"West," Elias said. "That is where the truth waits."

"West?" Abraham spoke followed by a cough, "We still need convincin' the wives and the children. Their near adults now and have minds of their own, especially them boys of yours." He then glanced toward Solomon, "Present company exclude."

Elias then gazed upon his old friend Abraham.

"I have a plan, and a vision. Bring your family to Whitmore Manor and they'll witness prophesy."

* * *

Let the spy choose his road.

The manor's smokehouse was silent, low to the ground like a waiting beast. The moon hung thin above the trees.

Hiram didn't resist when Elias entered the small smokehouse where he was being held. His hands were unbound now, his coat returned to him.

Elias set a lantern on the floor and sat on the overturned crate opposite him.

"I know what you are," Elias said. "And I know who you've been writing to."

Hiram said nothing.

"I'm not here to punish you. That would be a waste."

He pulled a folded letter from his coat—the cipher. He placed it between them.

"You've been compromised," Elias said. "Even if you ran, even if you made it back to Charles Town in the west, the Union wouldn't trust you now. They'd assume you flipped."

"You're a traitor," Hiram said.

"I'm a visionary," Elias replied. "And right now, I see one path left for you."

A pause stretched between them.

"I'm offering you exile," Elias said. "With us. Into the old valley. Into something different."

"You want me to follow you?"

"I want you to witness what comes next. You'll ride freely. But you'll be watched. If you stay, you live. If you run, you disappear."

Hiram looked at the letter, then back at Elias.

"You're mad."

"Maybe," Elias said. "But madness is where the new world begins."

He rose.

"Think on it. Tomorrow at dusk, we meet the Mercers."

Hiram didn't speak. But he didn't try to flee when the door opened.

And that, Elias knew, was enough.

2

CHAPTER 2 – THE GATHERING OF THE CHOSEN
The westward wind returns.

The road to Whitmore Hall lay shrouded in the hush of the Virginia countryside, a dark ribbon stretching beneath the weight of the night. A full day had passed since the lodge had been broken and the spy offered his path. The manor, a lone sentinel at the valley's edge, stood with its windows ablaze, lamplight spilling into the surrounding gloom like the glow of a beacon. The house, with its formidable stone foundation and timeworn shingles, bore the weight of generations—its walls thick with secrets, its corridors steeped in the quiet authority of men who shaped destinies in whispered councils.

Whitmore Hall was a fortress of contrasts. Its stone facade held the cold gray of approaching twilight, and shadows pooled beneath the eaves, softening the edges of its gabled roof. The building's silhouette cut a jagged line against the sky, the gothic arches of its windows casting elongated shadows like fingers reaching into the earth. Dark ivy climbed the walls, its tendrils curling into the stone as if the house itself had grown from the ground, a natural extension of the land's quiet power.

Unlike the simple wooden homes of the valley, Whitmore Hall stood as a testament to southern wealth and permanence in the mid-19th century. Above the arched doorway, the Whitmore family crest glimmered in the fading light. The stone relief, carved with vines, serpents, and an all-seeing eye, had been brushed with gold leaf that caught the last threads of sunlight. It cast a warm glow against the cold stone, a promise—or perhaps a warning—to those who entered beneath its gaze.

Atop the highest spire, a weather vane turned slowly in the breeze. Its golden surface, polished and gleaming, caught the sun's last light, casting a spear of brightness against the twilight sky. It pointed westward—always westward—like a compass that knew more than it should.

A wrought-iron fence encased the property, its gate left slightly ajar, as if in quiet invitation—or warning. Beyond the manor, the plantation stretched toward the mountains, where the wilderness began.

Inside, the house breathed in muted tones. The halls were dressed in deep greens, the color of forest shade, and the rich blues of a sky before a storm. Heavy drapes framed the windows, their fabric the color of midnight, swallowing the lamplight in soft folds. The walls bore dark wood paneling, the mahogany polished to a dim sheen that caught the candlelight only in narrow streaks.

Amidst the dark, the color gold whispered through the house—subtle, deliberate. Gold trim lined the edges of the framed portraits that gazed down upon the room, their eyes following those who passed. The candle sconces held gold filigree, the metalwork curling like tendrils of flame. And on the chandelier that hung above the grand hall, gold beads threaded through crystal, catching the light and casting fractured rainbows against the walls.

The air was thick with the mingling scents of oil lamps, aged wood, and the cloying trace of tobacco that clung to the wainscoting like an old memory. Servants passed through the dim corridors, their footfalls hushed against polished floors. Trays of wine and untouched bread moved from hand to hand, but no one ate.

In the shadowed curve of the grand staircase, Solomon Whitmore stood shrouded in darkness, watching. Listening. His blue eyes—bright and cutting, as sharp as the cold morning air—watched the arriving guests with quiet calculation. Of the four sons of Elias, he was the third-born, yet the favored one. Shaped by his father's hand.

He knew why they had come.

* * *

The summons was silent, but heard by all.

By the time the Mercer wagon rattled to a stop at the entryway, the sun had fallen behind the hills and dusk had soaked the valley in violet shadow. The horses shifted, their breath fogging in the cold air.

Abraham Mercer stepped down first, the worn leather of his boots sinking into the damp earth. He adjusted the folds of his heavy coat, his fingers working the buttons with unconscious precision. A trader by nature, he was a man accustomed to risk, to weighing cost against gain. Yet, tonight, uncertainty swashed in his chest. This was different. This was something beyond trade, beyond reason.

Lucy Mercer descended next, her shawl wrapped tight, her movements careful as if bracing against more than the cold. Then came their daughters—Hannah, Eleanor, Eliza, and Virginia—moving in practiced quiet, their faces unreadable.

Hannah kept her hands folded before her, her expression composed but tight at the edges, as if holding her breath. Virginia, the youngest, shivered, though not from the chill. Her fingers curled in the fabric of her skirts, her eyes darting toward her father, seeking some silent assurance.

They had heard the whispers. They had listened to Elias Whitmore's words before. And now, they stood before the man who would ask them to abandon all they knew.

The great doors opened before they could knock. An enslaved steward, his features composed in careful neutrality, stepped aside to usher them in. The warmth of the hall wrapped around them, but it did little to ease the cold knot in Abraham's chest.

Solomon, still shrouded in the stairwell's shadows, felt his pulse quicken.

Something was coming. Something that would change everything.

* * *

The hall was vast, its wooden floors gleaming beneath the glow of brass chandeliers. The walls bore the scent of burning oil, aged parchment, and lingering tobacco, remnants of discussions that had once shaped the valley's future.

A long wooden table dominated the center of the room, its surface worn smooth by years of deliberation. Tonight, it was bare, save for a single oil lamp. Its flickering light sent restless shadows crawling up the walls, dancing over maps with curled edges and faded ink.

At the far end of the hall, Elias Whitmore stood waiting.

He did not speak immediately, yet his presence filled the room.

He was a man who did not need to raise his voice to be heard, his silence as weighted as scripture. The dark wool of his coat clung to his frame with precision, tailored and deliberate, a quiet testament to his wealth. His hands, clasped before him, were still. Steady.

Hannah felt the certainty in his stance, the quiet power in his gaze.

Abraham let his eyes drift across the room, taking in the cold hearth, the empty chairs—the absence of comfort. Finally, he exhaled.

"You called for us."

Elias inclined his head. "That I did."

"For what purpose?"

Elias stepped forward, his boots making no sound against the polished floor. He studied Abraham for a long moment before speaking.

"To ask you to leave this place behind."

Only the faithful will see the city.

The lamp flickered. A draft moved through the hall, shifting the air just slightly.

Abraham's expression did not change, but his voice was careful. "Tell us why."

Elias's gaze did not waver. "'Cause I seen what's comin'."

Silence gathered around his words.

From the folds of his coat, he withdrew a leather-bound book, its pages brittle with time. He opened it with practiced reverence, revealing lines of inked prophecy—words that had shaped his vision.

He placed his palm flat against the aged parchment, his fingers steady.

"I've seen the city we're meant to build," Elias said, his voice low but resolute. "A place beyond the reach of wicked men, beyond the grasp of those who'd bury the truth. It rises from the earth like somethin' placed there by the hand of God Himself. A sanctuary for those who'll endure what's comin'."

Virginia's breath caught in her throat.

Solomon gripped the railing of the staircase, his knuckles white.

His father's voice filled the great hall, heavy with certainty.

"In the final days, the chosen'll be hunted like prey, their wealth scattered among the heathen. The righteous'll hide the sacred word in the hidden valley, deep in the mountains, where the divine race is preserved—where none but the faithful'll ever find it again."

Abraham exhaled, slow and steady.

"You believe now's the time?"

"It ain't belief, Abraham. It's knowin'." Elias's fingers traced the inked lines of the manuscript. "The signs are here. Charles Town is filled with Union sympathizers. Virginia may split. Right through our plantations. Secret societies conspire in the shadows." He held up a red string, clenched it in his fist, his knuckles whitening with the force of it. His gaze flicked, just once, toward the far side of the room. The firelight caught on the brass buttons of Hiram Sloane's coat.

Abraham followed Elias's glance. Hiram stood near the window, his posture rigid, his expression unreadable. The fire cast long shadows across his face, but Abraham noticed the frayed edge of his coat collar.

Elias's fist tightened once more before he threw the string into the fire. The thread ignited with a sharp snap.

Virginia flinched. And then she noticed Solomon.

Solomon's chest ached with the weight of those words.

He wanted to believe.
He wanted to feel what his father felt.
But he did not.

* * *

Faith can be forged in silence.

That night, long after the Mercers had departed, Solomon waited until the house had fallen silent. Then, with slow, careful steps, he slipped into his father's study.

The candle on the desk had burned low, its wax pooled beside the base. The seer stone lay next to the brass scrying bowl, its surface smooth and unassuming.

Solomon's hands hovered over the stone, hesitating. For the first time in his life, doubt crept in.

"Let the unseen be revealed."

The words were barely a whisper.

He pressed his palms to the stone, the bronzed ridges etched with strength yet sculpted by refinement, willing something—anything—to happen.

The water in the bowl remained still.

The shadows in the room did not stir.

Nothing.

Not a sign. Not a whisper. Not even a flicker.

His broad, sculpted chest tightened, the muscle beneath his linen shirt flexing instinctively, as if bracing against an unseen weight. He had been shaped by his father's expectations. His father had seen Empyrean. His father had spoken with certainty, and men had followed him. Why not him?

Was he not chosen?

Or had his father been wrong all along?

The thought made his stomach twist.

Slowly, he pulled his hands away.

And yet—when morning came, he would face his brothers, and he would not speak of failure.

* * *

Blood listens for the voice of vision.

The great hall was cast in soft, golden light, the embers of the hearth still glowing faintly from the night before. Solomon stood tall, shoulders squared as he faced them.

Gideon, the eldest, was first to meet his gaze. He was broad-shouldered, not unlike Solomon, but where Solomon's hair gleamed gold, Gideon's was a deep chestnut, tousled with an almost untamed quality. His hazel eyes burned with quiet intensity, his jaw sharp, his features carved with an unspoken weight. He was his father's firstborn, but not his favored. Despite being overlooked by Elias, he had never wavered in his quiet conviction, a steadiness that perhaps came from their mother, Rebecca.

Ezra stood just beside Gideon, only a year younger, watching Solomon carefully. He had a lean frame, quick hands, a mind that was always calculating. He followed Gideon in all things, almost reverent in his devotion, a shadow to his older brother's steps. While their father had never offered him much affection, Ezra had been bound to the warmth of their mother's presence, and it had given him something the others lacked: empathy.

Nathaniel, the youngest, stood just past them, barely into his twenties, his expression wide with admiration. He looked more like Solomon than their other brothers, sharing his golden hair and blue eyes. There was something softer about him—something untested, unshaped by the expectations that had hardened the others.

Solomon took a breath. He would not fail here.

"Our father has seen the vision," he said, voice steady. "He has seen Empyrean, the place we are meant to build, the sanctuary where we will be safe."

Gideon's brow furrowed, arms crossing over his broad chest. "And you believe him?"

Solomon did not hesitate. "I do. Because I have seen it, too."

A silence stretched between them, weighty, uncertain.

Ezra watched Gideon, waiting for his response. Always following his lead. Nathaniel leaned forward slightly, eager, hopeful.

Gideon exhaled, measured, skeptical. But he did not challenge Solomon outright. "Then tell us," he said. "Tell us what you saw."

Solomon's pulse thrummed. He knew that if Gideon did not believe him, Ezra would not either. And if Ezra turned, Nathaniel's admiration would waver.

So he told them.

He wove the vision into words, shaping it as Elias had spoken, as though it had burned into his own mind. The valley, the city, the sanctuary where the chosen would find refuge. He told it with conviction, with certainty.

And in the end, they believed him.

Or at least, they followed him.

CHAPTER 3 – THE DEPARTURE

We did not walk toward myth. We build it behind us.

The house had been silent in the final hours—no farewells spoken, no second chances offered. The servants moved like ashen ghosts through the halls, finishing their last duties, their faces unreadable in the dim lamplight. Elias had not slept. Neither had Solomon.

From his window, Solomon watched the lanterns sputter against the blackened glass, each flame a whisper of light against the looming dark. Final preparations were made—horses saddled, provisions packed. He listened to the faint murmur of his father's voice, steady even in the late hours, speaking with Abraham Mercer one last time.

In the stillness of his mind,

"Will I have a place in this new world? Will my brothers rule over me or will I rule over them?"

When the candle in Elias's study finally died, Solomon exhaled, his breath fogging the glass.

By sunrise, they would no longer belong to this world.

The road ahead cut westward through the early mist, little more than a scar through the wilderness, winding its way toward an uncertain horizon. Behind them, Front Royal faded into mist, its rooftops and fences dissolving into nothing.

The past was no longer a place they could return to.

Hooves struck damp earth in rhythmic silence. Breath plumed in the cold air, vanishing into the gray light of morning. No laughter. No idle chatter. Only the weight of departure—the quiet resolve of those who had severed ties with the world they had known.

Solomon rode just behind Elias, close enough to listen, to learn. His father's back was straight, his posture unwavering. If he felt doubt, he did not let it touch him.

But Solomon felt it.

He had spoken the words. He had given his brothers the vision they needed to hear. And now, he rode alongside them, carrying the weight of a lie.

His hands tightened around the reins.

"Now faith is the substance of things hoped for, the evidence of things not seen."

The verse drifted through his mind, a whisper from long sermons and quiet lessons. His father had taught him that faith did not require proof—that the very act of believing could shape the world.

But what if the evidence remained unseen because it did not exist? What if the substance of his hope was nothing more than smoke and pretending, held together by his will alone?

Perhaps belief could be built like a structure—stone by stone, lie by lie. Perhaps if he repeated the vision enough, shaped it in the minds of others, it would cease to be a lie at all. Perhaps, in the end, even he would believe it.

Perhaps, if he upheld the magic long enough, it would cease to be a lie at all.

As they traveled, the landscape began to shift. The forests thinned, the hills flattened. The road stretched ahead, winding westward.

Somewhere beyond the horizon, Empyrean awaited.

Rebecca rode at the center of the caravan, her presence as steady as the sun. She did not falter, nor did she look back.

She was leading them now.

And they would follow.

Rebecca clutched the reins of her horse, her fingers stiff with cold. She turned once, taking in the town one last time—its familiar rooftops, the narrow streets, the life she had known. Her wealth, her comforts, her legacy. And then she faced forward, toward the raw, untamed land ahead.

She ushered Elias to the front so he felt he was leading them, his gaze fixed on the road ahead.

Gideon walked beside his horse, his steps measured, his gaze flicking from face to face. He did not speak his doubts, but they traveled with him, whispering in the wind.

Ezra walked a step behind, his pace unconsciously matching Gideon's. He had always followed his elder brother—not out of doubt, but out of trust. When Gideon glanced toward Elias, Ezra's gaze followed. When Gideon tensed, Ezra's hands curled into fists.

But now, he wasn't sure what he was supposed to feel.

At the rear, Hiram Sloane rode with an ease that belied his sharp attentiveness. His eyes, dark emerald green and knowing, measured each follower carefully. He was not a man of faith, but he understood the power faith could wield. He had seen it before, in other men, in other times. He would watch. He would wait.

He was more a prisoner than a follower.

Some walked, some rode, but all moved forward. Each step into the wilderness was a step into something unknown, something they could not yet name.

No map guided them—only conviction and the promise of something greater.

By midday, the road had led them into the heart of the Shenandoah, where the valley opened wide beneath a sky bleached pale by the autumn sun. Golden fields stretched to the edges of the forest, their dry grasses swaying in the restless breeze. Towering maples and sycamores stood as quiet sentinels along the banks of Cedar Creek, their branches draped with the first blush of autumn, leaves turning brittle at the edges.

The creek itself cut through the land like a silver ribbon, its waters shallow but swift, whispering over beds of polished stone. Slender reeds bent low at its edges, their roots tangled in the dark, wet earth. A heron stood motionless near the far bank, its long legs half-submerged, its sharp eyes tracing the water's surface. Beyond the creek, the land sloped upward into rolling hills, dense with old-growth forest—oak, hickory, and pine—standing thick and solemn, their trunks gnarled with age.

The air smelled of damp earth and the faint sweetness of decaying leaves, a crispness in the wind that spoke of the nearing cold. Somewhere in the distance, a woodpecker rapped against bark, the sharp sound fracturing the quiet.

They paused here, their journey briefly stilled.

Nathaniel, the youngest of Elias's sons, lowered himself onto a fallen log at the water's edge. The bark had long since been stripped away, leaving the wood smooth and pale, as if the years had bleached it to bone. He folded his hands, fingers twined in quiet contemplation. His fair curls stirred with the breeze, catching the light like spun gold, and his blue eyes reflected the water's restless shimmer. There was something of the valley in him—an untouched gentleness, a quiet grace.

And yet, beneath the soft glow of youth, a shadow lingered. A quiet knowing. The burden of a past not his own, but inherited nonetheless.

Rebecca moved through the group, her presence a quiet balm. When she reached Nathaniel, she knelt beside him, the hem of her cloak brushing the dirt. Her fingers found his shoulder, steady and firm.

"Mother, are you sure about this?" Nathaniel's voice barely rose above the whisper of the stream. His fingers were white where they twisted together, the knuckles pressing hard against his skin.

Rebecca's hand tightened, an anchor against the drift of his uncertainty.

"We left behind a world that was dyin'. Would you rather return to it?"

Nathaniel's lips parted, but no words came. His gaze drifted to the water, as if hoping to find an answer in its mirrored surface. He was young, but not a child. The world had begun to shape him, but not yet hardened him. His beauty was a dangerous thing—innocence wrapped in temptation. He drew the eye, of the young women among them. His presence seemed to shift the air around him, drawing attention without intent.

Rebecca leaned closer, her breath warm against his ear. "We were chosen for somethin' greater."

Her voice did not waver. There was no doubt in it, no hesitation. The words were not her own—they belonged to Elias. And yet, she felt them as if they had always lived within her.

Nathaniel's shoulders sank. He nodded, the movement small, his acceptance fragile.

Across the clearing, Elias stood, watching. His face remained impassive, but he gave a single nod—approving.

The others shifted, their weariness hidden beneath thin veils of resolve. Virginia, seated a few paces away, stole glances at Solomon, her expression a careful balance of hope and restraint. She drew patterns in the dirt with the edge of a stick, lines and circles that led nowhere. Nearby, Hannah's eyes remained fixed on Nathaniel, though she masked it with the practiced neutrality of a girl who had learned not to show too much.

Solomon stood just beyond the edge of the clearing, his silhouette sharp against the line of trees. His expression was veiled, a quiet observer. He moved among the group, his presence both guiding and distant, as if ensuring all remained in place, though his attention lingered nowhere too long. His watchfulness cast a subtle tension over the camp.

As he approached Rebecca and Nathaniel, his steps slowed just slightly. His shadow fell over them, stretching long in the waning light. He reached out, his hand brushing over Nathaniel's curls, a brotherly gesture —a tousle, gentle and quick. But his fingers lingered a moment too long, the pads of his fingers brushing the nape of Nathaniel's neck as if caught by accident. Nathaniel flinched, only slightly, a ripple of discomfort beneath his otherwise calm expression.

Rebecca looked up, her face a practiced mask of patience. She said nothing, only shifted her hand to Nathaniel's shoulder, a subtle shield between them. The moment passed as quickly as it came, slipping into the flow of camp life, but it left behind a quiet echo—something unspoken and unsettling, a thread pulled just tight enough to hum.

The stream gurgled softly, water slipping over stones, a lullaby in the quiet. But beneath its song, another note lingered—something deeper, something that moved with the shadows beneath the water. And if Nathaniel felt it, he did not show it. He sat with his mother's hand upon his shoulder, his beauty a thing of light against the encroaching dark, and he did not yet understand what it meant to be chosen.

By late afternoon, the group passed through Strasburg. Elias didn't stop, but led the party toward a narrowed trial toward the foothills of the Alleghany Mountains. The wind was cool —a hollow, whispering thing.

Gideon moved closer to Elias, his voice low. "Where exactly are we bound?"

Elias did not turn. His voice was even, unwavering. "To the place what was revealed to me."

Gideon exhaled sharply, his frustration swirling in his chest. "That tells me nothin'. Are you takin' us on some old pioneer trail?"

Elias turned slowly, his gaze unreadable. From his saddlebag, he withdrew a small, gleaming device—the orrery.

The brass rings caught the fading light. The black stone at its center gleamed, and for a moment, it felt like something alive.

Elias held it up, steady, unshaken.

"The way has already been written."

The rings trembled, then turned—slow, deliberate, as if stirred by an unseen hand. The smallest arm extended, its needle-thin point aligning toward the distant ridgeline.

Ezra let out a breath, his eyes flicking to Gideon, expecting to see the same wonder. But Gideon's expression remained tight, unreadable. His fingers twitched at his side.

He was not awed. He was uneasy.

Solomon watched from behind, silent.

He had seen what no one else had.

The way Elias's thumb had moved—barely perceptible—along the base of the device.

A small motion. A shift so slight it might have been nothing at all.

A mistake? Or an unseen mechanism?

He knew his father had fashioned this device, pretending it to be a spirit compass.

His stomach twisted, but he forced himself to move on.

The followers had seen proof.

That was all that mattered.

Rebecca, realizing Elias was leading them off trail, looked back at the edge of the town.

"Elias, the sun's fixin' to set. We oughta make camp here for the night." Her husband reluctantly yielded. The group settled camp just outside Strasburg.

Rebecca quietly departed for the town with a pack horse. She intended to find supplies after noticing a flour mill and shops when they passed through Strasburg.

"Ms. Whitmore," Lucy called out in a soft voice with a deep southern accent. "May I join you? I'd like to help."

Rebecca smiled and nodded. "Let us hurry before it gets too late and shops start closin'."

The road back into Strasburg was narrow, winding through clusters of birch and poplar trees that whispered against the encroaching twilight. The women walked in silence, their skirts brushing against wild grass, their steps muffled against the earth. The town lay ahead, its outline soft against the purple sky, silver lamplight pooling on cobblestone streets with a dark green tint, as if the world itself had taken on a quiet, expectant hue.

Strasburg breathed with the hum of the evening—windows glowed with hearthlight, and shadows moved behind drawn curtains. The main street held the scent of fresh bread and smoke, a thin trail of chimney ash curling against the twilight. Rebecca moved with purpose, her eyes scanning the fading signs painted on shopfronts, her fingers brushing the small purse at her waist.

Lucy walked beside her, a broad and welcoming figure. Her dark green dress was richly appointed, with silver trim catching the lantern light and silver lining peeking from beneath the folds of fabric. She moved with a soft elegance, the sway of her skirts accompanied by the gentle clink of silver buttons. Her hair was pinned up with a silver comb, the intricate design of vines and leaves glinting beneath the dying light.

In contrast, Rebecca's frame is thin and elegant. Her attire was more subdued but no less deliberate. Her dress was a deep charcoal gray, practical and unadorned, but at her throat was a brooch—a crimson stone set in a simple silver clasp. The color drew the eye, a dark red that seemed to pulse with its own heat against the cool palette of the evening. Her cloak, lined with a rich, wine-colored satin, shifted with each step, flashes of red visible in the folds as if she moved within a shadow touched by fire.

"There's somethin' mighty strange about campin' this close to town," Lucy said, her voice a warm, buttery drawl. "Feels like we're betwixt and between, neither here nor there. Like ghosts, I reckon."

Rebecca's lips quirked into a small smile. "Better here than further into the mountains with the night comin' on. I'd rather face a shopkeeper than a bear."

Lucy let out a laugh, soft but full, the kind that warmed the air around her. "Ain't that the truth. Though I reckon I could charm a bear if need be. Just gotta bake him a pie and tell him a good story."

Rebecca chuckled. "And if he don't take to your pie?"

"Oh, I'd just sweet-talk him into a nap. It works on my Abraham, and he's twice as stubborn as any creature God ever made."

The women turned down a narrower lane, the shop windows dimmer here, their displays covered in a fine layer of dust. Lucy's eyes caught on a telegraph office, the silver wires coiled behind the glass, the brass fittings gleaming faintly. Her expression shifted—something quiet and thoughtful beneath the jovial façade—but she moved on, her steps brisk to match Rebecca's.

The general store sat at the corner, its door slightly ajar, the warm light spilling onto the stoop. Inside, the shelves were lined with tins and tools, sacks of flour, and jars of preserves. The keeper, a wiry man with a frayed vest, looked up with tired eyes.

Rebecca approached the counter, setting down a small list. "Flour, salt, and oil, if you've got it."

The man nodded, moving with the slow efficiency of someone who had seen the end of the day and perhaps, the end of something more.

Lucy drifted through the aisles, her fingers grazing over metal tins and glass jars. She hummed softly, a tune that wound through the quiet store, her presence a gentle balm to the shadows.

She found Rebecca near the back, comparing prices on sacks of grain. "What do you reckon this town thinks of us?" Lucy asked, her voice low but light. "A whole pack of wanderers settin' up camp just outside their gates."

Rebecca considered this. "I imagine they think we're runnin' from somethin'. Or toward somethin'."

"Or both," Lucy said. She pulled a small jar from the shelf, studying the label. "I suppose it don't matter much. Folks always find a way to tell stories, whether they're true or not."

Rebecca's expression tightened just slightly, a shadow of the weight she carried. "We'll give 'em somethin' true to tell."

The women finished their purchases and stepped back into the cool evening. The town behind them seemed to breathe, its shadows stretching long. They walked together, their paces matching, their silences overlapping.

As they moved down the quiet lane, silver light fell across Lucy's green skirts, casting a faint shimmer over the fabric. The cobblestones beneath their feet seemed to hold the green of twilight, a quiet echo of the woods they had left behind.

Lucy spoke again, her voice softer. "Do you think we'll find it, Ms. Whitmore?"

Rebecca did not answer at once. Her steps did not slow. "I think we'll find what we were meant to."

The path ahead led into the dark, but neither turned back.

As they approached the camp, the quiet hum of conversation faded. The fire cast long shadows, silver and crimson dancing against the trees. Lucy tightened her shawl, the silver trim catching the light, while Rebecca moved ahead, her silhouette sharp and unwavering. In the distance, the mountains loomed—a dark promise against the stars.

4

CHAPTER 4 – NEMACOLIN'S PATH
The road forgets nothing

Dawn seeped into the valley, pale and hesitant. The camp stirred in silence, breath clouding in the chill air. Rebecca rose first, her cloak a dark ripple against the gray. She moved quietly through the camp, a shadow among shadows, nudging the embers of the fire to life and setting a pot to boil. She woke the others with a gentle hand on shoulders, her voice a soft murmur that cut through the last threads of sleep. One by one, they stirred—Solomon with a quick stretch, Ezra blinking against the dim light, Gideon already half awake, his instincts sharp.

Rebecca's presence wove through the morning camp, a quiet but persistent force. She tightened straps, redistributed packs, and whispered encouragement where fatigue had settled into bones. The group moved under her guidance.

By the time Elias rose, the camp was already shifting toward readiness. Rebecca met his gaze, a brief exchange—no words, just the acknowledgment of a morning well begun. She felt the weight of his stare, a silent reminder of the roles they played—the Prophet and his keeper.

The path ahead led upward, into the mountains, where the earth held its breath.

The land grew wilder, untamed, as if it had been waiting for them all along. The roads dissolved into jagged inclines, swallowed by the creeping wilderness. Each mile pressed harder, their bodies bowing under the journey's weight. The night before had carried omens—the hush of the blackbirds, the unnatural chill that slithered through camp, the wind that did not whisper, but wailed. A sign, some had murmured. A warning, Gideon had thought. But morning had come, and Elias had not wavered.

They pushed northwest, entering the foothills of the Allegheny Mountains. The mountains reared before them like silent sentinels, their jagged peaks clawing at the heavens. The easy road had been left behind, replaced by a ruthless ascent of uneven stone and shifting earth. The wind cut through them like a blade, thin and sharp, whispering through the chasms below. Each step was deliberate, each breath a reminder of how much farther they had to climb.

As the path narrowed, the group fell into a quiet formation—one that did not feel entirely accidental.

Ezra found himself riding beside Eleanor. They had barely spoken in the days since leaving, but she had been placed near him, whether by the gentle guidance of the mothers or by something unspoken among the men. He glanced at her once, but she kept her gaze ahead.

Nathaniel walked near Hannah, though he did not seem to mind. He still carried a boy's admiration for those older than him, and Hannah—sharp-eyed and bold—had already begun treating him like a younger brother.

Only Gideon was unpaired. Whether by choice or by quiet defiance, he had positioned himself apart.

Elias led, his horse steady despite the treacherous footing. He moved with the same certainty that had carried them this far, his posture unbowed by the strain of the climb. He did not look back. He did not slow. The path ahead was his to follow, and he asked no permission from the earth beneath him.

Rebecca moved among the weary, her voice a quiet anchor. She whispered words of encouragement, steadied hands that trembled from fatigue. She believed. Even now, even as the road turned cruel, she believed.

But Gideon—Gideon saw what Rebecca would not. He watched the hesitation growing in the eyes of their followers, the exhaustion weighing down their steps. Their faith, once bright and fervent, now flickered like a flame starved of air. The road was no longer a promise—it was a crucible.

Ezra followed closely behind his older brother, matching his pace without thinking. He always had.

At the rear, Hiram Sloan rode with an air of detachment, his dark eyes unreadable. He took note of those who faltered, those who walked with uncertainty in their strides. A leader was only as strong as his weakest disciple, and Hiram made it a habit to know which ones might break first.

The mountains loomed above them, silent and indifferent.

By sundown, the sky was bleeding gold and crimson, casting long shadows against the rock. They found shelter in a narrow clearing, a shallow cave offering little against the night's creeping chill. The fire that crackled in the center of camp was small, its warmth barely enough to chase away the cold.

The murmurs started here, in the quiet spaces between breath and fatigue.

Nathaniel, his face pale with exhaustion, finally gave voice to the thought that had been growing among them all.

"This path feels like a punishment."

The words landed heavy, an unspoken fear brought into the open. The fire flickered, and for a long moment, no one spoke. Rebecca stiffened. Solomon's gaze flicked to Elias. And in the dim light, Hiram smirked.

Elias did not turn. "You doubtin' me, Nathaniel?"

Nathaniel hesitated, but he did not look away. "Ain't seen no sign of the city. The land's wild. How much farther?"

Elias remained still for a moment, his gaze distant, as though seeing something beyond the fire's glow. Then, in a voice that carried the weight of prophecy, he spoke.

"Faith don't reckon with distance, boy. It walks where the Lord commands."

The silence stretched, thick with expectation. Nathaniel lowered his gaze. A few heads nodded, reassured, though their conviction was not as strong as it once was. Others looked away, uncertainty brewing at the edges of their thoughts.

For now, Elias' answer was enough.

But doubt, once spoken, does not fade so easily.

The moon hung low and bright, a silver eye peering down upon them as Gideon found Elias standing at the edge of the ridge. Below, the valley stretched wide and empty, the darkness swallowing all trace of a path forward. The Lost River whispered somewhere below, a secret voice beneath the earth, winding through unseen caverns. Its waters moved in silence, disappearing into the stone as if the land itself had taken a long, slow breath and held it.

The river's legend lingered in Gideon's mind. How it vanished into the earth, only to emerge miles away as the Cacapon River—a transformation hidden from the eye, a truth buried beneath rock and shadow. It felt too close to the truth of their journey, the way Elias guided them into the dark, promising that faith would lead them back to the light.

Gideon stepped beside his father, the silence heavy between them before he finally spoke.

"You gave the boy an answer, but not the truth."

Elias remained still. "And what truth is it you're after, Gideon?"

Gideon exhaled sharply, frustration weaving through his ribs. "Where are you taking us?"

A long silence. Then, Elias turned, his face unreadable in the moonlight.

"Careful not to set yourself against what's been ordained," he said. "It's written before us, and we must walk it."

Gideon's fingers wrapped into fists, the nails biting deep into his palm. He wanted to walk away. No—he wanted to turn them back, to shatter this illusion before it was too late. But faith, once spoken, was like a stone cast into a river. The ripples had already spread. And even if he shouted now, even if he tried to break the spell Elias had woven, he knew—no one would listen.

Instead, the crunch of gravel behind him pulled his attention. Ezra emerged from the shadows, his features half-lit by the silver glow of the moon. His breath hung in the air, a small cloud between them.

"What's goin' on?" Ezra's voice was soft, wary. He looked from Gideon to Elias, his brow furrowing.

"Nothin'," Gideon said, his tone sharper than intended.

Ezra flinched, but held his ground. "Ain't look like nothin'."

Gideon's expression softened, the edge of his frustration dulling. "Go back to the fire. It's cold."

Ezra hesitated. His gaze lingered on their father, searching for signs—of anger, of truth, of anything that might anchor him in the uncertainty that gnawed at his chest. When none came, he turned to Gideon.

"We're gonna be alright, ain't we?"

The question hung between them, delicate as frost.

Gideon reached out, his hand closing over Ezra's shoulder. The gesture was rough but steadying, a brother's grip that held both strength and restraint. "I'll make sure of it."

Elias turned away, his silhouette a dark line against the pale sky. The orrery in his hand caught the moonlight, its brass rings turning slowly, the black stone at its center gleaming like an eye. "Faith walks forward," he murmured, as much to himself as to his sons. "Whether you see the ground beneath your feet or not."

He disappeared into the night, leaving Gideon and Ezra alone beneath the silver sky. The Lost River's hidden current murmured far below, its secrets safe beneath stone, its path a mystery neither of them could see.

Ezra leaned closer to Gideon, his voice a thin thread in the cold. "If the river finds its way, maybe we can too."

Gideon did not answer. But his arm remained around his brother, a silent promise as they stood at the edge of the world, with only the stars and the whisper of the unseen river to guide them.

Abraham woke just before dawn and noticed Elias already preparing his horse for travel. The camp lay still, shadows stretching long beneath the gray sky. Wisps of mist coiled around the tree trunks, and the dying embers of the campfire cast a dull, pulsing glow against the cold earth.

Elias moved with the patience of a man who knew time was on his side. His fingers worked the leather straps of the saddle, precise and methodical, as if each pull and knot was part of some quiet ritual. He did not acknowledge Abraham at first, allowing the silence to stretch, to weigh. Finally, as he cinched the last strap, he spoke.

"Couldn't sleep?"

Abraham stepped closer, his breath fogging in the chill. He drew a cigar from his coat, its wrapper dark and worn. The match flared, a brief orange glow in the dim morning, and soon smoke rose, curling around his head like mist. 'Not with that Yankee sleepin' so close by.' His voice was low, his words careful. 'You certain bringin' the spy along ain't a mistake?

Elias's hands stilled. His knuckles whitened against the leather, but when he turned, his expression was as calm as ever. "And what would you have me do, Abraham? Spill blood in front of the children? In front of Rebecca?"

Abraham stared at Elias and with sarcasm in his voice,

"Our kids are grown, my friend" he spoked in his deep voice. Then side eyeing Hiram, "He's a snake," Abraham muttered. "Knows too much. Saw too much. We ought to have buried him where he stood."

A shadow passed over Elias's face, there and gone like a cloud over the moon. "You think I don't know that?" His voice remained soft, but something coiled beneath it—something cold and sharp. "The Red String Band sent him to root us out. If we'd killed him, they'd have more men at our door by now. No, takin' him with us keeps his secrets buried."

Abraham glanced over his shoulder, where the dim outline of Hiram's figure lay among the sleeping. His coat, worn and threadbare, rose and fell with shallow breaths. The spy slept close to the fire, but the heat did not seem to reach him. Shadows clung to him, as if the night itself refused to let him go.

"What if he don't stay?" Abraham's drawl had softened, a thread of unease woven through the words.

Elias's gaze did not waver. "He will. The Knights got him bound tight. Fear is a better chain than iron." He drew a small brass object from his coat—the orrery. Its metal arms shifted gently, the spheres within turning with a whisper of gears. The device seemed to breathe in the dawn light, casting faint patterns on the ground—stars and constellations that moved, though no hand touched them.

Abraham's eyes narrowed. "And if he don't?"

Elias held the orrery between them, letting the dim light glint off its polished edges. "Then we deliver him to the Sons of Liberty. They'll know what to do with a Red String."

The name hung between them, heavy and cold. The Sons of Liberty. A breakaway faction of the Knights, hardened men who believed the coming war would burn away the weak, leaving only the righteous to rebuild. Men who would see Hiram's blood spilled as easily as water.

Abraham breathed deeply, his broad chest rising and falling like the bellows of a forge. "So Martin County, Indiana, then."

Elias did not answer immediately. His eyes remained on the orrery, the way the metal spheres spun slowly, guided by some unseen force. "We go where the orrery leads," he said at last. "Nothing more, nothing less."

But his tone held a lie. Abraham heard it—a quiet note of deception, buried beneath the cadence of faith.

"You ever wonder if it's leadin' us wrong?" Abraham asked, his voice almost too soft to hear.

Elias's expression did not change, but the light in his eyes cooled. "A man who questions the path finds only darkness. It is the blind who are blessed, for they walk without fear."

A silence settled over them. From the edge of the camp, Hiram shifted, his shadow bending in the half-light. For a moment, Abraham thought the man's eyes were open—watching them. But when he looked again, Hiram lay still, his breath slow, his expression empty.

Elias's lips curled into the faintest of smiles. "Keep your faith, Abraham. And your silence."

Then he turned away, the orrery cradled against his chest, its metal arms still turning, whispering secrets only he could hear.

The remainder of the party arose from their sleep. Rebecca moved the group along to continue their journey west. Just after dawn, they found themselves standing before an abyss.

The gorge cut deep through the forest, its edges veiled in mist. The bridge that spanned it was old, but sturdy—wide enough for the wagons to pass, if slowly, and strong enough for the weight of horse and rider. The ropes had weathered years and though they groaned when touched, they held.. The rocks at the bottom waited like open mouths.

They gathered at the edge.

Elias said nothing. He only studied the bridge with the calm of someone who had seen worse in vision than in flesh.

Solomon stepped forward, testing the first few boards with the toe of his boot. They groaned under his weight, but held.

"This wasn't in the maps," Gideon muttered, squinting through the trees.

"No map shows what it costs to cross," Elias said quietly.

The first few crossed carefully—Solomon, Ezra, Gideon. The bridge swayed, the ropes creaking in protest, but they made it across.

Then Abraham stepped forward.

He wiped sweat from his brow, though the air was cold. His coat clung to him, damp at the collar, and his breathing had grown loud, unsteady. Still, he gripped the rope railing and placed one foot on the planks.

Lucy called out from behind. "Wait. Let someone help you."

"I'm fine," he growled. "I've crossed worse in my day."

But the bridge did not care for his pride.

With each step, the wood groaned louder beneath him. Halfway across, he stopped—legs trembling, chest heaving.

The wind picked up. The bridge swayed.

Below, the white noise of the river echoed off stone walls, rising into a hiss.

"Abraham," Elias called from the other side, his voice steady, calm. "Turn back. Let Solomon come for you."

Abraham shook his head. "No. No, I've got it."

He took another step.

His foot caught—just slightly—on a raised board. His body pitched forward. He grabbed for the rope but caught only air.

A cry rang out from behind.

"Hold on!" Solomon shouted, already running back onto the bridge.

But Abraham's fingers were slick with sweat. His breath came in choking gasps.

Abraham stumbled sideways, arms windmilling, the weight of him too great to recover.

Then, over the side.

No scream. Just a dull, thick thud below. Silence.

Lucy turned her face away, one hand clamped over her mouth.

Solomon stood at the halfway point, staring down, unmoving.

Elias closed his eyes.

Behind them, no one stepped forward.

The bridge swayed, empty now, haunted.

The sickening thud of his body striking the unseen depths below sent a jolt of horror through those who stood at the edge.

Eliza sobbed, reaching for the broken ropes, but Solomon grabbed her wrist, pulling her back. "He's gone," he whispered.

Eleanor turned to Ezra, eyes wide, searching. She said nothing, but her hand briefly touched his arm, fingers tightening just slightly before pulling away. As if she had reached out by instinct. As if she had already accepted that in the absence of a father, there must be another.

Ezra swallowed, unsure of what to say. Unsure of what he was supposed to be.

Rebecca did not cry. Did not gasp. The breath left her lips in a slow, measured exhale, but inside, something cracked—something deep, something final. Her fingers twitched at her sides, instinctively reaching for something—someone—but there was nothing to hold. Nothing but the silence that followed a man's last scream. Then she opened her eyes, and she walked.

Lucy remained at the edge, her body a silhouette against the chasm. Her hands were empty, her arms slack at her sides. She did not move, did not breathe, until the others had pulled away, their backs turned to the broken bridge, to the darkness below. Only then did the sound escape her—a raw, fractured moan that slipped past her lips and into the wind.

Her daughters stood beside her, their faces pale, eyes fixed on the darkness below. Lucy reached for them, her fingers intertwining with theirs. The gesture was small, but in it lay the weight of shared loss—the silent understanding that everything had changed. They stood together at the edge, a line unbroken, even as the chasm yawned beneath them

Rebecca approached, her shadow folding over them. She crouched, her hand a steadying weight on Lucy's shoulder.

"We have to go," Rebecca said. "Its not safe here."

Lucy did not look up. Her fingers tightened against the fabric, the silver threads woven through her sleeves catching the dim light. "Your husband, Elias. He didn't even look back."

"No," Rebecca agreed. "He didn't."

Lucy's breath shuddered. "What if he's right?"

"Then we keep walking," Rebecca said, her voice unyielding. "And if he's wrong, we walk still."

* * *

The fire had burned down to embers by the time the camp settled again. The group lay scattered beneath the open sky, the stars sharp and cold. Lucy sat apart, her daughters beside her, their faces turned toward the dying fire. They sat shoulder to shoulder, a quiet line of mourning, none of them speaking. She did not sleep. Neither did Gideon.

Gideon noticed his father alone and approached him as the camp slept. The fire had burned down to embers, casting the world in shades of ash and shadow. His voice was sharp with fury, his green eyes seemed to glow with anger.

"You talk of faith, but shut your eyes to what's plain. This is madness."

Elias did not flinch. "Faith don't reckon with fear, nor does it shrink from sacrifice."

Solomon watched from the shadows, his form half-hidden by the lean of a tree, his face a mask of quiet observation. Doubt simmered within him, a dark undercurrent that he held tightly beneath the surface. His secrets were his own—whispered thoughts, forbidden desires, the unsettling pull of questions he dared not voice.

He had always understood the power of belief. Faith was not a promise of truth but a structure built on hope, brick by brick, lie by lie. It was Paul in Corinth, standing before those who had waited a lifetime for a prophecy that had not come. It was the soft voice that turned the unseen into evidence, the whisper that made the hollow echo of an empty tomb a sign of resurrection.

"*I am Paul,*" he thought. The words settled into his bones, heavy and certain. The mantle had not been given to him—he had taken it. Like the prophets of old, he would not ask permission to lead. He would be the voice that shaped the world. But beneath the thought lay a shadow, a whisper of something sharp—a delusion draped in scripture, the first brushstroke of a portrait not yet fully seen.

Solomon stepped forward, his movement deliberate, his voice firm. "Enough, Gideon. If you doubt, then doubt in silence. Don't sow fear among the faithful."

Gideon's hands bound into fists. "You're leading us to ruin."

Solomon did not move. His shadow stretched long across the cold earth, a bridge between Gideon's anger and Elias's unyielding calm. He spoke again, softer, but with a weight that cut through the night. "Faith doesn't require the path to be clear. It only asks that you walk it, doubting nothing."

And with those words, the true division began.

The night swallowed their mourning, and when the dawn came, it found them hollowed, their grief woven into the mist that clung to the earth.

5

C HAPTER 5 – THE WIDOW'S ROAD
"We carry the weight of the dead by walking."
– *Old Appalachian Saying*

Dawn broke cold across the spine of the Allegheny Mountains, brushing pale light over the travelers who had left blood behind them. Four days had passed since departing Front Royal, whispers of unease had begun to spread, and the shadow of death loomed on Elias's vision and journey to Empyrean.

The mountains behind them loomed tall and unmoving, indifferent to the grief that pressed into the bones of those who traveled beneath them. Dawn stretched pale fingers through the trees, but the morning brought no warmth. Abraham was gone, yet his presence lingered in the spaces he once filled—the bare patch of earth where he had knelt by the fire, the indentations of his boots in the morning frost. He had been loud, unwavering, and now, the silence he left behind pressed against them all, like a waiting storm.

Lucy Mercer walked with her daughters in the shadow of the others. Her grief had hollowed her, drawn fine lines beneath her hazel eyes, deepened the silver strands in her thick brown hair. She had spent years following Elias's vision, trusting in her husband Abraham, believing that faith and obedience would be enough. But Abraham was dead, and Elias had not even turned back.

Her daughters walked on either side of her, their steps in rhythm with hers. Virginia's face was set, her expression hard beneath the brim of her violet bonnet. Hannah moved with a quiet grace, her hands clasped before her, eyes downcast. They were their father's daughters—strong, steady, but their paths had begun to diverge, even if none of them saw it yet.

Gideon had always been a man of steady conviction. He was broad-shouldered, his chestnut hair tousled from the wind, his sharp features cast in flickering firelight. His hazel eyes, once unwavering in their faith, had begun to darken with something unreadable. He had barely spoken since the ravine, but his silence carried weight. Ezra, ever his shadow, followed his lead.

Where Gideon burned with quiet intensity, Ezra was a restless flicker, always shifting, always watching. His lean frame carried the ease of someone who never quite settled. His gray eyes, quick and discerning, were different from Gideon's—more calculating, more knowing. There was no fire in them, only embers waiting for a gust of wind.

And Eleanor had begun to notice.

She had once believed, without question, in Elias's path. But now, she found herself drawn to Ezra's silences, to the way his mouth twitched when someone spoke of Elias's visions, to the way he lingered near Gideon when he thought no one was watching.

Eliza had always admired Gideon. But admiration had begun to shift into something else. She was cautious, always cautious, but she watched him now not just with faith, but with longing.

The road west was slow, winding through forests thick with bare branches and valleys still slick from the recent autumnal rains. There was no clear path, only Elias's orrery, his hands moving the brass spheres as he murmured his interpretations.

Gideon watched, silent.

As the sun began to set on their day of travel, Rebecca called the group to gather for camp.

"Gideon," Ezra whispered to his brother as they watch the sun's final breath sink below the horizon, *"Are we headed where I think we're headed?"*

Gideon shook his head and mumbled, "The Ohio, I hope."

At night, when the camp settled, he remained awake, staring into the fire. Ezra sat beside him, saying nothing.

"You're troubled," Ezra said at last, his voice low.

Gideon exhaled, slow and steady. "I don't think he knows where he's goin'."

Ezra did not answer, but his jaw tightened.

Eleanor lingered at the edge of the firelight, her hands busy with the worn edge of her shawl. She watched the brothers, her gaze slipping from Gideon's steady silhouette to Ezra's restless form. She did not approach, but when Ezra's eyes found hers, she offered a small, hesitant smile.

Eliza sat beside Lucy, her fingers twisting the silver cross that hung from her neck. "Mother, do you believe him?"

Lucy's breath shivered, a soft cloud in the night air. "I don't know, child. Thought I did. But faith is a quiet thing. It can slip through your fingers if ya ain't careful."

Virginia and Hannah sat a few paces away, their heads bowed as Solomon led evening prayers. They did not look up. They did not question.

Virginia lingered at the edge of Solomon's words, arms wrapped tight around herself, the violet ribbon in her hair limp with dust. Hannah sat beside her, silent, her face lifted in prayer.

Solomon noticed. He knelt beside her, she did not look at him.

"My father died," she said. Not as grief, but as fact. Her voice had the clarity of glass. "And nobody wept long."

Solomon's gaze rested on the flames. "There's a time for mourning," he said softly, "and a time for building what must come next."

Virginia's lip trembled, just once. "You didn't even speak his name."

"He was a good man," Solomon offered. "He walks with vision now. He understood what was asked."

Something cracked behind her eyes, maybe the aching need for something to hold onto. Her fingers twitched against her skirts.

"I don't want to be left behind. I want to understand the vision," she whispered. "I want to *see*."

Solomon turned to her then. His hand moved gently—too gently—and tucked the loose strand of hair behind her ear. "Then walk beside me," he said. "And I will show you what Empyrean requires."

Her breath hitched, but she did not pull away.

Eleanor found herself drawn closer to Ezra. Not just to his doubts, but to his quiet certainty. To the way he showed quiet empathy, without words.

Eliza, torn between loyalty to Solomon and the pull of Gideon's quiet strength, wavered.

Lucy listened.

She had spent her life listening.

But now, she had begun watching Elias with different eyes.

The morning sun lifted, and the air had changed.

The group continued their journey, moving west from the Alleghenies.

The deeper they pressed into the Monongahela Wilderness, the less the world seemed familiar. The towering oaks and sycamores stretched their gnarled limbs toward the sky, their canopies knitting together so tightly that only fragments of pale, anemic sunlight trickled through. Moss smothered the rocks and tree trunks, and the ground, still slick from the last rain, swallowed their boots in sucking gulps.

The trees here were older, their roots thick and coiled like the veins of the land itself. Ancient, untamed. The underbrush, tangled with vines and briars, reached out in gnarled fingers, snagging at skirts, tearing at stockings. The path—if it could even be called that—narrowed into a twisting corridor of shadow, forcing them into single file.

Lucy Mercer's breathing had grown labored, her skirts darkened with mud up to the hem. She pressed a hand against her lower back, stealing a glance toward the sky, but there was no open horizon here—only trees upon trees, pressing in on all sides.

"This ain't a path," she muttered under her breath, adjusting her bonnet. "It's a grave waitin' to be filled."

No one answered.

The journey had stretched them thin. Abraham's absence was a wound no one spoke of, but it bled into every moment. The silence had grown more pronounced, the conversations sparse. At night, they huddled around their dwindling fire, and even prayer had become a hushed, weary thing.

But Solomon was thriving.

He walked beside Elias, his voice soft but steady, reciting verses under his breath. He spoke not to his father, but for his father, filling the spaces where Elias no longer needed to. Rebecca watched it happen, saying nothing.

Behind them, Virginia and Hannah stayed close, nodding along to Solomon's murmured words, their faith deepening with every hardship. They had begun echoing his prayers—not Elias's, but Solomon's.

And Gideon noticed.

Gideon had lagged behind for most of the morning, his shoulders tense, his breath short with frustration. Ezra, ever his shadow, matched his pace, watching him out of the corner of his eye.

Gideon thought to himself. *We need to stop. We need to turn toward the Ohio River.*

Up ahead, Elias led them deeper inland, avoiding the obvious routes. The Ohio lay somewhere beyond the hills, unseen but closer than Elias wanted to acknowledge. The easiest road westward followed the river—a known path, well-trodden. *That was where they ought to be,* thought Gideon.

Instead, Elias had led them into the worst of the wilderness, forcing them over broken terrain, slowing them with steep climbs and tangled forests. Every extra mile, every unnecessary detour, sapped their strength.

It didn't have to be this way.

Finally, Gideon broke.

"We're wastin' time."

Elias did not turn.

Gideon quickened his pace, stepping over the thick roots that sprawled across the forest floor. He moved beside Elias, his voice sharp.

"The river's down the main road," Gideon pressed. "That's where we oughta be. We could follow it—rest, resupply, even—"

"The river is not our path," Elias interrupted. His voice was quiet but firm, the weight of finality in it.

Gideon exhaled sharply. "And why the hell not? There's food there, water. And if we need to, we could even take passage—"

"No." Elias stopped abruptly, his pale eyes fixing onto his son. "The river is watched."

Gideon felt his frustration twist into something hotter. "By who?"

Elias's hand rested over the orrery tucked into his coat, fingers tracing its metal edges.

"The river carries men both righteous and unclean," Elias said. "It carries soldiers, Unionists, lawmen, and spies. It carries sickness and death. And it carries those who would hunt us down, given the chance."

This was different.

Gideon expected his father to say the river was *cursed*, or *unholy*. But instead, he spoke of practical dangers—of enemies, of being seen.

"And yet we're goin' west, ain't we?" Gideon challenged. "We can't just avoid it forever."

Elias's expression remained unreadable. "We will cross when the Lord commands it."

We will cross.

That was different from *we won't go near it at all.*

6

CHAPTER 6 – THE DARK ROAD WEST
The fire burns lower, but not out.

The fire burned low, casting shadows across the weary faces of those gathered. Solomon led the longest prayers yet, standing before the dwindling flames, his voice calm and unwavering.

"The Prophet has shown the way," he said, his tone almost hypnotic. "And we'll not falter."

Virginia knelt beside Solomon during prayers, her voice rising with his, steady and clear. Hannah stayed close to her sister, her hands folded neatly in her lap, her lips moving with the practiced rhythm of prayer, her freckled face smiling with hope. Their faith was not blind, but it was anchored. Where others saw shadows, they saw only the path ahead.

Hiram Sloane sat apart from the others, sharpening an arrowhead with slow, deliberate movements. His hands—scarred from years of battle and survival—moved with absent precision, but his gaze was anything but unfocused.

Elias believed it was fear that kept him tethered.

But Hiram's motivations were his own. And if anyone had been watching closely, they might have noticed the way his eyes lingered on Rebecca when no one else was looking.

Rebecca dutifully managed the camp for the evening, realizing the supplies were running dangerously low. *We'll need to find a place to stock up supplies tomorrow,* she thought to herself.

Gideon sat at the edge of the group, his elbows resting on his knees, eyes dark. He wasn't watching Solomon. He was watching who was listening.

Ezra, sitting beside Gideon, kept his head down, but his fingers twitched where they rested against his knee.

Lucy, arms crossed, watched her daughters Virginia and Hannah nearly worshipping at the feet of Solomon, the whole thing felt horrific to her.

Eliza cast a glance toward Gideon but didn't move. She was caught between her mother and her sisters. Between faith and doubt.

Eleanor sat beside Ezra. Close enough to touch. She didn't say a word, but her presence was answer enough.

Solomon turned, catching Gideon's gaze across the fire.

And he smiled.

The road had already split.

They just hadn't reached the breaking point yet.

By the seventh day, the divide had begun to show.

Gideon did not challenge Elias. He did not need to.

The silence between them was enough.

Solomon saw it first.

His bright blue eyes watched his older brothers, Gideon and Ezra, with quiet calculation. He was everything his father had molded him to be—broad-shouldered, golden-haired, an image of the divine race.

"Gideon," Solomon's voice was even, measured. "You walk with hesitation."

Gideon, running his hand along the worn leather of his belt, did not answer immediately. "Perhaps I am waitin' to see if my hesitation is justified."

The wind shifted.

Solomon smiled, small and knowing.

"Then let 'em walk by faith. Watch closely, brother—soon enough, you'll see us headin' toward the Ohio. Marietta ain't too far."

Had Solomon truly convinced Elias? Or had this always been the plan?

Gideon clenched his jaw.

It was not leadership.

It was control.

His father would not listen to him. But he would heed Solomon's words.

The journey west had become a slow and steady erosion of certainty. The faithful still followed, but now, there were more glances exchanged, more hushed conversations just out of Elias's earshot.

They were nearing the outskirts of another settlement, moving carefully through the wooded ridges south of the river. They kept to the shadows, avoiding the main roads, avoiding towns where the wrong eyes might notice them.

The land was changing. The hills had begun to roll rather than climb, the dense forests thinning into a landscape shaped by rivers and trade.

Ezra, who had spent his childhood studying maps under candlelight, knew they were threading through old pioneer trails leading westward. The land still belonged to the South—but only barely. The Union pressed from the north, creeping downward like an oncoming tide.

And the river lay ahead—just as Solomon had smugly foretold, as if he'd carved it from the land himself.

They had not yet seen the water. But Gideon could feel it.

The air smelled different here—damp, earthen, carrying the faintest whisper of something unseen. The Ohio River was close now, winding ahead of them like a boundary between two worlds.

The last barrier.

As the wind shifted, Gideon turned his gaze over his shoulder, toward the distant lowlands where the trees thinned.

For a moment, he imagined taking a horse, riding ahead, and finding the river himself. He imagined the ferry, the long stretch of water gleaming in the afternoon light.

He imagined leaving all of this behind.

They were finally heading toward the river—but not because of him. Not because it was the logical choice.

Because Solomon had willed it.

A bitter taste curled at the back of his throat.

But he didn't stop.

Instead, he exhaled, slow and steady, and forced his feet forward.

Ahead, Elias rode in silence, his posture as straight and unwavering as the day they left Virginia.

He did not glance back.

He did not acknowledge the shifting wind or the distant scent of damp earth carried from low-lying valleys.

The world behind them was not for them.

To their right, a column of black smoke twisted into the sky. Ezra saw it first.

"Steamboat," he murmured.

Eleanor turned her head, following his gaze.

Just beyond the treetops, a dark plume rose against the horizon, curling and stretching into the wind. Somewhere beyond the hills, men were moving cargo—cotton, tobacco, wealth.

Industry.

The world they had left behind was still turning, untouched by their exodus.

Lucy Mercer caught sight of it as well. Her hands tightened in the folds of her dress, her thoughts undiscernible.

Her husband had died for this journey, and yet, the world beyond their path had not even noticed his absence.

Virginia and Hannah kept their eyes ahead, following Solomon, their faith unshaken.

Nathaniel trailed behind them, blindly following.

But Gideon—Gideon had seen the smoke.

And though he never spoke of it, though he never slowed his pace or let his doubt reach his father's ears, something inside him had already begun to drift, like a boat untethered from the shore.

As the evening approached, Rebecca knew they needed to find a place to rest and resupply.

And in the distance, she noticed a lonely building—perhaps a tavern.

7

CHAPTER 7 – ALE, SIN & THE STYX
Not all rivers cleanse. Some only carry the dead.

The tavern was nothing special at first glance. A weathered, single-story structure hunched low against the wind, its windows glowing softly in the night. Smoke curled from the chimney, blending with the damp air of the Ohio frontier. The sign above the door had long since faded, its letters swallowed by time.

Rebecca said nothing at first, simply adjusting her pace so that Elias would take note of it on his own. As expected, he did. And she whispered to him.

"We camp here," he announced, voice steady with authority as he acknowledged Rebecca's prompt.

He turned to Solomon and Nathaniel. "The faithful will remain at camp. We will pray, we will sing, and we will thank the Lord for the trials we have endured."

Nathaniel nodded, his face solemn, ever eager to listen to his father's words. Virginia knelt beside them, eyes closed in quiet devotion.

Rebecca bowed her head in quiet deference. "Shall I take some to gather supplies?"

Elias nodded absently. This, too, was part of their unspoken pattern—she handled the practical matters, ensuring the group had what it needed while he maintained their spiritual strength. He assumed she would take only Lucy, but tonight, others spoke up before she could reply.

"I'll go," Gideon said, shaking dust from his coat.

Ezra, standing beside him, crossed his arms. "Me too."

Eliza glanced between them and then to Eleanor. A silent decision passed between the two young women. "We'll help."

Rebecca met Elias's gaze, expecting protest, but he merely waved a dismissive hand. "Fine. But return quickly. I will not have distractions during our evening prayers."

Hiram said nothing, only falling into step beside Rebecca as they made their way toward the tavern.

* * *

The Rose Tree Tavern: fire, ruin, or revelation

The tavern was warm, thick with the scent of aged whiskey, burning tallow, and the musk of bodies long accustomed to the road. The low hum of conversation blended with the rhythmic drone of a fiddle, its bow scraping over taut strings in a melody both melancholic and wild. It was a song meant for restless men, a tune that spoke of roads left behind and the ones still ahead.

The fiddler played near the fire, his fingers dancing over the worn wood of the instrument, his boot tapping in time against the uneven planks. The melody curled through the air like ghosts rising from the embers, the kind of sound that settled into bones and stayed there.

Gideon stepped inside and exhaled slowly, shaking the tension from his shoulders.

Hiram, however, froze just inside the doorway. His eyes darted across the room, lingering for a moment too long on a man at the bar—a broad-shouldered figure with graying hair and a sharp, assessing gaze. A man who, upon seeing Hiram, barely reacted.

But Gideon saw it. The slight flicker of recognition. The way the stranger's fingers ghosted over his collar, just briefly, just enough to draw attention to the small **red** string threaded through the buttonhole.

A message. A quiet, wordless acknowledgment.

Hiram didn't flinch, didn't react. Instead, he met the man's gaze, his expression unreadable.

The bartender, seemingly unbothered, poured a drink and slid it across the counter to another patron. As he did, he murmured, "Been a long road, stranger. Time to rest?"

Hiram's fingers drummed lightly against the table—a slow, deliberate rhythm. His answer.

The bartender inclined his head, almost imperceptibly, before turning away. No further words needed to be spoken.

Gideon caught the exchange and narrowed his eyes. The two men seemed to know one another.

Hiram did know. A fellow. An unspoken ally. He could leave. Now. Slip away while the others were distracted, find refuge with his fraternity.

But then his gaze drifted to Rebecca.

She sat near the fire, her face half-shadowed in the flickering light, her voice low and even. She was conversing with the tavern keeper, her presence strangely calming in the chaos of the room.

She had no idea who he truly was. Not really.

And if he left, she never would.

He hesitated too long.

Lucy, meanwhile, had wasted no time. She sought only to drown her despair in the holy spirits she knew all too well. She sauntered into the room like a woman who had long since abandoned pretense, slipping seamlessly into the revelry, her laughter light and reckless. She threw an arm around the nearest man, stealing his drink without apology.

"You're a terrible host," she teased, tossing back a swallow of whiskey. "But I'll forgive you."

Lucy Mercer had taken off her considering cap.

Ezra chuckled, shaking his head. Gideon watched, unsure whether to feel amused or unsettled.

Eliza and Eleanor, for all their upbringing, were not far behind.

And soon, neither were Gideon and Ezra.

Rebecca continued near the fire, not drinking spirits but simply conversing with the tavern keeper, her presence strangely calming in the chaos of the room.

"Not much to offer," the tavern keeper admitted. "But I'll see what I can spare."

Rebecca nodded, accepting the limitations without complaint. "Flour, dried meat if you have it. Medicine. Anything that keeps well."

Hiram approached, hands resting casually on the edge of the counter. "I wouldn't have pegged you as the kind to bargain in a place like this."

She turned to him, arching a brow. "And what kind would you have pegged me as, Mr. Sloane?"

Hiram hesitated, then smirked. "The kind who never has to ask twice for what she wants."

Rebecca's expression didn't shift, but something flickered in her gaze. "You assume I always get what I want?"

"I assume you know how to get it," he countered.

The air between them shifted, the noise of the tavern fading just slightly. Hiram, who had been so close to escaping, found himself anchored in place.

Across the room, Lucy had begun to sing, off-key but fearless, making up lyrics to match the fiddler's tune.

"Oh, I once had a husband, but now he is dead, Gone off to the kingdom while I drink in his stead! Oh, I once had a fortune, but now I am poor, So pour me another and show me the door!"

The room erupted into laughter, boots stomping along with her improvised ballad. Gideon and Eliza sat nearby, locked in a quiet but charged debate about something neither seemed willing to concede. Ezra and Eleanor, meanwhile, were much less concerned with conversation—her fingers traced slow, idle patterns along his forearm as they leaned in too close, their words exchanged in murmurs meant for no one else.

And Hiram? He stayed and would seemingly follow Rebecca anywhere.

Rebecca finished her dealings with the innkeeper and glanced at her sons with a knowing smile. "Don't stay up too late," she murmured, though she already knew they wouldn't heed her.

Hiram walked with her as they took a slow path back to camp, the weight of the night settling around them. The distant hum of laughter and music faded into the rustling of the trees.

After a stretch of silence, Rebecca spoke. "I noticed the red strings tied to the men's collars."

Hiram kept his stride steady. "Did you?"

She nodded. "I remember when you wore one." Her voice was calm, but there was an undertone of something else—something knowing. "Before Elias tore it away."

Hiram exhaled slowly. "And you know what it meant?"

"I do." She glanced at him, her face shadowed in the low light, her voice a whisper. "*The Red String Band. The Heros of America. The men who stand against the old order.*"

Hiram gave a slight nod. "The Union has more claim to us than Richmond ever did."

"The Knights want to preserve the old order," Hiram said, voice low but steady. "The Red Strings want to burn it down. And the Sons of Liberty?" He smiled without warmth. "They just want to be gods when the fire goes out."

The silence that followed was heavy—not because it was untrue, but because it was.

Rebecca listened, her steps even, her expression thoughtful. "You were one of them."

"I was," he admitted. "I am, actually, still a member, technically." He lingered as he contemplated the fact that he has *allowed* Elias to keep him prisoner.

She studied him, then looked ahead, her lips pressing together briefly. "And this is why my husband called you a spy?"

Hiram smirked faintly. "A spy?"

A quiet chuckle escaped her, soft and low. "Maybe."

He turned to her then, something flickering behind his sharp green eyes. "And you? Do you respect me, Mrs. Whitmore?"

Rebecca met his gaze without hesitation. "I think I understand you."

They walked the rest of the way in silence, their footfalls light against the damp earth, the glow of the campfire flickering in the distance.

And for the first time in days, Hiram didn't feel entirely alone.

Rebecca slipped quietly into Elias's tent, settling beside him, her body still and composed as she drifted to sleep.

Hiram found a spot a short distance away, laying back against the hard ground, staring at the sky above.

As Hiram lay back against the hard ground, the distant echoes of fiddle music and laughter still lingered in his ears. The night air was cool against his skin, the scent of damp earth and smoldering embers filling his lungs.

His gaze drifted upward, tracing the endless black sky, speckled with distant stars that seemed just out of reach—like everything else he had lost.

Rebecca's voice still lingered in his mind. *"I think I understand you."*

He wasn't sure why that unsettled him more than anything else.

Understanding was dangerous. It meant seeing a man for what he truly was, not just the mask he wore. It meant acknowledging the choices he had made, the ones that had brought him here, chained to a cause that was not his own.

He remembered. A creek behind the tobacco mill—the way the water swirled around his brother's body like it meant to comfort him. But the mud had turned red, and the thread they found looped through his collar was torn, dirtied, soaked through.

They'd said it was deserters. Bandits, maybe. But Hiram knew better.

The Knights never left clean wounds. They left symbols.

He had knelt there in the shallows, hands shaking, watching the way the current tugged gently at his brother's sleeve—like even the river couldn't bear to keep him.

That night, he tied his own red thread. Tight. Vengeful. Certain.

But threads wear thin. And faith, if twisted too long, becomes a noose.

With that final thought, Hiram closed his eyes and let the night take him.

* * *

Even sin can be sanctuary, if the candles stay lit.

The morning was still and gray, the mist of the night before lingering in the air as Elias stirred awake. The campfire had burned out, the only sound the faint rustling of wind through the trees.

Rebecca lay beside him, her breaths slow and even, her body curled in the warmth of their shared blankets. For a moment, Elias simply watched her, his mind slow to shake off sleep. He exhaled through his nose and sat up carefully, his movements practiced and quiet.

The camp was silent. Solomon, Nathaniel, Virginia, and Hannah were still asleep, as were the others. He assumed everyone had returned in the night.

He pulled on his coat and stepped away, his boots crunching softly over damp earth as he made his way toward the tavern.

The tavern smelled of stale whiskey, pipe smoke, and bodies that had settled in too long. Elias stepped inside, his posture straight, his pace deliberate. The air was thicker than it had been the night before, heavy with the remnants of indulgence and revelry.

He approached the bar with quiet authority, his gaze sweeping once over the dim room. A few men still lingered, some barely stirring from their slumped positions against the tables.

The bartender glanced up, nodding in greeting.

"Coffee," Elias said, his voice even.

A steaming mug was placed before him, the aroma sharp and bitter. He took a slow sip, letting the warmth settle in his chest.

And then—movement.

At first, he barely noticed, but the shift of shadows at the top of the stairs drew his eye.

Ezra stumbled from the upstairs hall, blinking against the morning light that filtered through the dirty glass windows. He wasn't properly dressed—his shirt was half-buttoned and misaligned, the sleeves still wrinkled from having been tossed aside the night before. His bare feet padded unevenly against the wooden stairs, and for a moment, he gripped the railing hard, trying not to trip.

Behind him, Eleanor emerged, still smoothing her dress, her hair unkempt in a way that left little room for interpretation.

Elias's grip on the mug tightened.

A quiet, simmering rage stirred beneath his ribs, but he did not move. Not yet.

Ezra reached the last step and ran a hand through his hair, oblivious to his father watching him with smoldering, unspoken fury.

Before Elias could fully react, his attention was drawn to a heavy groan from across the room.

His eyes snapped toward the sound—Lucy Mercer, sprawled across the piano, her body draped over it like a forgotten sack of grain.

And something else.

The fiddler beneath her was pinned to the bench, his arms limp at his sides, his head tilted awkwardly against the keys, as though he had simply accepted his fate.

Lucy stirred slightly, one hand swiping at the air as if trying to bat away the morning.

The barkeep chuckled. Someone at a nearby table muttered, "Damn shame. She was the life of the party."

Elias's jaw clenched. His stomach churned.

This was not his flock. This was depravity. A sickness. A festering rot.

And still—it got worse.

His gaze flicked back toward the far side of the room. Another stir of movement.

A table near the hearth—Gideon, stretching, half-dressed, boots kicked aside.

Eliza beside him, her hair loose, the two of them unmistakably having spent the night in each other's company.

There was no shame in Gideon's expression as he sat up, rubbing the back of his neck. No guilt.

And that was what broke something in Elias.

His heart pounded hard in his chest, his fingers tightening around the mug until the heat of the coffee no longer registered.

His sons. His people. And they had been lost to this place.

He pushed back from the bar—but then he saw it.

His eyes flicked to the bartender.

The thin **red** thread was knotted through his buttonhole, barely noticeable unless one knew what to look for.

Elias's breath hitched—and then he saw it everywhere.

Not just the bartender. The other men sitting at tables, the ones who had stayed late into the night.

The subtle, quiet mark of allegiance.

The Red String Band.

A den of Unionists. Abolitionists. Enemies.

His pulse roared in his ears.

He took a slow step back, his body rigid, his mind racing. The walls felt closer now, the air too thick to breathe.

His fury boiled over.

"Gideon. Ezra." His voice cut through the morning stillness, sharper than a blade.

Both turned.

Ezra, blinking in surprise. Gideon, his expression shuttering.

"We leave. Now."

His voice left no room for argument.

Eleanor hesitated, gripping Ezra's arm. "Elias—"

"Now!" he snapped.

Lucy groaned from the piano, shifting her weight.

"And get that fat woman up."

Gideon and Ezra stiffened but obeyed. Ezra grabbed Lucy under one arm, grunting under her weight as Gideon took the other.

Eliza hurriedly gathered what little they had brought in, her expression unreadable.

Elias did not look at the bartender again.

He did not look at the men in the room.

He only turned, stepping out into the morning light, his entire body coiled with rage.

The camp was still sleeping when they arrived, the fire burned down to embers.

Elias strode to the camp like a storm.

"Up." His voice shattered the quiet.

Nathaniel and Solomon stirred immediately, sitting up in confusion. Virginia blinked awake, startled.

Rebecca sat up as well, her brow furrowing. "Elias—what's—?"

"We leave."

Rebecca rose fully now, stepping toward him. "What happened?"

He did not answer.

"Elias," she pressed. "What did you see?"

Still, he ignored her.

"Break camp," he ordered, his voice tight, controlled. Barely contained.

And as the others scrambled to gather their things, he turned his back on the tavern. On the sin.

They would never speak of it again.

But they would remember.

They would all remember.

Elias glared at Rebecca,

"We head westward, away from these settlements, but we must cross the Ohio first. I trust you have procured enough supplies for several days."

Rebecca stilled. His words weren't a question. They were a warning.

Her fingers tightened in the folds of her cloak, but she only nodded. "We have enough."

Elias didn't respond, only mounted his horse, his body tense with unrelenting anger.

The sky hung low over the river, a heavy gray pressing down against the slow-moving current. The wind carried the damp scent of earth and woodsmoke, mixing with the sweat of those who stood waiting at the river's edge.

Elias had forced them to march hard after the tavern, his jaw clenched, his eyes dark and distant. He spoke little, except to command their steps forward. No one dared question the urgency in his voice.

They finally approached The Ohio River, they stood at the crossing—a ferry landing at Marietta, Ohio, where the wide expanse of the river stretched before them like a barrier between past and future.

A handful of travelers had already gathered, waiting for the flat-bottomed ferry that rocked against the current. The ferryman—a broad, weathered man with a thick beard—stood at the dock, eyeing the newcomers with a mix of suspicion and calculation.

"Westbound?" the ferryman asked, his voice rough as river stones.

Elias gave a tight nod, keeping his voice measured. "Yes."

The ferryman's eyes flickered toward the group—toward Hiram, toward Gideon, toward Lucy's disheveled state. Then, his gaze settled on Solomon, standing at Elias's side, stiff-backed and alert.

"Two silver pieces per person. Extra for the horses."

Money was not an issue for the Whitmore or the Mercer families. Elias stepped forward, drawing out a small velvet pouch from his coat.

He dropped the required sum into the ferryman's hand.

The ferryman weighed the coins in his palm, then spit into the water before nodding toward the boat. "Load up."

* * *

The river Styx

The ferry was large enough for the group but crowded once the horses were led aboard. The deck creaked beneath the shifting weight, and as the ferryman pushed away from the dock, the boat lurched into the current.

The river was wide, deep, and slow-moving, but its surface shimmered with unseen depth. A thick silence hung over the crossing, broken only by the rhythmic push of the long oar guiding them forward.

And then, a voice rose from the far end of the boat.

A gaunt man stood near the stern, wrapped in a tattered coat, his boots worn from long travel. He clutched a leather-bound book to his chest—not a Bible, but something else, something unfamiliar. His face was sharp, his eyes wide with fervor. His voice carried over the hush of the river, neither loud nor soft, but eerily certain.

"The Destroyer rideth upon the face of these waters."

Elias stiffened.

Gideon turned slightly, glancing at Ezra, who arched a brow.

Rebecca, however, did not turn. She kept her gaze forward, her fingers tightening around the folds of her cloak.

The ferryman said nothing, only watching the water with a steady, practiced eye.

The man's voice dropped lower, almost to a whisper.

"It is not God who watches these waters."

Something in the way he said it sent an unnatural chill through the air. Even Lucy, groggy and disheveled, shifted in her seat, rubbing her arms.

The Mormon preacher turned then, his gaze locking onto Elias. A flicker of something crossed his face—not recognition, but something deeper. Understanding.

"Ye lead them west," the man said, his voice reverent, almost hushed. "And yet ye do not see. Ye do not see what is coming for them."

He took a slow step forward, his fingers tightening around the book with gold embossing on the front at his chest. "I have seen the land where the rivers do not run. I have seen the valley where shadows walk at midday."

The ferry rocked slightly beneath them.

Elias's jaw tightened, but he did not respond.

The preacher's lips parted as if to say more, but then, as suddenly as it had come, the moment passed. His gaze drifted beyond Elias, past him, toward the unseen road ahead.

"Go on then," he murmured. "It is already waiting for you."

He turned away.

Hiram exhaled, slow and steady. The words had rattled him more than he liked to admit, but he wasn't thinking about Elias.

His green eyes flicked toward the ferryman, then toward the other passengers—the way they shifted, the way one man's fingers brushed against his collar, where a red string might have been.

He should have been worried about Elias's reaction. He should have been wondering if crossing into Union territory meant the preacher's warning had some truth to it.

But he wasn't.

Instead, his thoughts turned to Rebecca.

She had said nothing to him this morning. She hadn't looked at him once.

What was she thinking?

She knew now. Last night, he had told her. He had spoken the truth in a hushed moment beneath the trees, admitting what he had hidden since the beginning.

"I was one of them," he had said. "I am, still. A Red String. A member of the Heroes of America."

And she had listened. She had not gasped, nor recoiled, nor whispered his name in horror. She had simply met his gaze, her dark eyes unreadable.

Now, as they drifted toward the opposite shore, he could not help but wonder—did she regret knowing?

Rebecca caught the change in his expression. She moved closer, her voice barely a whisper. "What is it?"

Hiram's jaw tensed, but he only shook his head. "Nothing."

The far bank grew closer, the trees lining the shore twisting upward like silent sentinels. The ferryman worked the oar with slow, practiced movements, but his eyes never left the group.

When the ferry scraped against the opposite dock, he stepped forward, holding out a hand to steady the horses as they were led off first.

Elias disembarked without a word, his boots striking solid ground with purpose. He did not look back to see if the others followed.

Rebecca exhaled, guiding her own steps forward. But as she passed the ferryman, his voice, low and deliberate, reached her ear.

"Not all men in these parts serve the same master," he murmured.

She stiffened.

Before she could respond, the ferryman had already turned back to his boat.

The group moved inland, the weight of the river behind them—but the knowledge that they had been seen, marked, traveled with them.

Elias had reason to fear.

8

CHAPTER 8 – THE HOOPIE
Crossing into the unknown

They pushed westward, leaving the last traces of the river behind. The air carried the damp breath of the Ohio, but the water was now only memory, swallowed by towering ridges that rose and fell like sleeping beasts.

The land grew denser, tangled in thick woods, the soil rich with centuries of decay. Each step deeper into Unionist territory marked a break from the world Elias once ruled—and a slow drift toward something unnamed.

They passed through what some called the Old Works—earthen mounds and burial sites of long-dead peoples, rising in quiet defiance of time. Some whispered of giants buried beneath them. Others said they were the graves of gods.

The trees stood taller here. Their roots curled deep into the land, as if they remembered what had been forgotten. The air felt heavy, haunted. Even the Gideon faction, normally drawn to quiet, felt the press of unseen things. History whispered in the rustle of leaves. This was not their land—and it knew.

They had crossed the river.

But they had not escaped the feeling of being watched.

They rode together, but apart.

Gideon, Ezra, Eliza, Eleanor, and Lucy moved in rough formation through the woods, the weight of the night before still thick between them.

Lucy felt no guilt.

If anything—freedom.

As the horses moved, she stretched in the saddle and sighed. "Strange, isn't it?" she said, glancing toward Gideon and Eliza. "We go to bed as people, and wake up fugitives."

Gideon's jaw set. He didn't reply.

Eliza held her reins too tightly and stared straight ahead.

Ezra, however, chuckled. "And here I thought you just woke up with a headache."

"Oh, I did," Lucy smiled, rubbing her temple. "But also with clarity. And a newfound hatred for that sanctimonious bastard leading us."

Eleanor shook her head, smiling despite herself. She nudged her horse closer to Ezra's, their bodies leaning toward one another—intimacy without effort.

Eliza remained silent.

Gideon rode beside her, unspeaking, unwilling to meet her eyes.

It was easier that way.

The trail narrowed beneath darkening trees. The light thinned. The earth grew damp.

Solomon rode beside Elias, upright in the saddle, waiting for his father to speak.

Elias did not.

He had not spoken since the tavern. Not to Solomon. Not to anyone.

Finally, Solomon asked, "What happened back there?"

No answer.

Only a slow exhale through Elias's nose.

It was the first time Solomon felt him slipping.

At the rear, Hiram watched everything.

He noticed Elias's twitching fingers—always near the pistol.

He noted the silence. The hardening edge in the man's movements.

The Red Strings. The tavern. The Union. They had rattled him.

Hiram had seen fear take shape before.

Some men turned cautious. Others turned violent.

He was beginning to understand what kind Elias might be.

By nightfall, the sky cracked open and spilled rain.

Thick droplets tapped against leather and leaves. Elias raised a hand.

"We camp here."

Relief swept the group—brief, heavy.

"No fire," he added. "No talking. Camp. Sleep. We move at first light."

There was no warmth in the command.

Solomon furrowed his brow. Even he was unsure.

Rebecca shifted in her saddle.

"Elias—" she began.

"Go to sleep, Rebecca," he said. "And stay away from that hoopie."

He didn't look at her.

She obeyed. But for the first time in years, she was afraid of him.

The camp moved under rain and silence.

Hiram lay still, listening to the trees weep.

Gideon sat beside his horse, staring into the dark.

Ezra and Eleanor whispered softly, ignoring the orders.

Lucy watched the sky, soaked, furious.

And Rebecca—Rebecca lay beside a man she no longer trusted.

Elias closed his eyes.

But he did not sleep.

He was planning.

By morning, fog had swallowed the trail.

The Knobs rose and fell around them—rugged hills, sharp limestone, trees crowding in from every side.

Mud clung to everything. Horses slipped. Packs dragged. The rain did not stop.

They crossed into Indiana without joy, only dread.

No one spoke unless required.

Not because of obedience.

But because of fear.

That night, they made camp on a limestone shelf above the valley. The rain slowed but did not stop.

Elias built the fire high. Its flames flickered against the rock like ghosts.

The group gathered slowly. Warily.

Elias stood beside the fire and let the silence stretch.

Then he spoke.

"There is a traitor among us."

The words cracked like a rifle.

He drew his LeMat revolver—ivory-handled, Confederate-made, unmistakable.

And he pointed it at Hiram.

"Stand."

Hiram did.

Rebecca rose, but Elias barked, "Stay where you are."

She froze.

Elias gestured to Solomon and Nathaniel. "Bind him."

Solomon obeyed without hesitation. Nathaniel followed.

They tied Hiram to a thick tree, rope at his wrists and throat.

"A warning," Elias said. "A reckoning."

He looked around the circle of faces.

"You will vote."

He drew a box from his saddlebag.

"One white stone for innocence. One black for guilt. One black—and he is guilty."

One by one, they stepped forward.

Solomon did not cast black.

He ensured no one else did either.

The vote was counted.

All white.

Elias's jaw clenched.

"One of you is a liar."

He gripped the pistol tighter.

Solomon stepped forward.

"Father. Listen to me."

Elias stared.

"The people are afraid. But fear can be useful."

"They are not ready to break."

"They can still be shaped."

Silence.

Then Solomon gave the final blow:

"Declare him guilty. Keep him bound. But deliver him to the Sons of Liberty. Use him."

Elias inhaled slowly.

Then nodded.

Solomon turned to the others.

"There are others who must be judged."

"Tomorrow, we hold another trial."

Ezra stood at the edge of the circle, a little removed, his face bathed in the glow of the fire. Some had settled into prayer—Solomon's voice rising like smoke, measured and smooth.

Gideon sat beside the hearth, silent, eyes sharp.

Ezra watched his older brother for a moment—watched the way his hands moved slightly, as if bracing for something he couldn't name. Then his gaze drifted to Solomon.

He was good at this.

Now Solomon's voice carried the gravity of conviction. Ezra had heard his father speak this way. Now Solomon did it better.

He looked down at his hands, flexed them once, then again. They were shaking, just faintly. From cold, maybe. Or something else.

Behind him, Eliza stirred. Her presence had become a strange comfort—one he hadn't asked for, but hadn't pushed away.

Ezra closed his eyes. Just for a moment.

The night ended heavy and unbroken.

And the ninth day closed in silence.

9

CHAPTER 9 – THE BREAKING POINT
"And the price of revelation was always exile."
— *Collected Sayings of the Prophet Elias, Lost Journals*

The camp still held the shape of judgment.

Smoke swelled upward in faint spirals from the last of the coals, dissolving into the cool breath of morning. Dew clung to the grass and the folds of blankets, but no one stirred to shake it free. Not even the wind dared to move.

Hiram sat slumped against the tree where they had left him—tethered, not broken. His eyes were closed, but he was not asleep.

Elias stood alone at the edge of the clearing, hands clasped behind his back. The fog reached for him in pale fingers. His gaze was fixed on something beyond the trees—something none of the others could see.

Solomon emerged from the mist with a slow, deliberate gait. His boots made no sound on the wet earth.

"It's time, Father."

Elias didn't turn. Didn't blink. The fog moved around them both, thick and unmoving.

At last, his voice came low and unshaken. "We hold the second trial tonight."

Behind them, others stirred—but no one spoke. A breath passed through the camp like a warning.

* * *

The hills had grown cruel with each step westward, and the path now climbed without mercy.

Ridges rose like broken ribs from the forest floor, the land folding in on itself. Every incline scraped at bone and breath. The Knobs of Eastern Indiana were no longer a place—they were a punishment.

No one spoke of the trial. But it followed them, coiled beneath their silence.

Gideon felt it in the way Solomon watched him now—not with suspicion, but with strategy. Ezra sensed it in the slack of Eleanor's grip on his arm. Lucy felt it in her spine, in the way her horse shivered despite the spring air.

The rain had passed, but the air remained thick. A kind of pressure settled between their ribs.

Rebecca rode quietly behind Elias. Her presence had once been a mirror to his—now it was a shadow. She did not speak. She did not reach for him.

Hiram, bound and trailing, was not offered food. He did not ask for it.

Solomon scanned the line as they crested another ridge. The ground here was raw limestone, cracked in places like the surface of an old tooth. Ahead lay a clearing hemmed in by jagged stone spires—pale, angular, ancient. A natural amphitheater.

This was the place.

The fire reached skyward in sudden, angry tongues as the evening approached.

Its heat stretched into the clearing like breath into a cold lung, casting flickering shadows across the waiting crowd. The slabs of limestone behind Elias made him seem larger, sharper. His coat clung damply to his frame, as though even fabric now obeyed his will.

"Last night," he said, "we found one traitor among us."

His tone was calm, but the sharpness in his gaze sliced cleanly.

"Tonight, we will find the rest."

Gideon did not flinch. Ezra stood beside him; his fists clenched tight enough to shake. Lucy's jaw was set.

Elias raised his arms.

"Let those with faith kneel. Let the Lord reveal the forsaken through our prayers."

Nathaniel, Virginia and Hannah quickly kneeled.

Gideon straightened. Ezra mirrored him. Lucy folded her arms, defiant.

Solomon stepped forward from the firelight, voice steady. "Come forward."

Gideon did not.

"You've turned your back," Elias said. "You've lost the path."

"Or maybe I see it more clearly than you," Gideon answered.

Ezra stepped closer to him. Eleanor followed without hesitation. Eliza wavered, then crossed the line.

Lucy stepped forward last, her voice shaking as she turned to Elias. "You're a real son of a bitch."

Gasps stilled the air.

Lucy continued her confrontational tone,

"Abraham died, and you didn't even turn back."

Virginia and Hannah remained kneeling, their hands clasped tightly, their lips moving in silent prayer.

Rebecca moved, shawl slipping from her shoulder. "Elias—"

"Silence!"

His voice was iron. His stare, fixed.

"You have led others astray," he said, staring directly at Gideon. "But unlike Hiram, I offer no trial. I already know the truth."

A hush fell as his hand drifted to the polished grip of the LeMat.

"You are exiled. You will not return."

Lucy's mouth formed a sarcasm. "That's it? We're free?"

Elias's eyes narrowed. "You are forsaken."

He stepped forward into the firelight.

"You are without name. Without shelter. Without faith. The Lord will judge you, and the mark of your failure will cling to your blood."

The wind shifted. Sparks leapt upward into the trees.

His voice dropped into ritual.

"Vos, qui viam veritatis reliquistis… signum feretis in carne… et in sanguine."

The wind shifted. The fire flinched.

Above, a streak of fire tore across the sky—a lone meteor, burning against the night, leaving a deep silver scar.

Elias opened his eyes.

"Your children and your children's children must never mingle with the elect," he declared, his voice rising. "You are cursed. And the sign of that curse shall live in your skin—making you abhorrent to the sons and daughters of the chosen."

He stepped forward, the flames casting his shadow long and flickering across the stones.

"Let it be known—your bloodline is defiled," he continued. "Your skin shall carry the mark of your rebellion, and your descendants shall be loathsome in the eyes of the chosen. They shall not mingle. They shall not marry. They shall wander."

The words hung like smoke, thick and choking.

Rebecca's breath caught in her throat.

Ezra stared in disbelief. "You speak madness."

Gideon moved toward the edge of the clearing, not bothering to look back. "I ain't afraid of your riddles."

Lucy took Eliza's hand. Ezra reached for Eleanor's.

Solomon's voice was final. "You are cursed. You are no longer among us."

The embers burned low. The clearing had emptied of its warmth.

Rebecca moved like a woman dreaming—silent, disbelieving. Her hands worked quickly, almost on instinct. She gathered bread, dried meat, lavender wrapped in linen. A flask of water. Her fingers moved without her heart.

She set the bundle beside her bedroll and went in search of balm, of salt, of hope.

Solomon waited until she stepped away.

He moved quickly.

From a pouch at his side, he withdrew a fine, gray powder. Spores. Almost sweet in scent. He dusted the bread. Let it sink into the water flask. Then he stepped back into the dark, silent.

If his father cursed them, he would make the curse real.

Rebecca returned unaware. She gathered the bread, the flask, the herbs.

At the horse, she fastened the pack with trembling fingers. Her son's survival stitched into every knot.

She packed the bundles with care, checking the clasp, the knots, the rations. Whispering blessings into each fold.

When she finished, Gideon approached. His hands covered hers, strong and steady. His face, chiseled and broad, carried the echoes of her own features—her high cheekbones, the quiet strength in the line of his jaw. His hazel eyes, sharp and steady, mirrored hers, a shared hue that bound them beneath the pale dawn.

"Stay close to each other," she whispered, her voice thick, the words sticking in her throat like wet cotton. "And keep warm. You know how the night steals the heat."

Her fingers wrapped into the fabric of Gideon's coat, lingering there for just a moment too long—like she could hold him there if she just held on tight enough. But she had to let go.

Gideon held her gaze, the warmth of his hazel eyes meeting the deep well of hers. "We'll be a'right, Mother. I promise."

She nodded. Her eyes filled with tears. Her heart broken. Her body remained rooted, her feet unwilling to carry her back to the fire where Elias stood with his cold, hollow stare. She felt his gaze on her, a weight pressing into the tender parts of her heart.

Ezra stepped forward, his lean frame shivering beneath his threadbare coat. He offered her a small, hesitant smile, the kind he used to give her as a boy when he thought a simple gesture could mend a broken world. Rebecca cupped his face, her thumbs brushing the faint shadow beneath his eyes. "My gentle boy," she murmured, pulling him into her arms. His hair, the same rich hue and thick waves as his mother's, jostled. His breath was warm against her neck, and she held him tight, tighter than she should, until she felt him pull away.

Elias shifted in the distance, a reminder—a shadow that loomed over her. She forced herself to release Ezra, to let him step back, to let the space between them grow.

Lucy approached; her daughters close behind. Eliza clung to Eleanor's arm, their faces pinched with fear, with a grief too large for their young hearts. Rebecca touched their shoulders, a fleeting press of warmth. "You take care of each other," she said, her voice a thin thread of strength. "And of Gideon and Ezra."

Lucy nodded, her lips pressed into a fine, trembling line. "We will."

Rebecca's hands fell to her sides, empty and cold. She wanted to say more, to spill all the words that crowded in her chest, but Elias's presence gnawed at her resolve. Her sons needed strength, not her grief.

"Go," she said, her voice barely more than a breath.

She stood there as they turned away. As the shadows swallowed them. As the wild, unyielding dark became their only guide.

When she finally turned back to the fire, to Elias, she drew heavy wool blanket around her shoulders and bit down hard against the sob that threatened to escape. Her love remained with them, trailing behind like a ghost in the dark. But her body stayed, obedient, at the side of the prophet.

The coals pulsed in silence, blood-red and vein-thin, as Solomon sat apart from the others—his knees drawn close, his palms spread open like a man awaiting judgment. Around him, the world exhaled softly, trees whispering in tongues he dared not name.

Once, he had prayed by firelight and felt the air change—whether spirit or fear, he couldn't say. Now the fire was just fire. Smoke, heat, light. And still he spoke as if it burned with truth.

If you say a lie enough times, does the soul forget it's lying? Or does it rot beneath the words, quietly, slowly, like an apple left too long in the sun—golden on the outside, black at the core?

His fingers twitched. He thought of Nathaniel's face. Of his mother's silence. Of the night his father first placed the orrery in his hands and called him chosen.

"I am Paul," he whispered again, but this time the words fell hollow in his mouth.

10

CHAPTER 10 – THE CURSED
The Exiles in the Wilderness

The night split them in two—those who remained in the firelight and those who vanished into the dark.

The wind cut across the open land, scraping low over roots and stone. The sky stretched wide above the exiles, cold and godless, swallowing the last heat of the place they'd left behind.

Gideon walked at the front, his breath a steady mist in the frigid air. With every step, they pushed deeper into the unknown. The hills of the Knobs loomed in the near distance, crouched like sleeping giants.

They carried little. A single horse. A rationed pack. A bundle of supplies Rebecca had prepared in secret.

A loose stone turned underfoot. Eliza stumbled. Her knee hit the ground, but she made no sound. Eleanor and Lucy were there, catching her, steadying her without a word.

Ezra lingered behind them, watching Gideon.

"We should go back," Eliza whispered, voice rough with cold and fear. "We were better off in Front Royal."

Gideon turned. His face was shadowed, unreadable. "There's no goin' back."

He paused.

"We left the land. We left the slaves. The valley's splittin'. Union's already watchin' every ridge. You think they'll take us in?"

Lightning crawled across the sky behind them. The wind shifted, sharp with the scent of the storm.

Ezra pulled the water flask from the pack and drank first. Eliza's eyes lingered on Gideon—his quiet strength, the way he wrapped his coat around his brother's shoulders, the gentleness he hid behind his silence.

Solomon had strength too, but it was cold, precise. Gideon's was something else. Gideon's strength offered refuge.

* * *

Rebecca did not sleep.

She sat by the fire, arms wrapped around her knees, staring at the path where her two eldest sons had disappeared.

Elias sat beside her, an aging prophet lost in his world of magic. The embers pulsed, their glow unable to dispel the darkness gathering at the edges of the camp.

She had made her choice. And yet, as Elias lifted his hands to the sky, she felt the weight of it pressing against her ribs, as if something unseen wrapped tight around her chest, pulling her back toward the fire she could not sit beside.

Across the camp, Solomon stood tall, his voice calm as he addressed the daughters of Abraham and his youngest brother, Nathaniel. The flames flickered over his face, lending his expression an almost ethereal quality.

"Those what ain't meant for the Kingdom have gone," he declared, his voice low, certain. "We press on."

At the edge of the firelight, Hiram Sloan remained bound and tethered, the flames licking at his silhouette. His wrists sore and the rope around his neck slowly cutting sores into his skin, but his smirk—small, knowing—betrayed the truth between them.

"Not what you expected, is it?" His voice was low, amused.

Rebecca said nothing. Only tears filling her eyes. But she did not look away.

* * *

Rain found them before dawn.

Gideon led the group beneath a stand of trees as the storm opened its jaws. Branches shook. The air turned black with wind.

Then came the sores.

They started as small black spots beneath the nails. Ezra was the first to weaken. He tried to hide it, but his breath grew short, and his limbs unsteady.

Lucy moved fast. She built a fire under cover, coaxed heat from wet wood. Gideon wrapped Ezra in his coat and held him upright, murmuring low reassurances.

Eliza watched from the shadows.

This was the curse, she thought. But not the one Elias believed in.

This one had hands. It held them in the dark.

* * *

Solomon led them through a narrow valley, the cliffs pressing in from both sides. The air was still. Too still.

A single, massive tree stood in the center of the path, its gnarled roots clawing into the earth. Its branches stretched wide, and perched among them were crows—hundreds of them.

Silent. Unmoving.

Rebecca's fingers straightened at her sides. The presence of the crows, the unnatural silence—it set something uneasy in her chest.

Then, without warning, the birds took flight.

Wings erupted in a chaotic flurry, blotting out the sky. Hannah gasped. The others shifted.

Rebecca turned to Elias.

"What does it mean?" she whispered.

Elias did not move for a long moment. Then, finally, he spoke.

"It means we are close."

But Rebecca wasn't sure if she believed him anymore.

* * *

The morning sun cast a gentle warmth over Gideon and his exiles, filtering through the thick canopy of leaves.

The first signs came slowly.

A dark shadow under the fingernails.

A bruise that would not fade.

The ache beneath the skin, deeper than bone.

Ezra rubbed at his arm, his breath sharp.

"It's just the cold," he muttered.

But they all saw it.

The curse had begun.

* * *

At a certain distance away, beneath the restless omen of crows in flight, Elias and his chosen pressed deeper into the unknown.

Rebecca hesitated.

Behind her, the dwindling line of loyalists - her youngest son Nathanial and Lucy's daughters, Virginia and Hannah - wound back into the woods, faces stern, eyes rimmed with dust and fear.

They moved through the undergrowth like a dark thread weaving through green.

Ahead, Elias moved with the weariness of an old king, his back beginning to hunch, his white beard catching the last light of day.

Rebecca hesitated again.

And at the horizon, through the parting trees, she saw it.

A faint ember against the dark.

Another fire burned.

The Gideonites' camp.

Her breath caught.

Two fates unfolding—one lost, one blindly following.

And between them, the forest breathed, ancient and indifferent.

11

C HAPTER 11 – THE RITUAL STONE
The valley keeps what it is given.

The Gideonites moved in silence, ghosts on the edge of dawn.

Before them, bathed in the hush of first light, lay The White River.

It curled like a silver serpent through the basin, its glassy surface rippling in places where the current quickened. The river was wide—wider than Gideon had imagined. The mist hovered over the water's edge, rising in soft, undulating waves.

Beyond the river, the land stretched in a tapestry of shadowed trees and pale fields, as if caught between waking and dreaming.

And there, where the river broke into Hindostan Falls, the water churned itself into white foam, cascading over a broad shelf of limestone, pouring into the depths below like distant thunder. The falls weren't high—only a few feet—but they stretched wide, their breadth giving the illusion of something far grander.

Gideon's breath came slow, steady, measured.

He had spent nights wondering what lay ahead, what wilderness they would be forced to carve a life from.

But this—this was something different.

"God above," Eliza exhaled beside him, her voice barely a whisper.

Lucy adjusted the shawl around her shoulders, her gaze sweeping over the river's edge.

"It's beautiful."

But there was something fragile in her voice—like she didn't trust the words.

Eleanor stepped forward, the weight of exhaustion momentarily forgotten.

Ezra, weak from sickness, wiped the damp from his forehead, staring at the horizon.

"Doesn't feel real," he murmured.

Gideon remained silent.

Because beneath the beauty, beneath the shimmering light on the river's surface and the soft whisper of water over stone, there was something else.

Something still.

Something waiting.

Nestled along the riverbank stood the remains of a settlement.

Houses. A church with a tilted steeple. A doctor's office with its sign half-sunk into the earth. The structures hunched together like abandoned husks, their wood darkened with time. A frayed cloth from a fence post, tattered by wind and rain.

Ezra exhaled, his voice barely above a whisper.

"What is this place?"

Eleanor turned to Gideon.

"Where are we?"

"How long have we been traveling from home?"

Gideon's voice was quiet, uncertain.

"Maybe two weeks."

The group hesitated.

Gideon knelt, brushing his fingers over the damp earth.

Footprints.

Many of them.

Some deep. Hurried.

All leading away.

None returning.

Lucy shuddered beside Eliza, her grip tightening on her sister's arm.

"This place is cursed," she breathed.

Gideon's eyes lingered on the footprints.

He wasn't sure she was wrong.

* * *

Far beyond the tree line, Elias Whitmore pressed forward, leading the group toward something ancient—something waiting.

The air thickened the deeper they walked. The sound of their footsteps softened, swallowed by the vast stillness pressing in from all sides.

Then, it appeared.

A monolith of stone, towering and ancient, stood sentinel over the valley.

Wind and time had carved their mark, yet the symbols remained—spirals and sigils, older than written word.

The wind moved through the pass in slow, uneven gusts, carrying something more than air.

A whispering.

Not words, but shapes of sound—echoes of something waiting to be heard.

Rebecca hovered at the threshold, breath shallow.

The weight of something unseen pressed against her ribs.

She could not read the symbols.

But she felt them watching.

Looking back.

Elias stepped forward, his voice smooth, unwavering.

"This is it. The passage to Empyrean."

The Chosen shifted.

Some exchanged glances, their unease rising.

Hiram Sloane tethered and bound to the horse behind Elias.

His thoughts turned darkly:

"He's convincing, isn't he?"

The wind shifted.

A deep hum vibrated through the air—so subtle, it could have been imagined.

Solomon hesitated.

Rebecca saw it.

And that, more than anything, unsettled her.

* * *

Inside the abandoned church, dust hung thick in the air.

The wooden door groaned as Gideon pushed it open, revealing a sparse interior—empty pews, a broken lantern, and a podium.

And on it, a book.

A leather-bound journal lay closed, its cover embossed with a name:

Shelmire.

Gideon's fingers brushed over ink stains that bled like bruises into the brittle pages.

The handwriting trembled.

A leader. A promise.

And then—the disappearance.

His eyes moved to the final entry.

The ink was smudged, hurried.

"We followed the book to this place.

We thought it would lead us to the kingdom foretold—the true kingdom.

We were wrong.

Some of us entered the valley. Some of us did not.

No one came back.

A sickness.

A curse.

The manuscript is lost or stolen.

If it is ever found again—it must not be trusted.

"The valley is not land. It keeps what it is given. It is alive."

Gideon's breath turned sharp.

His pulse drummed a steady, hollow rhythm.

His fingers flipped back through the journal, skimming the earlier entries.

No mention of Empyrean.

No name for the valley.

But the manuscript?

Geheimnisbücher Moses.

The Book of Abramelin.

The Lost Books of Moses.

The same symbols. The same promises. The same prophecy of a divine race.

But the Shelmire Journal told a different truth.

The prophecy did not belong to Elias.

It had belonged to someone before him.

And it had led them all here.

"No."

Ezra shifted beside him.

"What does it say?"

Gideon turned, voice breaking under the weight of it.

"They're going to die."

Lucy moved closer, her expression tightening.

"What do you mean?"

Gideon exhaled sharply, closing the book.

"There is no kingdom. There never was."

His voice cracked against the silence.

"It takes them. The valley—it takes them, Lucy. Just like it took the ones before."

The truth unraveled inside him, thread by thread, until he could see the whole terrible design.

Gideon stood, the journal clutched to his chest.

As if holding it could anchor him.

As if it could keep him from being swept away by the flood of realization.

He moved toward the doorway, the light of the dying sun spilling over him, casting long shadows across the dusty floor.

"Gideon?" Lucy's voice was small, a thin thread pulled taut.

He turned, his eyes wide, urgency crackling beneath his skin.

"I need to leave. Now."

Lucy stepped forward, her voice trembling.

"What are you going to do?"

Gideon exhaled sharply, closing the book.

"I have to warn them. I have to warn my mother."

His gaze swept over the others—Ezra, Eliza, Eleanor.

Ezra was pale. His hands shook where they gripped the pew.

Eliza and Eleanor stood close together, fingers interlaced.

They looked young in the dim light.

Too young.

"Gideon, wait."

He couldn't take them with him.

Whatever lay beyond the valley—whatever waited between him and Rebecca—he would not risk them.

Gideon turned to Lucy.

Her expression was steady. A quiet strength beneath the surface.

But he saw it—the flicker of fear in her eyes.

She understood.

"Lucy." His voice was low but firm.

"Keep them here. Keep them safe."

She nodded, her jaw set.

The Southern gentleness of her demeanor hardened into resolve.

"I will."

Gideon's gaze swept over them once more, committing each face to memory.

The curl of Ezra's hair.

The soft curve of Eliza's hand against her sister's.

The way Eleanor's lips moved in a silent prayer.

He needed them to be here when he returned.

He needed to believe he would return.

"I will come back," he said.

Then he was gone, the wooden door groaning shut behind him.

The others stood bathed in the pale light of the dying day.

* * *

Elias stood before the monolith; his silhouette carved from shadow.

The slab loomed, cold and inert, framed by jagged stone like a half-opened maw.

Beyond it, the world was nothing but darkness—an open mouth waiting to swallow the light.

The air held a stillness that felt unnatural, the silence so deep it pressed against the skin.

Elias raised his arms.

The mist swirled around him, settling like restless spirits.

His voice broke the quiet, the words heavy and wet, as if dragged up from the earth itself.

"Zirdo, Uo Uuoi, A L Zodameta!"

The language slithered through the air.

Not English. Not Hebrew. Not Latin.

Something older.

Something neither holy nor damned—but something in between.

Each syllable seemed to bruise the silence, leaving trails of sound that hung and shimmered like heat.

The gathered Loyalists flinched, their breath coming in tight, sharp gasps.

The monolith remained lifeless.

Cold stone.

No light.

Elias's lips pulled back, baring teeth in something not quite a smile.

He beckoned.

"Rebecca."

A summons.

Not a request.

She stepped forward, her feet heavy against the ground.

Her eyes never left the archway.

The closer she drew, the more the monolith seemed to breathe.

The carvings along its surface began to shift, their edges softening, writhing, as if something beneath the stone had started to wake.

Elias's voice rose again.

This time, deeper.

"Vpaahi, od Zodameta! Zodamran, od Iadnamad!"

A crack of sound.

The monolith shuddered.

A thin seam of golden light split across its stone face.

At first, it was just a thread.

Then, the light erupted—

A deluge of molten gold that flooded the clearing.

The shadows fled.

Drawn into the light's greedy pull.

The Loyalists stumbled back, faces bathed in the glow, their expressions soft and gilded.

Around the circle, gildelumes sprouted from the rock—twisted iron sconces that seemed to bloom from the stone, their glass orbs filling with a slow, liquid glow.

The aureflames within burned, their light shifting like oil on water, casting ripples of gold over the ancient carvings.

Rebecca stood at the threshold, her outline swallowed by the aurelight.

Her breath misted the air, a soft cloud that lingered too long.

She lifted a hand.

The light curled around her fingers.

Warm.

Alive.

She turned.

Her eyes met Hiram's.

His smirk was gone.

His lips a thin line of dread.

Elias's arms lowered, and the aurelight pulsed—

A heartbeat made of molten gold.

His eyes gleamed, alight with reflected fire.

"Tonight, we will be sealed to Empyrean."

The Chosen stood rigid, their faces flickering with aurelight and something else—

Hope.

Fear.

Surrender.

The archway yawned before them.

Dark.

Endless.

"Step through," Elias murmured, his voice threaded with the hum of old magic.

"Enter, and be remade."

A hesitation.

Then she began to step forward.

Her pulse drummed against her ribs.

This was what she had made her purpose, wasn't it?

A calling.

Called to be his helpmate.

She would not only follow him—

She would legitimize him.

She felt something waiting.

She took a half-step forward.

Then—

She stopped.
Hiram's gaze flicked from behind.
A gust of wind carved through the pass.
The ground trembled beneath them.
Beyond the archway, the darkness moved.
Shapes twisted in the shadows—
Tall.
Thin.
Their edges curling like smoke.
A presence pressed against the light,
A vast, hollow thing that watched with
a thousand unseen eyes.

* * *

The fire burned low in the old hearth, its flames flickering against the church's hollowed walls.

Ezra sat closest, his breath shallow. His skin had taken on a strange undertone, something unnatural in the pale glow.

Eliza and Eleanor watched their hands. Beneath their nails, dark spores had begun to spread—thin veins of something growing. Something unwelcome.

Ezra stirred, shifting uncomfortably.

Lucy moved cautiously, her skirts brushing against the dust-covered floor.

"You stay by the fire," she murmured, already making a decision. "I'll return."

She slipped outside, closing the door softly behind her.

The main road stretched before her, a forgotten scar of packed earth and stone.

She looked to the far end of the street.

A sign dangled from a rusted chain, its paint long faded.

The Telegraph Station.

Lucy's eyes flicked to the left.

A doctor's office—its windows dark, its door half-hidden behind the weeds.

I need both, she thought.

Her feet carried her forward, moving swiftly toward the telegraph station first.

She pushed through the door. The wood groaned.

Dust hung thick in the air.

The room was a relic of past urgency—wooden counters, neat rows of brass telegraph keys, glass jars filled with brittle paper slips.

But Lucy's attention went elsewhere.

Tucked behind the counter, lined against the back wall, stood a row of glass jars.

Inside them, suspended in stagnant liquid, were copper and zinc plates.

Thin wires coiled between them.

Telegraph batteries.

Once used to power the line, now dormant—but not beyond revival.

Lucy's breath caught.

Her fingers brushed the glass, feeling the age in them, the weight of years.

Copper and zinc... I can work with this.

She gathered what she needed and moved on.

The doctor's office.

The narrow building leaned with age.

Lucy pushed the door open, stepping into stagnant air.

The remnants of a life once lived lay scattered—glass vials, a leather-bound medical tome open to a page on purgatives.

Her eyes flicked to the silver instruments in a dark velvet case.

They gleamed unnaturally.

Perfect.

She took what she needed.

Silver scissors.

A scalpel.

A pair of fine silver wires.

With these, she could create the electrolysis setup she envisioned.

The process would not be swift.

But desperation had a way of stretching time.

She set up the jars she has taken from the telegraph station and rigged a make shift battery.

The air thickened with the sharp bite of metal.

Copper and zinc sparked to life.

The scent of wet pennies and distant thunder curled through the dark.

Lucy's fingers flexed over the wires.

A faint hiss—

A pop—

And then—

Pale blue arcs of light crackled along the silver wires.

Green light pulsed in thin, twisting threads.

The doctor's office windows shimmered, glowing like foxfire in a dark wood.

The room shifted, caught between past and present—an alchemist's chamber where science and sorcery blurred.

She stood in the center of it all, her face aglow in the unearthly light.

If this works—if the silver solution can halt the infection—then perhaps...

Perhaps the curse of Elias Whitmore might be lifted.

She stepped back into the street, the doctor's satchel slung over her shoulder.

She moved with new purpose, her shadow long against the empty buildings.

The deep green of her gown fluttered in the breeze, trailing behind her like the robes of an old-world apothecary.

The silver choker encircled her neck, its intricate filigree a lacework of moonlight and shadow.

At its center rested a cabochon of dark stone, set within spinning silver tendrils, as if the metal had grown organically around it.

Her black hair, swept back with precision, was crowned by a diadem of silver leaves, their edges sharpened like the petals of a frost-kissed rose.

Together, the pieces transformed her.

She was no longer just Lucy Mercer.

She was a pioneer of science.

A keeper of ancient secrets.

A woman who could sew flesh and weave shadows with the same steady hands.

In the gathering dark, Hindostan seemed to breathe again, a soft intake of breath—

As if the town, too, had been waiting for this moment.

She stepped inside.

The fire had burned low.

Ezra sat near the embers, his breath shallow.

His skin—

Gray.

Lucy knelt beside him.

She reached into the satchel, her fingers closing around the silver.

"You'll drink the silver infusion," she whispered.

Ezra turned his hand over, staring at the darkening veins beneath his skin.

His voice was raw.

"The silver slows it?" he asked.

Lucy nodded.

"But I can feel it," he admitted. "What if... whatever's in there... can't be stopped by the silver?"

Lucy exhaled, steady.

"Then we fight it another way."

* * *

Gideon ran.

The cold air sliced against his skin, burning in his lungs, but he didn't stop.

Ahead, the faint flickering lights of The Chosen danced like specters in the mist.

He had kept his company close enough to follow. But now, as the landscape twisted into unfamiliar ridges and shadowed cliffs, the distance between them felt impossible.

The words from the journal clawed at his thoughts, each syllable a stone sinking in his gut.

The valley is not land.

It keeps what it is given.

It is alive.

The wind shifted. The trees whispered.

He stumbled, catching himself against an outcropping of rock.

Ahead, the cliffs rose—tall, jagged, swallowing the horizon. The world narrowed into this one place, this final threshold.

Gideon stared toward the valley where Elias had led his people.

Where his mother still was.

They were walking into something that would never let them leave.

His pulse hammered.

Rebecca—

Elias—through her—was leading them inside.

Would they ever come back out?

Gideon tore forward.

But the valley was waiting.

And it had been waiting a long time.

12

CHAPTER 12 – THE VALLEY

Some doors do not open. They erase the world behind you.

The aurelight bathed Rebecca's skin, winding over her throat, her hands, her wrists—like something alive. It moved with unnatural purpose, wrapping around her fingers before dissolving into the void. The air thickened, humming with a low, guttural resonance. It did not belong to her. The pulse beneath her skin faltered, caught in something else's rhythm.

The archway stood like a wound in the world, its jagged edges swallowing the liquid light from the gildelumes, devouring everything that passed beyond it. The stone around it was slick with shadow, the gold veins seeping into the cracks, filling them with a strange, honeyed light that dripped and pooled like sap.

Rebecca hovered at the threshold, her breath uneven, each exhale a fragile cloud against the cold. The space beyond the archway was more than dark—it was absence, a perfect, gaping silence that gnawed at the edges of reality. The aurelight curled into the void and vanished, as if consumed by a vast, hollow mouth.

Behind her, the embers of the old world smoldered. The dying light licked at the stones, but even fire seemed small here, reduced to embers in the presence of something that could unmake the world. She could feel the weight of the others behind her—their quiet, stuttering breaths, the shift of feet against stone, the soft rustle of foot steps.

Her fingers dragged against the stone, leaving faint smudges of blood where the rough surface bit into her skin. The gilded light ran over her foot and into the darkness, swallowed whole. She stepped forward.

The aurelight bathed Elias in liquid gold, transforming his clothes into white robes trimmed in gold as he followed Rebecca into the void. His mouth moved, lips shaping words that did not make sound. The ancient language unraveled in the air, its syllables twisting and stretching, threads of meaning that frayed at the edges.

Solomon came next, his eyes half-lidded, his body moving with the slow, dreamlike grace of a man entranced. His foot slid forward, the archway's edge cold and slick beneath him. His pupils were blown wide, black seas that swallowed the gold.

Virginia, Hannah, and Nathaniel were last. The Chosen moved like specters, their feet skimming the ground, aurelight running over their clothes in thin, molten streams. One by one, they vanished into the black. And last of all, the horses followed with Gideon tied to one of them. His breath fogged in the cold, his handsome face barely visible in the flickering light. His expression was drawn, eyes darkened emeralds beneath the shifting light of the aureflames.

The moment Rebecca crossed, the warmth vanished. The world tightened around her, the air pressing against her ribs—thick, suffocating, like unseen hands were closing in. Her breath came short and sharp, each inhalation a struggle against the crushing weight.

The light behind her winked out, and for an instant, there was nothing but weight, silence, and the deep, unfathomable black. Her senses folded in on themselves. The edges of her vision folded inward, a soft, darkening halo. She felt the brush of stone beneath her feet, the cold lick of air against her skin, the shallow drum of her heartbeat echoing back from somewhere impossibly far away.

Then—

A breath.

Not her own.

A shiver of air moved over her skin, bringing with it a scent—wet stone, iron, and something sweet, like crushed flowers. The darkness began to shift, thin strands of light threading through the void, weaving pale patterns across the backs of her eyelids.

Rebecca opened her eyes.

She stepped through, and the world swallowed sound. Her ears rang—sharp, unbearable, then hollow. The pressure of the void lifted, leaving behind only the weight of silence.

There was no ground, no sky, only the suggestion of both. Light slithered through the air like smoke, moving in slow, deliberate spirals, but the light did not cast shadows. Rebecca's body remained untouched by it, as if she had never arrived at all.

She exhaled—watched the breath curl before her, and then fade, absorbed into the emptiness.

The ground beneath her feet was not solid but soft, a stretch of white that rippled with each step, as if she stood upon the surface of a lake made of frost. Her footprints dissolved behind her, erasing any trace of the world she had left behind.

Shapes twisted at the edges of her vision—tall, thin things with limbs that bent too many times, their forms half-glimpsed shadows against the white expanse. Their faces were blank, skin a perfect wash of light and shadow. They moved through the Chosen, slipping between bodies without touch, as if they occupied a plane just beyond reality.

Hiram felt the rope unravel from around his neck. His hands became unbound as he walked through the void. Then his fingers brushed against someone. It was her. Rebecca. Warm. Human. She tightened her grip, his touch a thread of warmth against the cold void. His skin stood out against the landscape—alive, imperfect, a defiance of the monochrome world.

Elias moved ahead, his figure stark against the endless white. His robes, once gilded with aurelight, had dulled to ash, the gold leeched away by Empyrean's hunger for absolutes. His voice rose, the words stretching through the air and unraveling like mist. The shapes around him leaned in, their faceless heads turning, their bodies bending in ways that defied the natural order.

Solomon followed, stepping with measured grace—as if something unseen guided him. He did not stumble. He did not hesitate. His lips parted, tasting the air like a priest inhaling incense.

As he moved, the fabric of his clothes darkened, stiffened, the white draining into something too deep, too absolute—beyond black, beyond shadow.

The ground beneath him did not shift. It did not ripple, as it had for the others. It accepted him.

The Chosen moved as one, their bodies swaying in time with the slow undulation of the light. Their clothes had shifted to white, edged in black, as if Empyrean had stripped them of all color, all individuality. The aurelight that had once pooled at their feet was gone, swallowed by the starkness. Now, only shadows stretched around them, long and thin, bending in unnatural arcs.

Rebecca felt the pull of the place, a soft tug at her bones, a whisper that slipped into the creases of her mind. It pressed against her thoughts, turning them pale and translucent, as if her very identity were being worn thin by the sheer blankness of the world.

She had crossed the threshold.

But she did not know if Empyrean would let her leave.

The ripple of her footfall spread like breath through wet earth.

Rebecca stumbled.

She found her balance against soil that smelled of rain. The sky overhead stretched indigo and endless.

The valley yawned before them, flanked by cliffs that loomed like dark sentinels. A river wound through the center, its waters too still, as if time had pressed a glass pane over the world. Nothing moved. Not a bird, not a breeze. The silence pressed against her, a weight, a hand at her throat.

It was pristine. Untouched.

Elias stood with arms lifted, his silhouette sharp against the pale light. His voice slipped through the quiet, a thread of reverence. *"This is the final place."*

Solomon dropped to his knees. His body struck the earth with a dull, final sound, as if surrendering to gravity. Nathaniel hesitated, the tight line of his shoulders betraying him, but he followed, kneeling in the damp soil beside his brother.

Rebecca's legs gave way, and she knelt too. Her fingers pressed into the nothingness of the ground. The soil felt soft, but beneath it was a hardness that didn't belong—like skin stretched over stone.

Virginia and Hannah remained standing. Their eyes turned back, searching for the archway, for the golden glow of the aurelight, but it was gone. Only a smooth wall of stone remained, indifferent and silent.

Though Hiram was now free, Solomon and Elias ignored him, or forgotten him. But in this strange new world, he was remained a prisoner still.

A hush settled over them. No wind. No birds. Just the weight of expectation, the breathless pause of a story waiting to see if it had an ending.

Hiram exhaled sharply, his voice a cut in the silence. *"Well, isn't this a pretty little cage."*

Solomon turned, his eyes dark, his voice a low hum. *"This is our promised land."*

Rebecca wasn't sure if she believed.

* * *

Gideon tore through the trees, the underbrush clawing at his legs, branches snapping against his skin. The Shelmire journal was clenched in his fist, its leather damp with sweat. His breath came in ragged bursts, his lungs raw and burning, but he pushed harder. His mother was just ahead—she had to be.

"Mother! Stop!"

His voice fractured against the night, the syllables splintering in the cold air. But the forest swallowed the sound, the trees standing mute and indifferent.

Too far.

Too dim.

The clearing yawned before him, empty and still. The fire had burned down to its last embers, thin tendrils of smoke swirling against the dark sky. Shadows pooled around the stones, their edges soft and uncertain, as if the world itself were already forgetting those who had passed through.

His breath hitched.

"No. No, no, no!"

He stumbled forward, his boots skidding against damp earth. His momentum carried him to the edge of the archway—his fingers grazing the cold stone—

And then—

The entrance vanished.

Light flickered once, a brief, golden shiver that painted his outstretched hand in molten gold. And then—nothing. The aurelight died, and with it, the world stilled.

The air hung heavy and motionless. The trees, which had whispered and swayed just moments before, stood as silent as stone. Even his own breath seemed to echo, small and thin, in the void.

"Wait!" he shouted, his voice shattering the silence. It echoed back at him, twisted and hollow, as if the forest itself mocked him.

There was no answer.

Gideon's knees hit the ground. Pain flared, sharp and bright, but he barely felt it. His hands pressed against the stone, the cold seeping into his skin. He pushed, scratched, struck the unyielding surface until his knuckles split, and blood smeared across the rock—dark, wet streaks against pale stone.

"Where did they go?" he whispered, his voice hoarse and small.

He didn't know.

The archway remained—a slab of stone, its carvings dull and lifeless. No door. No path. Just a wall where the world had once opened.

The journal slipped from his fingers, landing with a soft thud in the dirt. Pages fluttered open, revealing ink-stained secrets and brittle, yellowed paper.

A chill wind stirred the edges of the clearing, carrying with it the scent of ash and old earth. The last ember of the fire winked out, and the darkness swallowed everything.

Gideon sat in its jaws, alone, with nothing but the echo of his own voice and the unyielding stone that had swallowed his family whole.

* * *

The valley was too still.

Rebecca felt it the moment they arrived—the weight of something pressing just beyond perception. The air was thick, as though the land itself had inhaled and was waiting, suspended.

Elias Whitmore stood at the heart of it.

His gaze lifted toward the cliffs, his fingers twitching at his sides. Something was wrong.

Rebecca knew him—knew his posture, his mannerisms, the way he held himself like a man who had already seen the end of the story. But now, for the first time, he looked unsure.

Solomon walked beside him, his jaw set, his eyes sharp. "We have arrived, Father."

Elias's lips parted—but no sound came.

A flicker of confusion crossed his face, and he staggered.

The collective inhaled.

Solomon moved quickly, catching him before he collapsed. Rebecca took a step forward, but an unnamed instinct stopped her.

No one else moved.

The hush deepened.

Rebecca's stomach twisted.

Elias's breathing turned shallow. His fingers pushed into the dirt as though trying to hold onto something unseen. A golden hue flushed the whites of his eyes. His lips moved. Solomon bent close.

No one else heard what Elias whispered before he died.

Only Solomon.

And then—he was gone.

No great suffering. No final proclamation. Just silence.

Rebecca's breath shuddered. Her heart pounded. This wasn't how it was supposed to happen.

Not like this.

A single black bird cried in the distance—sharp and sudden, the only movement in the unnatural stillness.

Then, Solomon rose.

He did not wail. He did not shake his father or beg the heavens for an answer.

Instead, he exhaled.

And he was different.

Rebecca saw it. The others saw it.

Solomon turned his head, just slightly, as if listening to something the rest of them could not hear. His expression did not betray grief, nor shock, nor hesitation.

Just understanding.

He looked down at Elias's still body. Then, slowly, he lifted his gaze to the gathered.

And he spoke.

"We do not grieve as those who have no faith."

Solomon's voice was steady. Measured.

Rebecca stiffened.

Somewhere among the gathered, a murmur rippled—hesitation, unease. But the Chosen simply listened.

The fire crackled. Someone sniffled.

And then Solomon smiled.

"Elias has walked his path. Now, we must walk ours."

Rebecca's breath came shallow.

This was too fast.

Too seamless.

Elias had barely fallen cold. And yet, Solomon stood before them, not as a grieving son, but as a man who had always been meant to stand in this place.

A chill crawled up Rebecca's spine.

Solomon's hands remained steady. He did not reach for Elias. He did not kneel.

And he stepped over Elias's body.

A moment stretched—heavy, unnatural.

Then, one by one, heads bowed.

But none defied.

Except Hiram.

Rebecca's stomach twisted.

Solomon had become the prophet.

And Empyrean had already accepted him.

They burned him at the river's edge.

The flames licked the sky, devouring the old prophet as the group stood in eerie silence.

Solomon placed a hand upon the firewood, murmuring words no one else recognized. A ritual of his own making. His fingers brushed the wood with reverence, as if he were not just lighting a fire—but sealing something unseen. The flames licked at his skin, but he did not flinch. A ritual of his own making.

Nathaniel stood close by, wide-eyed, motionless. The youngest son, watching his father burn.

Rebecca reached for him, but he did not react.

He did not cry.

Did not move.

Did not blink.

He only watched, clinging to Solomon.

As the funeral ritual begins, Nathaniel refuses to let go of Solomon's arm, pressing his forehead against it like a child clinging to a parent.

Rebecca watches with unease, but Solomon does not push him away. Instead, he places his hand on the back of Nathaniel's head, fingers threading through his hair.

As Solomon anoints himself as prophet, Nathaniel whispered,

"I will follow you. I will obey."

For a moment, Solomon didn't respond. His fingers lingered in Nathaniel's hair, slow, thoughtful.

Then, he smiled—soft at first, then fuller, as if he had expected nothing else.

"Of course you will."

Rebecca felt something twist in her gut.

Solomon was not just his brother anymore.

He was his father. His guide. His prophet. *or something else.*

And Nathaniel belonged to him now.

Night pulled the sky closed over them. The fire's glow clawed at the darkness, stretching shadows long and thin over the gathered faithful—if they could still be called that. The pale earth gleamed in places where the firelight kissed it, but beyond the circle, the blackness of Empyrean pressed in, vast and unbroken.

A fire burned at the center, stretching long shadows over the gathered faithful—if they could still be called that.

Solomon stood before them, his presence unwavering, his voice calm.

"We have arrived. This land is sacred. We will build our home here. And we will call this place, Empyrean."

Then he turned to them, eyes searching each face in turn.

Rebecca, still wrapped in the quiet weight of Elias's death.

Nathaniel, vacant, staring at the fire but seeing something else entirely.

Virginia, still and cool beneath the weight of all that had happened since leaving her home.

Hannah, breathing too softly, too carefully, like prey waiting to be noticed.

Solomon exhaled slowly, then stretched out his hands. His voice lowered—not gentle, but absolute.

"Virginia, Hannah, Nathaniel and," looking toward Rebecca with some hesitation "my mother—" his voice breathed into the night, his fingers outstretched like a shepherd welcoming his flock. "We are The Chosen."

His words lingered in the silence. They did not speak them back.

Hiram only observed.

But still, Solomon smiled.

"The Chosen are not meant to be the last."

A flicker of something passed through Rebecca's chest—too quiet to name, too familiar to ignore.

Solomon lifted his chin. The firelight flickered against his skin, the glow catching in his eyes like embers waiting to ignite.

"We will build Empyrean," he said. "And we will forge the divine race." The words hung in the air, heavy and absolute. No one spoke. Not because they agreed—

But because they did not yet know how to refuse.

No one responded.

Hannah shivered.

Virginia exhaled, steady and slow.

Nathaniel did not move.

Rebecca swallowed hard, and turned her eyes toward the fire.

They were too tired to question it. Too cold, too lost, too afraid.

One by one, they lay down by the fire.

Nathaniel was the last to move, curling onto his side, his face half-hidden in the glow.

Solomon stood a moment longer, watching them—watching his mother—as if measuring something unseen.

Then, at last, he lay beside them. The fire burned low, its embers sinking into the earth, its warmth barely reaching the edges of the group. The valley watched them, silent and vast, stretching its emptiness over them like a shroud.

13

CHAPTER 13 – THE WHISPERING DARK
Some silences listen back.

Rebecca Whitmore woke to a silence so deep it felt alive.

Not the hush of an early morning, where wind rustled through leaves and birds filled the dawn with song—no. This was a stillness that did not belong.

No rustling leaves. No chirping insects. Not even the faint shift of breath from the others sleeping around her.

The air pressed against her ears, thick and absolute, as if the valley itself were holding its breath.

She sat up, scanning the valley in the pale light of dawn. The land stretched out before them, untouched, pristine. Too untouched. The grass lay undisturbed, unbent by the wind. The trees did not sway. Not a branch bent. They stood like sentinels—untouched, as if wind had never passed through this valley at all.

Her eyes drifted to the stream—a perfect ribbon of water cutting through the valley. It shimmered in the early light, so clear it looked frozen.

Rebecca moved to the edge, crouching beside it. Slowly, she dipped her fingers into the water.

Cold. Crisp. But wrong.

She pulled her hand back, staring. No silt disturbed. No ripples spread. The water remained perfectly still, as if her touch had never been there at all.

A shadow flickered in the reflection.

She looked up.

Solomon was watching her.

His expression was serene, eyes bright with conviction.

"This land is pure," he said simply.

Rebecca forced a nod, but he gut wrenched at the strange gaze coming from her son.

* * *

Gideon had returned to the abandoned town of Hindostan. He had fallen asleep with the journal open in his lap overnight. The pages were worn, the ink smeared, but the words still whispered their warning.

"The valley keeps what it is given."

His fingers brushed the leather jacket of the journal, tracing the embossed name, *Shelmire*.

"Mother," he breathed.

The journal gave nothing back.

No coldness.

No warmth.

Just emptiness.

Ezra entered the room where Gideon has slept.

"How you feelin'?" he asked in a low town.

Gideon stumbled from the bed, his eyes wide, and the journal in his hands.

His vision blurred from the tears welling in his eyes. The edges of the world softened, and he fell to his knees.

"They're trapped."

* * *

Something had changed overnight within Empyrean.

At first, no one noticed.

Stirring from their bedrolls, rubbing sleep from their eyes, Virginia and Hannah ventured to the stream, intent on splashing fresh water on their faces. Nathaniel and Hiram followed.

Solomon bustled around the camp, murmuring to himself while he stepped off areas for future buildings.

Virginia returned from the stream, her gaze lingering on Gideon just a little longer than usual.

Hiram returned from the river and noticed Rebecca standing quietly at the edge of the camp.

Rebecca sensed something in the valley—its stillness, its unnatural order—unsettled her.

Something wasn't right.

As Hannah and Nathaniel returned from the stream, it was Nathaniel who noticed first.

He turned in slow circles, his breath coming short.

Rebecca saw him hesitate, his gaze darting around, and frowned. "Nathaniel?"

He turned to her, face pale.

"Where's the firepit?"

Rebecca blinked, looking past him.

The firepit was gone. Not scattered. Not smothered. Just... gone. As if it had never been there at all.

Not disturbed. Not moved. Gone.

The ground where it had been lay smooth and untouched, no sign of ash, no burned-out wood. The earth was pale, pristine—like nothing had ever marred its surface. The blackened wood, the scorched embers, the warmth of flame itself—gone.

A hush fell over the camp.

Solomon stepped forward, his face unreadable.

"We must have misremembered its place."

Nathaniel shook his head. "No, I built it myself."

"Perhaps you were mistaken," Solomon said, voice calm. "Empyrean is a land of renewal. It wipes away the old to make way for the new."

Nathaniel looked upon Solomon with confusion.

Rebecca looked across the camp. There was more.

The tents had shifted. They were in the same positions—but not quite.

The walking sticks and tools they had left out were still there—but their arrangement was... *wrong*.

The ground was too smooth, as if their footprints from the night before had been erased.

And then there was the thing no one wanted to acknowledge.

Where the firepit had been, something else had taken its place. A wooden altar.

Pale. Smooth. White. The wood was too perfect, too untouched—like something carved not by hand, but by something that did not understand imperfection.

Simple. Roughly constructed. But undeniably real.

The wood was white—too white. As if the valley itself had stripped it clean. No knots, no imperfections, its surface smooth as bone.

But beneath the surface, something darker pulsed. The base, where the legs met the earth, was shadowed—not by the firelight, but by something else. The blackness clung to it, untouched, as if the night itself refused to give it shape.

Rebecca's throat tightened.

Someone built this.

Or something.

She turned to Hiram, expecting to see his usual smug amusement. But his expression was dark, his gaze fixed on the altar.

"Well," he muttered. "That's new."

Nathaniel continued looking toward Solomon with confusion,

"Did you build that thing overnight or somethin'?" he asked Solomon.

Solomon stood perfectly still. Not confused. Not surprised. Just... watching.

Staring at the Altar.

Silent.

His gaze traced the rough wood, slow and deliberate. His lips parted slightly, but he made no sound.

A long moment stretched before he turned, as if waiting for something unseen to answer.

A breeze stirred through the valley. A whisper—soft, distant.

A sound that hadn't been there before.

That night, the group gathered around the new firepit, its flames crackling low, unfamiliar. No one spoke of the altar. But no one dismantled it either.

Rebecca sat apart from the others, staring into the flames.

Solomon's voice rang through the camp, steady, unwavering.

"We are meant to be here. This is a land untouched by corruption, by history. A land where only the faithful remain."

Hiram exhaled a slow breath. "Or a land that erases anything that doesn't belong."

Rebecca turned sharply to him, her pulse quickening.

He understood.

Hiram met her gaze, eyes sharp. He saw what she saw.

And for the first time, Rebecca was certain—Empyrean was not empty when they arrived.

The fire burned low.

The group settled down around the fire for the night.

One by one, all had fallen into the depths of their dreams.

Nathaniel stirred in his sleep, rolling onto his side.

Then—he froze.

A whisper.

Soft. Just beyond the fire's reach.

His eyes fluttered open.

The whisper was gentle, familiar.

Like a woman's voice.

Nathaniel blinked, staring into the dark beyond the camp's edge. He saw nothing.

But the voice was still there.

Close.

Almost... kind.

His breath caught.

"Come here."

A pause. Then, softer.

"You don't have to be afraid."

Nathaniel sat bolt upright, heart hammering.

The night was still. Silent.

He turned to the others. No one else had heard it.

But something was out there.

And it was waiting.

14

CHAPTER 14 – SOLOMON'S TEST
Faith is not tested by light. It is tested by whispers in the dark.

The fire burned low, but its color was all wrong.

Not orange. Not red. Not gold.

White.

Cold and sterile, the flames swirled upward in twisting ribbons, devouring the wood without crackle or ember. A strange warmth, no flicker—just a steady, consuming glow.

And yet, the smoke remained.

Thick. Heavy. Rising in slow, black coils that clung to the air as if reluctant to leave.

It did not drift or scatter—it hung above them, a deep, ink-dark stain against the pale light.

The fire was clean. But the valley remembered everything it took.

Beyond its reach, the valley stretched in absolute blackness, untouched by the light. The fire did not push the dark away—it simply sat within it, isolated, contained.

Rebecca Whitmore lay awake, her hands folded tightly over her chest.

The wind had died. The trees did not sway. The night held its breath.

And yet—

Something moved.

Soft as a sigh, just beyond the camp's edge.

A whisper oozed between the camp.

"This is part of the journey," Solomon had assured them. "There will be a voice. Calling. Calling some of you away for a greater purpose." Doing his best to pretend he understood what was happening.

But Hiram—Hiram was the first to say it out loud.

"Something is wrong here."

Rebecca turned her head, willing her eyes to adjust to the dark.

And then she heard it.

A voice. Soft, distant. Calling her name.

"Rebecca..."

Her breath caught in her throat.

Solomon sat across the fire, watching her. His mother, a leader amongst them. He did not know what the voice was. But— could he use this moment to prove his prophetic calling, and would she pretend along with him as she always did for Elias.

Hiram smirked, but his hands were tight on the edges of his coat.

Then the voice called again—closer this time.

"Rebecca... come see."

The group stared at one another, unsure of the sound they were hearing.

The others awoke slowly, drawn from sleep not by sound but by silence.

Something had changed in the air.

The group stared at one another, unsure of the sound they were hearing.

A strange voice?

Or something else.

Some looked at Rebecca for reassurance.

Solomon stood, hands raised, his voice low and fervent.

"Do not fear the voice," he said. "It is the voice of revelation."

The others listened, wide-eyed, some nodding, some rigid with doubt.

"The voice is here to prove our devotion," Solomon continued. "And some among us will be called." He attempted to eye his mother knowingly.

Rebecca noticed Solomon's stare. She pressed her palms against the ground. The words slid through the air like a trap tightening. She knew what Solomon was asking of her.

Then Solomon turned to her. "Mother, you heard it, didn't you?"

Silence.

She felt the weight of every gaze. She didn't want to admit it. But lying would be worse.

Slowly, she nodded.

Hiram shifted in the shadows, arms crossed. He saw what was happening. Solomon was molding the fear, shaping it like clay. *Was Solomon creating this trickery? Or was he trying to control something he was not aware of?*

And then, Solomon smiled.

Solomon's gaze sharpened.

"Tomorrow, at dusk, you will follow the voice."

A ripple of murmurs. The others watched her now—not with concern, but expectation.

Rebecca's pulse quickened. If she denied the voice, she denied her faith. If she obeyed, she walked into the dark alone.

There was no way out.

The voice had called her. And now, she would have to answer.

And Solomon would use it.

* * *

The abandoned church stood crooked in the gold-tinged dark of Hindostan, its wood bloated with rain and age. Dust hung heavy in the rafters. Fractured stained glass painted the pews in broken light.

The old church stood like a forgotten relic, its wooden beams swollen with time, the scent of aged wood and lingering incense clung to the air, a ghost of past congregations.

At the front of the church, beneath the shadow of the pulpit, stood the communion table.

It was a broad, sturdy thing, carved of dark walnut, its edges worn smooth by generations of hands. The scripture once etched into its surface had faded, but traces remained, whispering of sacraments long past. Tonight, it was no longer a relic of the old faith. Tonight, it was Lucy's altar.

Atop the table, a large ceramic bowl sat between two telegraph batteries, humming faintly, their crude wires submerged in the murky silver solution. The makeshift contraption flickered with occasional arcs of pale blue light, casting eerie shadows along the walls. A row of pints—one for each of them—stood ready.

Lucy Mercer presided over it all, her presence as grand as any queen's.

She did not sit—Lucy Mercer did not perch in corners like some frail thing. She stood, wrapped in the rich folds of her deep green gown, the silver choker at her throat gleaming in the candlelight. Her hair, dark as ink, was drawn back with the careful precision of a woman who still clung to her dignity, even here, in the wilderness. The diadem of silver leaves nestled against her carefully pinned curls, catching the glow of the lanterns.

She looked like a woman born to command. And so, she did.

She lifted her hands over the Moon Tonic, the silver swirling beneath the dim light, catching and bending the glow like liquid moonlight. Her voice, smooth and warm, filled the hollow church.

"The Lord gives us signs. He gives us wisdom. And He gives us a way forward. This here—" she gestured to the bowl, "is the way forward. The Moon Tonic will keep us clean. It will keep us whole. Y'all are gonna drink, and y'all are gonna live."

A murmur of agreement rippled through the pews. Some nodded solemnly. Others—like Gideon—remained still.

Lucy fixed them with a look.

"This ain't just some medicine," she continued, her voice softer now. "It's a blessing. A promise that we won't be taken by whatever foul curse Elias brought down upon us."

Her gaze swept over them. One by one, they would take their pint. And one by one, she would bless them.

Eliza rose with practiced elegance, her movements careful but unhurried. She did not rush toward the table, nor did she hesitate—she simply moved as if she had always known this moment would come.

The lanternlight flickered against her features, softening the fine lines of concern etched into her brow. Her warm hazel eyes, so much like Lucy's, carried something deeper—a quiet question, one she would never voice aloud.

Lucy knew that look well.

Her eldest daughter, always the careful one, the dutiful one. The girl who had never spoken against the faith but whose silence had never quite been agreement, either. Eliza had always toed the line between belief and hesitation, standing at the threshold of certainty but never quite crossing.

Lucy ladled the Moon Tonic into the pewter pint, the silver liquid swirling as it caught the dim light. Before she handed it over, she reached across the table, pressing her hands over Eliza's.

"I see your heart, child. And I know you think you carry the weight of doubt alone. But you don't."

Eliza's fingers twitched beneath her mother's touch, but she said nothing. Her lips parted, as if to speak, but then she simply pressed them into a thin line.

"This will keep you clean," Lucy murmured, her voice softer now. "And you will always have a place at my table, no matter what you choose to believe."

A flicker of something passed through Eliza's gaze—not relief, not quite trust, but something close. A shared understanding that, despite everything, her mother saw her.

Eliza took the pint with both hands, its weight cool and grounding in her grasp. She gave Lucy a small, hesitant nod before turning back toward the pew.

She did not drink as quickly as Eleanor had.

Instead, she lifted the pint to her lips slowly, deliberately, and drank as if trying to taste the truth in every drop.

Eleanor rose without hesitation, but without urgency. She did not fidget, nor did she hesitate at the edge of the pew like Eliza had. She moved with certainty, her deep crimson shawl trailing behind her like a banner of quiet defiance. The lanternlight softened the sharp lines of her face, but her storm-gray eyes remained unreadable, measuring the weight of the moment.

Lucy watched her closely.

Eleanor wasn't a child anymore.

She had always been the listener, the watcher, the one who knew when to stay silent and when to strike. She had inherited her mother's poise but wore her father's brooding spirit like armor. And yet, when she reached the table, there was something softer in the way she extended her hands.

Lucy ladled the Moon Tonic into a pewter pint, the silver swirling like captured starlight. But before she handed it over, she reached out, cupping Eleanor's hand in both of hers.

"You were always the one to listen first, child. But I reckon it's time you started speakin'—for yourself, for what you want."

A flicker of something crossed Eleanor's face—not surprise, but recognition.

She had made her choice long ago. It was only now that the world would begin to see it.

She accepted the pint without looking away from Lucy, the weight of their shared understanding settling between them like an unspoken promise.

And then, Eleanor turned on her heel, cloak swaying as she strode back to the pew, where Ezra sat waiting.

She did not sip. She drank deeply, fully, without pause.

Not because she feared the sickness.

But because she had already decided—she would live.

The wooden pew creaked as Ezra rose, his movements slow, deliberate. Unlike the others, he did not hesitate out of reverence or uncertainty—but because he was watching.

His gray eyes, restless and discerning, flickered across the communion table, the flickering lanternlight reflecting in their depths. Lucy's hands, steady and practiced. The Moon Tonic, thick and shimmering. The ritual, well-worn in its newness.

Ezra Whitmore did not put faith in ritual. He put faith in what he could see.

And what he saw unsettled him.

Still, he walked forward, his lean frame moving with a quiet ease, though he was never truly at ease. Not here. Not anywhere. He approached Lucy the way a man approached a thing he did not yet trust but knew he must partake in anyway.

Lucy, for all her warm presence, met his gaze with something knowing—not quite a challenge, but a quiet invitation.

She did not hand him the pint immediately. Instead, she studied him, her hands folded over the communion table.

"You were always the sharp one, Ezra," she murmured, voice low. "Too clever by half."

Ezra tilted his head, a flicker of amusement crossing his features, but he said nothing.

Lucy dipped her fingers into the tonic's surface, swirling it once, before lifting her hand and tracing a small cross of moisture at his brow.

"This ain't just silver, child," she said, her voice softer now. "This is the shield between you and the curse of your father. It will keep you from the curse that follows you."

Then Lucy paused, and spread her gaze toward the entire group,

"We must drink this Moon Tonic nightly, to keep the curse at bay. This is our Silver Ritual, within the sacred church of the cursed."

Ezra's jaw tightened—barely perceptible, but Lucy saw it.

The curse.

Elias's curse.

Ezra felt shame knowing it was his father that caused the blight upon them. He felt guilty for the sickness that gnawed at their bones.

Lucy pressed the pint into his hands. Firm. Assured.

"Drink, child."

Ezra exhaled, slow and steady. Then, with a practiced indifference, he tipped the pint to his lips and drank.

The tonic was thick, coating his throat in something that tasted like metal and moonlight. A cold fire slithered through his veins. His fingers twitched against the pewter.

He finished it in three long swallows.

When he lowered the pint, Lucy was still watching him. Then placed her plump hand softly on his cheek,

"Don't be 'fraid of me, dear boy. You might find me your mother-in-law soon enough." She winked then peered briefly toward Eleanor.

And so, for the first time in a long time, Ezra smiled.

He turned without a word, moving back toward the pews and sat next to Eleanor. And even as he sat, even as he wiped the back of his hand across his mouth, he felt it.

The Moon Tonic settling in his bones. Seeping into him. Changing something.

He wasn't sure, but a slight tint of blue seemed to pulse subtly beneath his fingernails.

Gideon was hesitant.

He rose slowly, his broad shoulders tense beneath the weight of expectation. He approached like a man approaching his own sentencing.

Lucy met his eyes and sighed.

"Boy, you're wearin' that look like you think you can fight this on your own."

Gideon set his jaw. "I ain't sick."

Lucy snorted.

"You ain't invincible either."

She took his pint and, unlike the others, she did not hand it to him immediately.

Instead, she reached forward and placed her hand on his cheek—firm, motherly, unyielding.

"You listen to me, Gideon Whitmore." Her voice dipped, low and steady. "You were chosen. Not by that madman Elias. Not by any sign or symbol. But by these people. By the ones who follow you. You don't get to falter. You don't get to fall. You drink, and you live. For them."

A heavy silence fell over the church.

"I don't need the tonic to be strong," he murmured.

Lucy arched a brow, unimpressed.

"No," she agreed, "but you need it to be whole."

A breath.

The words settled between them like an unspoken truth.

Lucy dipped her fingers into the tonic, the liquid swirling around her touch like mercury. Slowly, she traced a line down his forehead—cool, thick, a silvered blessing.

"You are the rock, Gideon," she whispered. "You are the foundation. The shepherd."

His throat bobbed, but he did not speak.

She pressed the pewter pint into his hands.

"You are the name upon this city, the city we will build together by reclaiming this abandon settlement."

The words should have sat heavy, but they did not. They settled into his bones, a weight Gideon had always known he would bear.

Lucy's voice rose, filling the old church.

"And so let this place be named Gideon. Let it stand because of him. Let it endure because of him."

The others bowed their heads.

The fire flickered.

Gideon swallowed, shifting beneath their gazes. The call to lead, to build—he had never sought it, but now it was his.

Slowly, he lifted the pint to his lips and drank.

The Moon Tonic burned cold, slipping down his throat in a rush of silver and steel.

The ritual was complete.

Lucy watched, satisfaction flickering behind her hazel eyes.

Gideon exhaled, lowering the empty pint. He turned back toward the pews, toward the people who now looked to him not as a man—but as something more.

He had been named. And now, he would have to become it.

Lucy watched him, pride swelling in her chest.

Then, she straightened, lifting her own pint of Moon Tonic.

"And so we claim this place." Her voice rang out, filling every inch of the hollow church. "This will be our home. And we will call it Gideon."

Then, she drank.

The name settled over them like an unspoken vow.

Gideon's face burned with quiet humility, his head ducking slightly at the honor.

As the last echoes of her words faded into the church walls, the Gideonites sat in silence, the silver settling into them.

Lucy exhaled, satisfied.

The ritual was done and would be done nightly thereafter and forever.

Their fate was sealed.

* * *

The sun bled out behind the cliffs, drowning Empyrean valley in gold and shadow.

Solomon had told Rebecca in secret that the voice was that of the dead *Elias*, that she must pretend until her faith made it real. She nodded. Now, she stood at the treeline, her heartbeat a drum in her ears.

Solomon nodded once.

"Go."

She stepped forward.

Later that morning, Rebecca stood at the treeline, her heartbeat a drum in her ears.

Solomon nodded once. "Go."

She took a step forward.

Then another.

The moment she passed into the shadows, the air thickened, pressing in like unseen hands.

She moved slowly, the world stretching and warping around her. The earth beneath her feet felt too soft, like something beneath the soil was shifting.

And then she saw it.

A figure stood ahead, back turned.

It was human—or close enough.

Its body stood rigid, arms too long at its sides.

Its head tilted, slow and unnatural, like it was listening.

Waiting.

The whisper came again.

A woman's voice.

"Come see."

Rebecca stopped breathing.

The figure moved.

Slowly, it began to turn.

15

❧

C HAPTER 15 – SOPHIA OF THE WOODS
She was not sent. She was waiting.

The air inside the valley was still. The sun spilled through the trees in thin, ghostly white beams—too pale, too perfect. Shadows pooled in the spaces between, untouched by the light.

Rebecca took slow, measured steps, her pulse hammering behind her ribs. The trees loomed around her, their branches twisting overhead like grasping fingers. Something had called her name. Not in a dream. Not in a hallucination. But out loud.

Was this Solomon's doing ? She thought. But the voice he expected her to witness was that of Elias. This was a real voice. A mysterious voice. A woman's voice. She should have turned back.

But she didn't.

She moved deeper into the woods. The darkness stretched wider, swallowing the rays of sun above her her.

Then—she saw it.

At the base of an old, skeletal tree stood a woman.

She was alone, shrouded in the dim glow of some other worldly light beyond the depths of the forest. Her posture was unnervingly still, hands clasped at her waist, eyes closed as if in deep prayer.

She did not speak.

She did not move.

Yet the space between them seemed to shrink, pulling Rebecca forward as if the very air had shifted around her.

The woman's dark dress stirred faintly in the unmoving air. Her hair, loose and unbound, cascaded over her shoulders in thick waves. Even in the shadows, she seemed *unreal*.

Rebecca swallowed, stepping forward. The woman did not react.

Then, as Rebecca crossed an invisible threshold between them—

The woman's eyes snapped open.

Rebecca stopped breathing.

The woman's gaze was dark, wide, and knowing. As though she had been watching Rebecca this whole time. As though she had been waiting for her.

Then, she parted her lips—

And whispered.

Not to Rebecca.

Not to anyone.

But to something else.

Back at the fire Solomon stared into the flames with steady eyes.

Rebecca had vanished into the trees. And still, Solomon did not move.

Hiram stood at the edge of the firelight, where the glow did not reach. The shadows moved around him, deep and bruised, streaked with something richer than black—indigo. His eyes flicked between Solomon and the woods, sharp, waiting.

A ripple of unease passed through the group.

Solomon finally spoke, his voice smooth, unwavering.

"She was chosen for this. She will hear *his* voice and return to testify."

Nathaniel, Virginia and Hannah nodded in agreement. But their eyes darted toward the woods, toward the place where Rebecca had vanished.

Even faith could not silence fear.

And Hiram saw it.

He thought, *He doesn't even know what she'll find.*

* * *

In Hindostan, Lucy Mercer traced silvered fingertips along the rim of the ceramic bowl. The ritual had been performed. Her daughters first. Then Gideon. Then Eliza anointed her in return. Lucy insisted the Silver Ritual be performed on everyone.

The Gideonites' fevers broke. Their strength returned. But beneath the relief, something else took hold. The sickness faded, but it left a mark—their skin, once flushed with fever, now bore a strange pallor, tinged blue. A silver shimmer beneath the surface. A quiet, creeping change.

Gideon heard footsteps on the road outside the church. He glanced at the others, urging them to stay inside while he investigated. Lucy did not obey, but rather followed Gideon outside.

The riders drew up short, hooves grinding against the gravel-strewn path. Their leader, a man with a hard jaw and a hat pulled low over his eyes, reined his horse close to Gideon. His voice rolled out, soft and dangerous.

"Strange place to make camp, friend. These parts ain't as empty as they seem."

Gideon kept his expression blank, his disciples still as shadows behind him.

'We're just passing through.'

The leader's lips curled. "Passing through to where?" he laughed then made a sarcastic expression, "you sure you're not here lookin' for that old iron pot of treasure, lost by the townsfolk who all died in this cursed town?".

One of the riders, a wiry man with a rifle laid across his saddle, leaned forward. 'We're looking for a man. Calls himself Hiram Sloan. You seen him?'

Gideon's silence hung between them. The leader shifted in his saddle, the hem of his coat lifting to show a metal pin, a circle enclosing a cross, etched in worn silver. The metal caught the gray light, and behind Gideon, Lucy's breath hitched.

Her fingers tightened around the worn hem of her shawl, knuckles white. She had seen that symbol before, hidden among Abraham's belongings, half-buried beneath old ledgers and prayer books. The circle and cross, a mark of his fraternity.

"Be wise, son. Those who help traitors find themselves bound by their fate."

Lucy's pulse thudded in her ears.

* * *

The woman in the forest whispered in a tongue older than breath.

Rebecca felt it in her bones before she understood it in her ears.

It was a chant—low, rhythmic, carrying on the wind like an echo of something ancient. The sound was both familiar and unknowable, settling deep into Rebecca's bones like a prayer she had never learned but somehow understood.

Rebecca's deep ruby lips parted. "Who are you?"

The woman's whispers stopped.

A long, unbearable silence stretched between them.

Then, she finally spoke.

Her voice was soft, yet it filled the space between them, wrapping around Rebecca like a veil.

"I have been waiting for you."

Rebecca's pulse stuttered.

The woman tilted her head, studying her. Not like a stranger. Like she already knew everything about her.

"You are lost," the woman said. "And you are not the only one."

The wind picked up.

Rebecca swallowed hard, her voice barely above a whisper.

"What are you?"

The woman smiled.

And in that moment, the world felt like it had shifted—just slightly, just enough to make Rebecca doubt she was standing in the same place she had been before.

The woman's smile was slow, knowing and, at last, the woman answered.

"I am the beginning."

Rebecca's breath caught. The words echoed through her, sinking deep, filling the spaces she didn't know were empty.

A shift. A change. Something had unraveled, and there would be no turning back.

16

CHAPTER 16 – THE GATHERING
Not all who return bring silence with them.

Rebecca stepped out of the trees, the weight of the valley pressing against her ribs. A thin line of blood traced her cheek, welling from where a branch had caught her on the way out. The red stood out—too vivid against the pale light, too real in a place that felt untouched by it.

The others stood waiting. Their faces warmed by the setting sun—shadows shifting over expressions of reverence and expectation. They wanted certainty. They needed it.

Solomon stood at the center, arms folded, his expression composed—too composed. He was waiting for her answer.

Hiram, standing at the edge of the firelight, tilted his head slightly. The indigo shadows stretched long behind him, his presence half in the dark, half in the light. Watching her in the way only he could. Caringly.

Rebecca swallowed hard.

She could still hear it. The voice. The way it played through the trees, wearing the shape of a woman who wasn't there. The figure or voice was not at all what Solomon said it would be, but had spoken with the celestial voice of a *woman*.

"You have heard it, you heard his voice!" Solomon said. Fully expecting his mother to support his fraud.

The hush around them deepened. The others leaned forward, hanging on her every breath.

Rebecca opened her mouth—then closed it.

That hesitation was enough.

Solomon's smile did not falter, but something in him shifted. It was microscopic, almost imperceptible. Almost.

"Now you understand," he continued.

Rebecca forced a nod. It was not agreement. But it was enough.

The tension snapped, the gathered exhaling in relief. "For behold, it is the voice of *Elias-* our father and prophet. His spirit attends to us, testifying we are in the right place." Murmurs of devotion swept through them, reassurance that all was as it should be.

Hiram did not murmur. He only smirked, shaking his head slightly. He knew Rebecca was only appeasing the mad prophet. She had not heard *his* voice, whoever *he* was.

Solomon's gaze lingered on Rebecca—too long. Too knowing. The smile never faltered, but something in his eyes darkened, calculating. Then, just as quickly, he turned away.

And from the outskirts of the firelight, another figure stood watching.

Someone new.

At first, she was just another shadow.

Then she stepped forward, and the fire caught her.

The Chosen stilled.

She was unlike anything in their world.

Her dark grey top hat – unusually tall for a top hat- adorned with a fan of peacock feathers - tilted slightly as she stepped onto the packed earth. Her gloves—lime green, unnatural, deliberate— flashed as she raised one hand. A color that did not belong here. A color that did not bow to Empyrean. A cane, elegant and black, tapped the ground with a slow, deliberate rhythm as she moved forward.

She did not need it to walk.

She carried it as one might carry a scepter.

Rebecca's breath hitched.

It was her.

The woman from the forest.

The one who had whispered like the wind and smiled like she already knew the ending of the story.

A murmur rippled through the gathered. Unease. Fascination. Fear.

But the otherworldly woman only watched. Her eyes—too knowing, too deep, the color of dark water—drifted over them, taking them in one by one.

Solomon did not flinch.

Hiram did not smirk.

The wind picked up slightly, rustling the edges of her long coat.

Then, at last, she spoke.

"Quite the gathering," she said. "I do believe I arrived just in time."

The air in the valley felt charged, alive with something no one could name.

Rebecca exhaled slowly.

The firelight reflected in Solomon's eyes. He smiled.

But Rebecca had known him long enough to see it.

For the first time, Solomon was unsure.

* * *

The fraternal order of men rode away, leaving the abandoned town behind. Gideon stood in the center of the road, watching as they departed. He gazed over the settlement. The buildings leaned in on themselves, doorways yawning wide, windows gaping like empty eye sockets.

The abandoned town was larger than Gideon had realized. In addition to the church, a tavern close to the white river. Several cabins. What looked like a saw or grits mill. And a doctors office.

It was no Promised Land.

But it was something.

Ezra slowly left the church and stood beside his brother, arms crossed, his face paler than before. The sickness had slowed, but his skin had taken on that — strange undertone — a silver sheen in certain light.

Behind them, Eleanor and Eliza moved out from the church, their hands brushing over broken walls, overturned carts.

Lucy ran a palm over a carved wooden post, her expression unreadable. "It seems many People lived here."

Eleanor knelt, brushing dirt from something small—wooden, rounded. A child's toy. Long abandoned. The carved surface was worn smooth, as if too many hands had held it. And for a second—just a second—she thought she heard laughter, distant and impossible.

Gideon exhaled.

"They don't anymore."

Ezra huffed. "You think that's a good thing?"

Gideon didn't answer right away.

But deep inside, he knew the truth.

The people who had lived here were gone. And whether they had died from a mysterious sickness—or had been taken—no one ever came back.

Still, they had no other choice.

He turned, taking in the remnants of the town.

"This is our home now."

Lucy placed her hand on Gideon's shoulder and said,

"We will name it The City of Gideon".

And slowly, one by one, they began to re-build.

* * *

The fire burned high in the Empyrean camp.

Solomon stood beside it, quiet as a stone.

McBride stood just beyond the firelight.

They had not spoken yet.

The group whispered among themselves. They had never seen a woman like her. Not just in dress, but in presence. She was something apart.

And she did not kneel.

She did not lower her eyes.

She simply watched.

Finally, Solomon broke the silence.

"What is it that you seek?"

She smiled. "Oh, I'm just here to listen."

Hiram scoffed, tilting his head. "People don't just show up here. Not unless they were called."

The woman's gaze flicked toward him. She smiled, slow and knowing.

"Oh, believe me," she said softly. "I was."

Rebecca swallowed.

Solomon leaned forward, his expression smooth as glass. "At least give us your name"

She answered, "I am Temperance McBride." she then looked toward Solomon, "and you are?" He was taken aback by her tone and grace. Stuttering he replied, "I am Solomon Whitmore, leader of The Chosen." Then motioning to his mother, "This is my mother and our matriarch- Rebecca Whitmore." Then nodding to his younger brother, "and this is my youngest brother. Nathaniel". Virginia stepped forward before Solomon could introduce her. " and I'm Virginia and this is my sister Hannah." The two girls were exited to meet this strange woman.

McBride made conversations with the girls and then Virginia turned to Solomon, "let her stay, please?"

Solomon stared at McBride,

"Then stay," he said. "Listen all you like."

McBride nodded, tipping her hat.

"Oh, I intend to."

And for the first time since stepping foot in Empyrean, Solomon felt it—a presence he could not command. He smiled, slow and measured, but in the fire's reflection, his eyes betrayed him.

17

CHAPTER 17 – THE FIRST CALLING
Empires begin not with war, but with weddings.

Night fell heavy over the valley of Empyrean.

The Chosen stood before Solomon in silent reverence. Their leader stood tall, his voice steady, his presence unshaken.

"Tonight, we move forward," Solomon declared. "Tonight, we take the next step toward the fulfillment of Empyrean."

Rebecca stood among them, the valley pressing her against her body, her soul. The air felt thick, unmoving. A silence that waited—not for an answer, but for acceptance.

"We heard my father's voice in spirit- witnessing to my mother that our calling to Empyrean is sure and elected."

McBride lingered at the edges, her gloved fingers lightly gripping the silver head of her cane. She did not speak. She did not move.

But she was there.

Solomon turned toward the gathered. "Empyrean must be whole. A city must have structure. A kingdom must have law. And a people must be bound together—body and spirit.".

Rebecca felt the shift before she heard the words.

Marriage.

She saw it coming before Solomon spoke it aloud.

"It is time we fulfill our design. It is time for marriage to be sealed within Empyrean."

There was no shock. No outcry. Only murmurs of anticipation.

Rebecca's pulse pounded in her ears.

Marriage meant permanence. It meant devotion not just to The Chosen, but to Solomon himself.

She turned, searching the crowd. Virginia and Hannah stood close together, as they always did. But tonight, beneath the pale firelight, their presence felt different – Virginia's gaze lingered on Solomon, her expression carefully composed, a shade of lilac deepening in the night. Hannah stood beside her, silent, softer – a whisper of violet caught in the shifting glow.

Nathaniel stood stiffly beside them, his thoughts locked behind an expressionless mask.

And across the fire, McBride tilted her head slightly, her dark eyes watching – not questioning, not doubting, but knowing.

Rebecca exhaled slowly.

This was happening.

And nothing would stop it.

The firelight flickered in uneven patterns, casting strange shadows across the faces of the gathered Chosen. Smoke exhaled upward into the vast black sky, where the stars stretched white and cold, watching.

Solomon stood before them, his posture regal, his expression serene. But the air around him—heavy, weighted, humming with something unseen—made the moment feel like something else entirely.

A proclamation.

A binding.

Rebecca stood still, her hands tight at her sides. She could already feel what was coming.

Solomon spoke.

"The time has come to solidify our covenant."

The Chosen barely breathed.

"Empyrean is not merely a place—it is a kingdom. And every kingdom must have its foundation. Its order. Its unions."

Virginia and Hannah stiffened.

Nathaniel exhaled slowly, his shoulders rigid.

Temperance McBride watched from the edge of the firelight, her presence quiet yet unshakable. Not a participant. Not an opponent. Something else entirely.

Solomon turned his gaze toward Virginia.

"You will be wed to me."

A ripple moved through the group. Not a gasp, not outright shock—just a subtle shifting. A murmur beneath the surface.

Hannah reached for Virginia's hand, fingers tightening.

Solomon's eyes did not waver.

"And Hannah will be wed to Nathaniel."

Nathaniel swallowed hard, his face carefully blank.

Rebecca's stomach twisted.

This was not a request.

Solomon smiled gently, his voice calm, absolute.

"These unions were foreseen. They are part of the divine order of Empyrean."

Virginia's expression was unreadable. She did not step forward. Did not speak.

Hannah's breathing had quickened, barely perceptible in the flickering light.

Nathaniel, his jaw tight, said nothing.

The moment stretched long, pulling at the edges of what was normal, reasonable, real.

Rebecca forced herself to speak.

"And when will these... unions be fulfilled?"

Solomon turned to her as if he had been waiting for the question.

"The stars have revealed the time." Then looking toward the heavens with an eerie expression,

"Tishrei, when the faithful are sealed and the unworthy are cast away."

The fire cracked.

"On the night of the next celestial crossing—when the Scales of Heaven tilt, when the Virgin sinks beneath the horizon and Orion ascends. On this night, the heavens align in the sacred pattern of Empyrean. The balance of day and night."

Silence.

Rebecca's chest tightened.

Temperance McBride liltingly hovered in the background far behind. She moved forward, as though she floated slightly above the misty ground, timeless. In an instant, Rebecca heard a whisper fall from Mcbride's lips and brush the back of her ear, *"The Harvest reckoning"*.

She only watched.

A slight tilt of the head. A faint, knowing smile.

Rebecca caught it— It would happen soon.

Too soon.

This was not merely a decree. It was an inevitability. A movement already set in place, winding forward like the workings of the orrery Solomon kept so carefully guarded.

A design already written.

The Chosen stood frozen in time. They just stood silently, absorbing the weight of the words.

A quiet certainty, as though she had seen this unfold before.

As though she already knew how it must end.

* * *

The moon hung low over the ruins of Hindostan, its pale light carving sharp lines through the broken windows of the abandoned buildings.

The Gideonites moved quietly through the crumbling streets, their shadows long, their voices low.

Gideon stood at the center of the town square, his back to the old church, its steeple a jagged silhouette against the night sky.

Ezra approached, his steps uneven, his breathing shallow.

"We're making good progress," he said, his voice lifted with hope. "We cleared out a couple of cabins and set up sleeping arrangement."

Gideon nodded, his expression tight.

Lucy, Eliza and Eleanor light lamps the hung at the entrance of the church and the cabins meant to be occupied for the night.

Ezra hesitated.

"Gideon," pointing to the cabin across the street from the church, "That cabin is for Lucy." He then pointed to the cabin on the left. "And that cabin is for me and," he paused "Eleanor".

Gideon eyed Ezra and remained silent.

"And that cabin on the right is for you and Eliza."

A pause.

Gideon's jaw tightened.

"You two don't have to stay in the same room. There are a couple rooms. Or Eliza can stay with her mother." Ezra said nervously.

"Thank you, Ezra." Gideon said with a calm and understanding voice.

He wrapped his arm around his younger brother and the two stood in the road, taking in the work they had accomplished. The city of Gideon had been a promise of refuge.

The church interior was cool and dark, the pews draped in dust, the altar bare.

Gideon knelt alone, his hands clasped, his forehead resting on the rough wood of the front pew.

"If you're out there," he whispered, "give me a sign."

Only silence.

The air hung still, the shadows close, and for a moment, he thought he heard a voice—

A soft whisper, barely more than a breath.

But when he opened his eyes, there was nothing.

Eliza entered, her footsteps careful.

"Come and see the cabins, it is getting late." she said.

Gideon rose, his expression closed, his hope buried.

"Sorry for my brother playing match maker." he said with some embarrassment.

Eliza curled her hands around Gideon's arm.

"It was my idea." she smiled.

And as they left the church, the shadows lingered, watching.

* * *

That same night, the fire's white glow cast deep black elongated shadows, dancing eerily across the faces of the gathered Chosen of Empyrean. The air was thick with the weight of Solomon's pronouncements, and an uneasy murmur rippled through the assembly.

Solomon stood tall, his eyes reflecting the flickering flames. He raised his hands, calling for silence.

"Brother and Sisters," he began, his voice resonating with authority, "through the sacred manuscripts and the divine guidance of the orrery, a new ritual has been unveiled to me—a ceremony that will bind us to the very essence of Empyrean."

They leaned in, apprehension etched on their faces.

"This is not merely a union of man and woman," Solomon continued, "but a fusion of souls, ensuring the purity and continuity of our divine race."

He gestured to the ancient orrery beside him, its celestial spheres glinting in the firelight.

"On the third night from now," he declared, "at the crossing of the heavens, we shall commence the Rite of Sacred Union."

A hush fell over the assembly as Solomon detailed the forthcoming ceremony:

"Purification" he started,

"At dawn, the betrothed will immerse themselves in the River of Sanctity, cleansing their bodies and spirits."

He continued with fire filling his eyes,

"Vestments of the Chosen — They will don garments of pure white linen, symbolizing their readiness to transcend the mortal plane."

Virginia and Hannah side-eyed one another, unsure how to react.

"Procession of Light — As dusk descends, the couples will proceed to the Temple of the Stars, each bearing a candle lit from the Eternal Flame, signifying the light of Empyrean guiding their path."

Hiram gazed toward Rebecca. His expression filled with concern.

"Oath of Eternal Blood — Before the assembly, they will recite vows in a sacred tongue—a blend of ancient languages—binding their souls to each other and to Empyrean"

Solomon would then raise his hands high above his heads and declare—

"Per hoc vinculum sacrum, nos coniungimur in aeternum, ut progeniem puram proferamus et Empyrean sanctificemus."

He then set his gazed upon the group,

"Being translated it is to say — through this sacred bond, we are joined forever, to bring forth pure offspring and sanctify Empyrean."

Rebecca was astonished. The Latin flowed from his tongue as though he spoke it as his first language.

"Sealing of the Covenant — A consecrated sigil will be inscribed upon their foreheads with the Oil of Anointment, marking them as eternal inhabitants of Empyrean."

Solomon paused. His face seemed to mutate subtle as he peered into the soles of each individual — Hiram first, then Rebecca, Virginia, Hannah and finally Nathaniel. His stared lingered upon Nathaniel.

"Consummation Directive — The final step, ordained and unbreakable. The newly bound must complete their union in flesh, ensuring the propagation of the pure lineage."

As Solomon's words settled over the congregation, a palpable tension filled the air. The gravity of the impending ritual was evident on every face.

From the periphery, Temperance McBride observed, her expression inscrutable. Her eyes, however, gleamed with a depth of understanding that surpassed even Solomon's fervor.

Rebecca's heart raced, a whirlwind of emotions churning within her. The path laid out before them was irrevocable, binding not just bodies, but souls, to a destiny she was no longer certain she could embrace.

The fire crackled, sending sparks into the night sky, then Nathaniel noticed a change. The valley had changed itself again.

Nathaniel's breath hitched.

"Look."

They turned. The altar was gone.

In its place stood something else—something that had not been there before, but had always been waiting. A shrine, its walls smooth and perfect, untouched by human hands. The air around it shimmered, as though the valley itself had bent and reshaped to accommodate Solomon's decree.

18

CHAPTER 18 – PRIESTHOODS
The divine begins not in temples, but in mental transmutation.

Morning broke over the valley like a held breath. The air was too still, the weight of Solomon's decree settling over the gathered like a stone pressed against their chests.

Virginia and Hannah stood apart from the others, side by side, their hands clasped so tightly that their knuckles had gone white. The firelight caught Virginia's face, washing her in pale lilac—soft, uncertain, hesitant.

Rebecca moved toward them, slow and careful, as if approaching wounded animals.

"Come," she said softly. "Sit with me."

For a long moment, neither sister moved. Then, Virginia exhaled, a sharp, trembling breath, and allowed herself to be led away from the firelight.

Hannah followed, her face unreadable, but Rebecca could see the tension in her jaw, the effort it took not to shatter.

They sat at the edge of the camp, near the sloping rise of the valley wall. Beyond it, the world no longer existed.

Virginia was the first to speak.

"I thought I would have a choice."

Rebecca reached for her hand. Virginia did not pull away, but she did not grasp back either.

"I know," Rebecca whispered. "I know."

Hannah let out a sharp breath, shaking her head.

"How can he say it was foreseen?" she said, voice tight. "We never spoke of marriage. He never—he never looked at me that way. And now I belong to him?"

Her voice broke on the last word, and Rebecca pulled her close.

"You belong to no one."

Silence stretched between them. The stars above burned cold and distant.

"I could run," Virginia said suddenly. "Tonight. I could leave."

Rebecca's stomach twisted.

"Where would you go?"

Virginia looked away. She had no answer.

A quiet chuckle broke the silence.

McBride.

She stood a few feet away, her cane tapping idly against her palm, watching. Not intruding, not demanding.

Just waiting.

"Running won't get you far," McBride said. "But neither will staying."

Hannah lifted her head, eyes narrowing. "And what do you suggest?"

McBride only smiled.

"I suggest you remember who you are before someone else tells you."

Rebecca's breath caught. The words landed heavier than they should have, as if laced with meaning beyond the surface.

Virginia and Hannah said nothing.

But something had changed.

Midday in Empyrean brought a silence that pressed inward. The shrine rose against a black backdrop of the valley's shadows, its smooth stone glinting bright white. The air around it pulsed, like breath against skin. It had not been built—it had been made.

Called forth. Willed into existence.

It should not have been possible.

Solomon stood before the altar within the shrine, running his fingers over the carved sigils, tracing their deep, intricate lines.

Hiram stood nearby, arms crossed, watching him.

Nathaniel was further back, his posture stiff, his jaw tight.

"The ceremony must be perfect," Solomon murmured, almost to himself. "The heavens will align, and Empyrean will seal itself."

Hiram scoffed. "You speak as if the valley itself is alive."

Solomon turned, his gaze sharp. "Perhaps it is."

Nathaniel exhaled sharply, shaking his head. "We should not be forcing this."

Solomon's expression did not change. "We are not forcing anything. We are fulfilling prophecy."

Nathaniel did not argue. But he did not agree either.

Hiram smirked, tilting his head toward Rebecca, who stood a distance away, watching the shrine with an unreadable expression.

"And what do you make of your mother's growing distance?"

Solomon's gaze flickered toward Rebecca.

"She will understand in time."

Hiram let out a quiet chuckle. "If you say so."

Rebecca met Hiram's gaze across the fire.

For the first time, she did not look away.

* * *

The streets of Hindostan whispered like old paper. The air in the abandoned town was different.

Gideon felt it the moment they awoke in the cabins. Not colder, not heavier—just... charged, as if the very ground recognized them now.

The wooden structures, long weathered by time, stood like skeletal remains of another era, waiting to be claimed.

Ezra walked out of his cabin stretching his arms with a waking groan. Eleanor moved past him, fingers brushing over a doorframe. A faint mark was left behind, something dull and colorless. Then, as the lamplight shifted—silver. The wood did not take on the color. The color had come from her.

The marks were grayish. No—silver.

Ezra saw it but did not react. Neither did she. They had all begun to change.

Lucy stepped out of her cabin, murmuring instructions to the others, her hands calloused but steady, a mother shaping a new people.

Ezra took a flask and drank deeply. When he pulled it away, the rim of the tin caught the light strangely against his lips.

Eleanor watched him, saying nothing.

The change was nearly complete.

And yet, no one questioned it.

This was the blessing of the silver ritual. A mark of their distinction, a curse. But now a sign that they had been purified. A silvery blue priesthood of their own.

Ezra exhaled and turned toward Eleanor. "I'll help with the foundations at the Tavern."

She nodded. Their hands hovered close—blue flesh and blue flesh.

Gideon looked toward Eliza, standing next to him as she exited the same cabin as he. She caught his gaze but said nothing. Respect. Admiration. Something growing.

Their city would rise.

And they would rise with it.

Marked blue in their skin. Bound. Gideonites.

* * *

It began at dawn.

Rebecca woke with a weight in her chest, her breath coming slow and shallow. A presence—unseen but undeniable—pressed against her ribs, curling like unseen fingers around her bones.

She was not alone.

Across the dim camp, Virginia and Hannah were already awake, their bodies stiff with the same silent knowing.

No words were spoken. No call had been given.

But still—they walked.

Beyond the camp, past the outer edge of the valley, McBride was waiting.

Not summoning.

Just waiting.

Rebecca's pulse quickened, but her feet did not falter. The pull was stronger than fear.

The valley around them shifted, the air thickening, stretching, becoming something else.

McBride stood at the farthest edge of the clearing, her dark coat catching the first pale sliver of morning light.

Her top hat cast a long shadow. Her gloved hands were outstretched, waiting.

She smiled. "You were always meant to come."

The words did not feel like hers.

They felt ancient.

Virginia inhaled sharply. Hannah's fingers listless. Rebecca's heart pounded.

McBride lifted her hands.

The sky responded.

The air pulsed, thick with something unseen, something vast. It was not the valley. It was not Empyrean.

It was other.

And then—light.

It did not burn. It did not blind.

It simply was, casting a color reflecting the lime green of Temperance's gloves.

A force without origin, without substance. A presence that was watching.

McBride's voice changed.

Lower. Resonant. Not entirely human.

"Έχετε δει. Είσαι γνωστός. Δεν είστε δεμένοι με τη γη, αλλά με τους ουρανούς."

Virginia trembled. Hannah clutched at her own chest.

Rebecca's breath caught as something unfolded around them—figures, neither man nor angel, towering and unknowable, their presence both terrible and beautiful.

Their shapes did not bend to the laws of the world. Their edges were blurred, shifting, as if seen through water.

Voices—not voices, but echoes of something older than language—moved through the space.

McBride tilted her head, listening.

Then the words came unbidden to her lips.

"Suffer not yourselves to be lesser than what you were made to be."

Rebecca felt it enter her.

Something new.

Something old.

It coiled around her spine, pressing into her marrow. A power, a force, an understanding that had no name.

She gasped.

McBride stepped forward, her movements slow, deliberate.

She reached for Virginia first. Her gloved fingers brushed Virginia's forehead—and the girl staggered.

A green glow—faint but unmistakable—rose beneath her skin.

She turned to Hannah next. Her fingers touched, and Hannah's breath hitched.

And then—Rebecca.

McBride's hand hovered over her brow, pausing just a fraction longer.

"You will know when the time comes."

The light pulsed once.

The figures—those things neither angel nor man—folded into the air, slipping away like mist.

The wind sighed through the valley. The sky stilled.

McBride lowered her hand.

She smiled.

Nothing more.

And when the three women returned to the camp, they were no longer the same.

Night fell quietly. Rebecca could not sleep.

She lay still beneath the heavy woven blankets, staring up at the sky, the stars unmoving—watching. Around her, the camp was silent. The others asleep, their breathing a rhythmic whisper against the hush of the valley. But something else stirred.

Something unseen.

She turned her head. The valley stretched wide and endless beyond the firelight, bathed in an unnatural stillness. The air felt heavier, charged, waiting. She exhaled slowly, closing her eyes.

Then—

Then—something split. A seam in the air. A fracture between worlds. And she was no longer in the valley.

The air around her shifted. The silence deepened, stretching into something vast and infinite. When she opened her eyes, the world had changed.

She stood in a city that should not exist.

It was not Empyrean.

She saw buildings.

A Tavern.

A Church.

There were structures half-formed but sturdy. The road was empty, save for the flicker of distant torches. And the sky — it was wrong. Not the deep black of the valley night, but a swirling mass of darkened silver, shifting like the surface of water.

She stepped forward, and the ground beneath her feet rippled.

Then she saw them.

Figures, moving between the church and the tavern. Their faces were familiar—Gideon. Ezra. Eleanor. Eliza. Lucy. The Gideonites. They were working, building their city, their voices hushed but determined. Their movements were deliberate, ritualistic. Silver powder clung to their fingers, to their skin. Lanterns lit the buildings and cabins, casting a blue hue across the wooden planks.

Rebecca's breath caught in her throat. Ezra.

She saw him clearly now, standing beneath the strange, silver sky. His skin had changed. It was no longer pale but deepened—tinted with an otherworldly hue, blue-silver beneath the firelight.

It wasn't just him.

The others bore the same mark.

Their skin glowed faintly in the moonlight, their bodies transformed in ways they had yet to understand.

Rebecca tried to move closer, but the air resisted her, thick like unseen hands pressing against her shoulders.

Then—Gideon turned.

His eyes locked onto hers. His breath hitched. His posture stiffened.

Ezra followed his gaze. His body stilled. His hands trembled.

One by one, they saw her.

Their expressions changed. Confusion. Recognition. Fear.

Rebecca's pulse hammered.

"They can see me."

She took a step back. The ground beneath her rippled again.

Ezra reached for her.

His blue fingertips brushed the edge of her vision—soft, real.

Rebecca gasped. And then—

The world snapped back. The valley. The fire. The silence.

But the memory of silver hands reaching for her remained. And she knew—

She had been seen.

The valley was still. The embers burned low. The stars above had shifted.

Rebecca sat up, gasping, her body cold with sweat. Her hands trembled against the blanket.

It had been a dream.

But she knew.

She had been seen.

19

C HAPTER 19 – THE WEDDING OF EMPYREAN
And what was once chosen may yet be undone – if the veil is lifted in time.

The dawn was too quiet.

Virginia and Hannah stood at the edge of the camp, staring into the open valley. The morning light cast long shadows, stretching across the land like unseen hands.

Rebecca watched them from a short distance, her heart heavy.

Virginia's arms were crossed, her expression carefully guarded, white light catching in her eyes—pale lilac, muted and soft. Hannah stood beside her, hands clasped tightly, her fingers like cold slate – stiff.

Neither of them had spoken since the announcement.

Rebecca approached slowly, the dry earth crunching beneath her feet.

"You don't have to be afraid." The words felt hollow even as she said them.

Virginia turned to her, her eyes dark and searching. "Do you believe that?"

Rebecca opened her mouth—then hesitated.

Hannah exhaled sharply. "Why us?" Her voice was quieter than Virginia's, but the tremor beneath it was unmistakable. "Why were we chosen?"

Rebecca wanted to tell them the truth. That there was no divine order to this. That Solomon's will had nothing to do with revelation, only control.

But what good would it do?

She reached out, gently touching Hannah's hand.

"You are not alone."

Virginia scoffed, shaking her head. "That doesn't mean we are free."

A rustling of fabric. A movement just beyond them.

McBride.

She stood just within the valley's edge, her dark coat rippling in the faint morning breeze. Her top hat cast a sharp shadow across her face, her gloved hands resting lightly on the silver head of her cane.

Virginia and Hannah stiffened at the sight of her.

McBride smiled, but there was sorrow in her eyes.

"You were always meant to come."

Her voice was calm, unshaken.

Rebecca swallowed hard. The weight of last night's vision still pressed against her ribs. McBride knew.

She always knew.

Solomon, Nathaniel, and Hiram stood before the great stone foundation, their hands stained with dust.

The temple was not built by ordinary means.

It had risen too quickly, stone by stone, as if guided by unseen forces. The towering columns, the intricate carvings—none of them had laid such careful hands to the rock, yet here it stood, as if it had always been.

Hiram ran his fingers over the stone.

It was smooth, too smooth—no marks of tools, no imperfections. It felt untouched, yet not untouched. Like something that had not been built, but had been waiting. He exhaled, his lips pressing into a thin line.

"This place ain't natural."

Solomon turned to him, his expression unreadable.

"It is ordained."

Nathaniel, standing apart, exhaled slowly. His fingers curled at his sides.

"Ordained or not," he muttered, "feels like it's watchin'."

Hiram smirked, but it was humorless. "Oh, it is."

They turned to look at Solomon. He stood before the great entrance, the orrery in his hands, its celestial rings shifting slowly.

He had not believed, once. Not fully.

But now?

Now the magic obeyed him.

Nathaniel's voice cut through the quiet. "And what if they refuse?"

Hiram chuckled darkly. "They won't."

But from the far side of the valley, beneath the shadow of the cliffs, McBride watched.

And she was smiling.

* * *

The city of Gideon was waking.

Lucy stood at the altar inside the church, her hands gripping the edges of a bowl filled with silver-laced water. The ritual had become second nature now. A necessity.

One by one, the Gideonites passed her, dipping their fingers into the liquid, brushing it across their foreheads, their wrists.

Ezra was among the last. His breath was steady as he pressed his damp fingers to his chest. Eleanor stood beside him, watching him carefully.

"It doesn't hurt anymore, does it?" she asked softly.

Ezra hesitated, flexing his hands. The silver sheen beneath his nails had deepened.

"No."

Eleanor studied him. She reached up, brushing the faintest dusting of silver from his jawline.

"You're changing."

Ezra's throat tightened. "We all are."

Gideon stood watching them. His gaze lingered on Eliza, who was helping Ezra drink from a small cup of silver water.

"Our mother came to us last night. How?"

Ezra asked the group, but side-eyeing Gideon.

No one spoke.

But something had begun.

And no one could stop it now.

* * *

The night air was heavy with incense across the valley of Empyrean.

The Chosen stood in two lines, their candles burning low. The white flames trembled, fragile in the heavy night, their light swallowed by the towering pillars of the temple. The wind did not stir. The air did not shift. Even the valley seemed to hold its breath.

Solomon led the way, his white ceremonial robes glistening in the firelight.

Behind him walked Virginia and Hannah, their faces veiled, their dresses woven in fine linen.

They moved forward in silence.

Nathaniel followed, his hands clenched into fists.

Hiram walked beside him, his smirk gone.

At the far edge of the procession, McBride stood just outside the torchlight.

Her gloved fingers tapped lightly against her cane, her hat casting a sharp shadow across her face. She did not move to stop them. She only watched, waiting.

The temple doors loomed ahead, waiting.

Rebecca exhaled, stepping forward.

This was it.

The temple loomed ahead, open and waiting. A door that had never been closed, because it had never needed to be. Once they passed through, there would be no turning back.

CHAPTER 20 – BOUND BY DIVINITY

When the altar breaths, the body obeys.

The temple had not been there before.

But now, as the first light of evening stretched across the valley, it stood—vast, smooth, and seamless, as if it had risen from the earth itself where the shrine once stood. But the altar remained inside at the center of a black and white checkered tile floor.

Its towering spires reflected the dying sun, their surfaces neither stone nor metal, but something in between. Something alive. The air around it pulsed softly, in perfect rhythm with Solomon's breath, as if the temple itself inhaled and exhaled through him.

The Chosen gathered at its base, their figures shrouded in white, their bare feet pressing into the unnatural smoothness of the temple steps.

A procession formed—silent, reverent, inevitable.

Solomon led them, his crimson crown pressed against his brow, the sash around his waist trailing like a river of blackened blood. Both Solomon and Nathaniel were adorned in the same strange attire—their white robes draped over one shoulder, leaving the opposite bare, exposing skin marked by past sun burns and the cool air. Their crimson crowns, woven from an unusual cloth with a sheen like dried petals, sat upon their heads, giving them the appearance of monarchs in some forgotten rite.

The aprons they wore were crafted from heavy, gold-hued silk, the fabric bearing the muted luster of age and ritual use. A deep crimson trim framed the aprons, its folds reminiscent of aged parchment, creating an unsettling contrast against the gold. The embroidery on the aprons depicted esoteric emblems—swirling vines, serpentine knots, and the ever-present reminder of mortality: a skull and crossbones nestled beneath the radiance of a golden sun and the cool gaze of a silver crescent moon.

Two deep pockets adorned the aprons, their placements mirroring the pillars of the Empyrean Temple threshold. The left pocket, embroidered with a corinthian pillar marked with the letter **N**, held a small pouch of emberstone powder—a ruddy, rust-colored powder with flecks of gold. The right pocket, bearing a doric pillar with the letter **S**, concealed silverviel dust. A fine, pale blue powder that shimmers with an ethereal glow. It is cool to the touch, leaving a gentle tingle on the skin.

Behind them, the women walked in veiled silence.

Virginia. Hannah. The brides.

Their golden veils covering their faces cascaded down their backs like molten sunlight, the delicate threads woven with symbols of fertility and birth. Tiny five-pointed stars, each stitched with thread as fine as spider silk, glimmered among the folds—pentagrams, ancient emblems of the womb, the earth, and the divine feminine. As they moved, the stars caught the light, casting subtle, shifting shadows on the ground, as if the heavens themselves bowed before them.

Their robes were pure white, but not the white of innocence—it was the white of bone, a shade that seemed to drink the color from the room. The fabric was gauzy and layered, giving them an ethereal quality, as though they hovered just above the ground. Beneath the outer robe, a glimpse of pale lavender and ash-gray silk hinted at twilight, the threshold between day and night, life and death.

Their aprons were strange, their color a hue that did not belong to this world, a soft, iridescent sheen like the underside of a raven's wing or the pearlescent flesh of an unearthly shell. The aprons bore embroidered sigils, a blend of botanical motifs and occult symbols—mandrake roots entwined with serpents, pomegranates split open to reveal seeds like droplets of blood, and the vesica piscis, the oval form representing the womb, the portal of life.

At the center of each apron, stitched in shimmering silver, was a five-pointed star, its lines interwoven with golden threads to create an endless knot. Within the star's center, a small, polished stone rested—a moonstone for Hannah, its milky surface veined with opalescent blue, and a sunstone for Virginia, warm and golden with flecks of amber. These stones, cradled in their settings, seemed to pulse faintly, as if echoing the rhythm of their hearts.

Hannah's fingers trembled at her sides, each movement causing the beads on her sleeves to whisper against the fabric, a soft, rhythmic sound like a chant. The tremor betrayed the weight of what lay ahead, the uncertainty woven through every thread of her attire.

Virginia's face remained stoic beneath her veil, her expression obscured by the filigree patterns cast by the lace. She stood with a stillness that defied reason, her form more statue than flesh, as if she had already crossed into the realm of the sacred, or perhaps the damned.

Behind them, the air grew heavy, as if invisible tendrils of incense smoke wound through the room, carrying the scent of myrrh and night-blooming flowers, a perfume of ritual and resignation.

They were no longer merely brides—they were vessels, altars, the embodiments of the sacred union between life and death, standing on the precipice of a ceremony that would transform them, body and soul.

Rebecca followed behind them, her heart pounding in her chest. Once inside, she stood near the edge of the temple chamber, the cold tile beneath her feet seeping through the thin soles of her ritual slippers. The robe draped over her shoulders was a soft alabaster, a shade of white that seemed to resist the flickering candlelight. It was an elegant garment, woven with threads that shimmered like spider silk, yet it rested on her like a shroud.

The high collar chafed against her neck, its embroidered symbols—interlocking circles and crescent moons—pressing into her skin.

Around her waist hung a sash of woven silver strands, each thread marked with tiny red beads like droplets of blood, a stark reminder of the sacrifices expected of the matriarch.

Rebecca's fingers traced the designs absently, her mind racing. She hadn't chosen this robe. None of them had. Solomon had summoned these garments from the air itself, his mind entwined with the power of Empyrean, his will knitting fabric from nothingness. She had watched in silence as the robes appeared, their folds settling over the shoulders of his chosen followers, as if they had always been there. She could still feel the cool brush of silk against her skin, the sense of unseen hands fastening clasps and tying knots.

This isn't mine, she thought, the words coiling in her mind. *None of this is mine.*

At the temple's rear, Hiram and McBride stood in their ordinary clothes. They were shadows at the edge of Solomon's world, as if the Empyrean's magic couldn't reach them—or refused to. Their faces were half-lit by the candlelight, their expressions hidden, but Rebecca sensed the isolation. Solomon hadn't banished them from the temple; he had simply forgotten them, his vision too narrow and bright to see the mundane edges of his own reality.

And from the edges of the gathering, McBride stood in stillness. Watching. Waiting.

Inside, the temple was silent.

No torches burned, yet there was light. It came from above, from the domed ceiling high above them, where celestial bodies moved in perfect synchrony—not painted, not carved, but real. The orrery of Empyrean, vast and alive, casting its ethereal glow across the waiting congregation.

The air smelled of frankincense, myrrh, and something older—something metallic, like the scent of deep earth before a storm.

Solomon stood at the center of the chamber before the altar - arms raised, his voice smooth as oil.

"This is the union foreseen," he said, his words rolling in cadence, practiced, perfect.

The Chosen whispered back, their voices weaving into the air like threads of an unseen loom.

"This is the will of Empyrean."

Nathaniel stood rigid beside Hannah, his hands tightening at his sides. His breath came shallow, uneven. He did not look at her.

His gaze stayed locked on the temple floor, as if looking up would shatter something inside him.

He stared ahead, unblinking.

Solomon turned toward the brides. His fingers dipped into a bowl of dark oil, thick and fragrant, pressing the symbol of the binding onto their foreheads.

The women did not flinch.

Not Virginia.

Not Hannah.

But Rebecca saw the way Hannah's throat moved, the subtle tremor of breath held too long.

She was afraid.

And Nathaniel—he was breaking.

Solomon raised his hands, and he lifted his voice.

Latin. Greek. Enochian. Words from somewhere older than time, curling through the air like smoke.

"Nos coniungimur in aeternum. Per hoc vinculum sacrum."

The women repeated it.

Their voices did not waver.

Solomon continued, his voice weaving the final strands of the ceremony.

"You are bound to Empyrean. Your bodies, your blood, your seed, your wombs—these are no longer your own. They belong to the kingdom."

Virginia remained still.

Hannah's fingers clenched at her sides.

Nathaniel exhaled sharply—barely a sound, but Rebecca heard it.

And McBride?

She did not speak.

She did not move.

But something in the air shifted around her, as if the temple itself recognized her presence.

As if it knew.

Rebecca had watched Solomon grow into this.

He had once been a boy, doubtful, untested, second to Elias's visions.

But now—now, he had become something else.

She watched him move with perfect certainty, the orrery above him shifting in time with his words, the unseen forces of Empyrean aligning with every step he took.

But this was not Elias's power.

This was Solomon's.

And that frightened her more than anything else.

She glanced toward McBride.

The woman's hands rested on the silver head of her cane, her eyes dark and deep as the abyss.

And Rebecca felt something coil in her stomach.

McBride knew.

Not just what was happening.

What was coming.

The ceremony was complete.

The temple hummed softly, its unseen presence pressing against them.

Solomon turned toward the newly bound couple. His hands rose once more.

"It is done."

They bowed. The words fell over them like a weight.

Nathaniel's shoulders were rigid.

Hannah did not look at him.

Virginia did not look at Solomon.

McBride, unseen by all but a few, slipped into the darkness beyond the temple doors.

Rebecca exhaled.

The Chosen rose as one.

And somewhere—somewhere beyond the valley, beyond the borders of Empyrean—something stirred.

Something had seen.

Something had heard.

And the world would never be the same.

The rite ended in silence.

Solomon turned to the assembly.

"It is done."

Nathaniel did not look at Hannah. Hannah did not look at anyone. Virginia's breath came shallow beneath the veil.

The temple doors opened to the night.

The Chosen stood, their white-robed bodies swaying in rhythmic prayer, their voices humming with the final echoes of the rite. The scent of oil and incense clung thick in the air, the aftertaste of something sacred and profane.

Virginia and Hannah stepped out first, their golden veils catching the moonlight, their hands trembling beneath the weight of all that had transpired.

Nathaniel followed, his crimson crown tilted slightly fastened by a red string to his bare shoulder, his gaze unfixed.

And last came Solomon.

His robe swept over the temple steps as he walked forward—then he stilled.

Rebecca, standing at the edges of the gathered faithful, followed his gaze.

A new building stood before them.

It had not been there before.

The valley had *risen* it from the earth.

A structure of seamless stone, smooth as ivory, without seams or chisel marks. A house that had never been built by hands.

It was waiting.

The Chosen did not question it. The valley provided.

But Rebecca felt it.

The way the air around it seemed denser, heavier, watching.

Solomon exhaled softly.

For a moment, there was hesitation—a flicker of something. Something almost like fear.

Then it was gone.

He turned to Virginia and Hannah.

"This is the Creation House."

Virginia's breath hitched. Hannah did not move.

"The valley has spoken," Solomon continued. "This is where the rite of creation will be fulfilled."

The pit in Nathaniel's stomach dropped.

It was meant to be a private union, a private room with his new bride. A consummation in their own time. Their own way.

But there was no privacy in Empyrean.

And Solomon was in control.

Virginia clutched her hands together.

"Alone?"

Solomon smiled.

And then, with absolute certainty, he answered.

"No."

The single word struck like an iron bell.

Nathaniel's fists rested at his sides. Hannah visibly swayed.

Solomon stepped closer to them.

"We will enter together."

Silence.

The weight of the moment pressed into flesh. Into bone.

Virginia's breathing grew sharp and uneven.

Hannah did not speak.

"The rite of creation," Solomon said, his voice rich with certainty, "is not merely an act of flesh. It is the binding of will. It is the continuation of Empyrean. It is divine."

Nathaniel exhaled sharply, his teeth clenched.

The valley watched.

Rebecca stepped forward, her pulse pounding.

She knew—if she spoke now, if she protested, it would break something.

Not the ritual.

Not the night.

But herself.

Solomon turned his gaze to his brother.

For a moment, they were only that. Brothers.

Then he smiled. And he was something else.

"Come," he said, his voice thick with purpose. "The house is waiting."

The doors to the Creation House opened.

A breath of air exhaled from within.

A scent—not of earth, nor stone, nor fire.

Something else.

Something alive.

Nathaniel and Virginia stepped forward.

Hannah followed.

And in that moment—

McBride spoke.

Her voice was low, almost inaudible beneath the hush of the gathered Chosen. The words lifted through the air, folding over themselves in ancient syllables.

"Γίνεσθε ό,τι προορίζεστε να είστε."

Virginia stiffened. Hannah inhaled sharply.

Neither of them knew what it meant.

Not yet.

But they felt it.

Then Solomon entered last.

And as they crossed the threshold, the doors closed behind them.

Sealed.

At first, there was nothing.

No sound. No movement.

Then—

A whisper.

Low. Distant. Unintelligible.

A rustling—not fabric. Not footsteps.

Something unseen.

Virginia shuddered violently. Her hands went to her veil, gripping the gold-threaded fabric like an anchor.

Nathaniel reached for Hannah—but he could not move.

The air itself had shifted, thicker now, charged with something unseen.

The whispering grew louder.

Something unseen touched Hannah's shoulder. She let out a sharp, *silent gasp.*

Then—

Their robes began to unravel.

The fabric moved on its own.

Thread by thread, inch by inch, it unraveled—not pulled, not torn, but undone.

As if the valley itself was stripping them of what little they had left.

All four of them stood nude, exposed, seeing each other and all their vulnerability.

And Solomon smiled.

The valley would take what it was owed.

21

CHAPTER 21 – THE FIRST WARNING
Ethereal vision and magnetic auras.

Rebecca woke in the hush before dawn. The air inside her tent was wrong.

Thick. Still. Holding its breath.

Her fingers twitched, the last echoes of movement lingering in the tendons, as if they had been writing long after the rest of her had fallen still.

She sat up slowly, pushing the deep red blankets from her skin. The candle at her bedside had burned down to the base, its last threads of smoke coiling through the stale air.

She could still hear the echoes of the marriage rites, the celestial oaths, the sealing of Virginia and Hannah into something they did not understand. The words clung to her, whispers woven into the marrow of her bones.

And the Creation House—it lingered. An unseen eye in the dark, its watchful presence a weight at the back of her mind. Though she had not stepped inside, it had seen her. She was sure of it.

Rebecca shifted her feet against the packed earth, and something cool brushed her skin.

Her breath caught.

Not just wax. Symbols.

Carved into the ground where the melted wax had pooled—sharp, deliberate lines that scored the earth itself.

She leaned closer, fingers hovering just above the etched shapes. They did not smudge. Did not bend to her touch. These marks were not made by human hands.

She had seen them before.

Not here.

Not in Empyrean.

But in her dream.

The one where she had seen Gideon.

Where she had seen Ezra.

Where she had seen their skin touched by silver and changed.

Her pulse quickened, a drumbeat against the hollow quiet. She drew her shawl around her shoulders, its fabric thin as old parchment, and stepped outside.

The camp still slept. The fires had burned low, their embers glowing like the last breath of stars. Shadows draped themselves over the tents, shifting as if stirred by an unseen hand.

And there—just beyond the dying fire—

McBride stood.

Her silhouette cut against the dim glow of the embers, a shape both present and not, as if she stood in the world and somewhere else at once. Her gown hung in still folds, and her hair, unbound and dark, moved despite the air's stillness.

Her hands were clasped at her waist, fingers curled like roots. Her eyes were closed, lashes dark crescents against her skin. She looked as if she were in prayer—or perhaps, in the act of listening to something far beyond the camp's edge.

Rebecca's feet stilled. She felt the earth breathe beneath her, the soil alive and awake.

McBride opened her eyes.

Pale. Unblinking. A quiet, unfathomable light within them.

"You felt it, didn't you?" Her voice threaded through the air, soft but unyielding, each syllable a hook beneath the skin.

Rebecca's pulse faltered.

"Felt what?" she asked, though the truth already curled inside her chest, sharp and cold.

McBride's lips curved, a slow, knowing smile. "The words."

Rebecca frowned. "What words?"

McBride did not answer. Instead, her gaze dropped, drawn downward with a weight that tugged at Rebecca's own bones.

Rebecca followed her line of sight—

And her stomach dropped.

Her fingertips were stained.

Dark. Inky black.

As if she had written something in the night.

Something she did not remember writing.

A gust of wind stirred the ashes at her feet. The embers in the fire pit flared—just enough to cast light over the dirt behind her.

Rebecca turned.

And there—scratched deep into the earth—

"The valley is not land. It keeps what it is given."

Her breath shuddered out of her, misting in the cool air.

McBride did not move. She remained as she was—still, clasped, watching. The forest behind her yawned wide, the trees a dark choir, their limbs swaying to a song just beyond hearing.

"Now," she murmured, "why would you go and write something like that?"

The ground beneath Rebecca's feet felt thin, a skin stretched over a yawning void. She had the sense that if she stepped back, even an inch, the earth would peel away and she would fall through—to where, she did not know.

Temperance McBride, the Sophia of the Forest, stood as if she had always been there, as if she were not bound by the same hours and seasons. Her presence drew the night around her, a cloak of twilight, and Rebecca felt the pull—the quiet, insistent tug of something ancient, something that moved beneath the world's skin.

Rebecca's mouth opened, but no sound came.

McBride's eyes softened, and for a moment, there was something tender in the way she looked at Rebecca—a sweetness beneath the shadow.

"Hush," she said. "The night has not yet finished speaking."

And somewhere, deep in the woods, the wind began to whisper.

Solomon stood alone in the temple.

The air inside was thick. Alive. Each breath tasted of smoke and iron, as if the very walls bled beneath the weight of what had transpired.

The marriage and creation rituals had bound the first of the unions. Virginia, Hannah, and Nathaniel were his now, more than ever. They had knelt before him, their eyes glazed with reverence, their bodies twisted into rhythms of devotion.

And yet—

The temple was not silent.

The orrery stood at the chamber's center, its brass rings and glass spheres catching the dim torchlight. It had begun moving on its own, the celestial bodies charting a path that he had not commanded. Each rotation set a low hum into the stone floor, a vibration that crept up through his boots, settling beneath his skin.

Solomon's fingers grazed the cold metal. It pulsed, almost imperceptibly, as if something beneath its surface stirred—something alive, something waiting.

The manuscript lay open on the altar beside him. Its pages quivered in the draft that wormed its way through the ancient stone, the words dancing in the fickle glow.

He knew them by heart. The prophecies, the commandments, the truths of Empyrean. He had etched them into his mind, whispered them to the faithful, and wielded them like a blade.

But now—

New lines had appeared.

Scrawled in the margins, cramped and hurried, the ink still wet. The words twisted through the familiar text, like a vine strangling a sapling, their shapes wrong, their angles biting.

They were not in his handwriting.

And they were not in the language of Empyrean.

His breath slowed. His chest tightened, his ribs locking like a trap closing in on itself. He reached out, fingers hovering above the ink—but stopped just short. His hands did not tremble. He would not let them. But something else did. The temple. The air. The space between the walls, pressing in.

The letters seemed to ripple, as if sensing his proximity, as if they might leap from the page and burrow into his flesh.

"You are not the first."

The voice was a sigh, a brush of air against the nape of his neck.

Solomon turned sharply, his robes snapping against his legs.

No one was there.

Only the temple. The altar. The book.

And the words, waiting to be read.

His lips moved, shaping the foreign script, the sounds thick and viscous, as if the air itself resisted him. His tongue felt heavy, leaden, as though the words turned to ash upon his mouth.

Images bloomed behind his eyes—a procession of faces, hollow and gray, their mouths sewn shut with wire. The creation house, its walls wet with blood, the marriage rites twisted into something ancient and hungry. Rebecca, her hands ink-stained, her eyes filled with shadows.

A warmth trickled down his lip. He touched his mouth, and his fingers came away red.

The temple watched him.

Its stones leaned inward, the shadows deepening in the arches. The orrery turned, its spheres grinding against one another, a sound like bone on bone.

Solomon swallowed the copper tang of blood, steadying himself. His mind sharpened, the blade of his will carving through the encroaching dark.

"I am the first."

The temple did not respond. But something shifted. The hum beneath his feet grew.

And the words, still wet upon the page, began to fade—soaking into the parchment, the ink bleeding like an open wound. The manuscript closed.

Solomon grimaced.

"The lost books of Moses," Solomon reads from the germanic words embossed on the cover of the manuscript.

He would rewrite them.

He would make them his own.

"Die verlorenen Bücher von Salomon," he thought in German.

"The lost books of Solomon," He smiled to himself.

And the people—they would never know the difference.

* * *

Gideon stood at the town's edge, the Shelmire journal still clutched in his hands. His knuckles had turned white against the worn leather, the sharp corner biting into his palm. He barely felt it. Pain had become a constant hum, a dull counterpoint to the sharper ache of truth settling into his bones.

Ezra sat nearby on a splintered log, the wood soft and damp beneath him. He had rolled up his sleeves, baring his forearms to the fading light. The skin there had taken on the same blue-silver hue as the others—a creeping stain, like frostbite, only colder.

Tiny veins of silver webbed beneath his skin, catching the dusk in glints and flashes. The discoloration had spread past his wrists now, creeping up toward the crook of his elbows. Each new inch lost felt like the winding down of a clock, the slow tick-tick of time slipping through their fingers.

Gideon turned back to the journal, flipping to the final entry. He had read it a hundred times—had worn the ink with his eyes, traced the letters in the dark when sleep would not come.

"The valley is not land. It keeps what it is given."

But now—for the first time—he wondered if the valley had been trying to warn them.

Not keep them out.

But keep them from going back in.

A shiver licked up his spine, as if the valley itself had exhaled against his skin. He clenched his jaw, forcing his breath to steady, though his ribs ached with each rise and fall.

"We're running out of time."

Ezra frowned, his expression soft despite the pallor beneath his skin. The blue-silver had leeched the warmth from his cheeks, leaving him a portrait half-finished, all shadows and sunken places.

"For what?"

Gideon exhaled. The words sat heavy in his throat, a stone he had carried for too long.

"To reach our mother."

Ezra's frown deepened, and for a moment, the boyishness in him broke through—the way he had once looked, bright and full of possibility, before the valley had marked them all. Before the silver, before the sickness.

The sky had turned the color of iron. The last light fell in narrow bands through the trees, casting stripes across the ground, as if the world itself were caged.

Ezra's hands tightened over his forearms, his nails digging into the skin. Where they broke the surface, dark beads of blood welled—silver-laced, catching the light.

"Do you think she's still alive?" Ezra's voice was small, a child's voice, though he had long since left childhood behind.

Gideon's chest constricted. His own arms itched beneath the sleeves of his coat, a phantom burn where the silver had not yet touched him. He knew it was only a matter of time. The sickness came for them all, slowly, with the patience of the earth.

"I don't know," Gideon said. "But if she is—we can't let her think we've forgotten her."

Ezra's eyes shone, and for a moment, Gideon did not see his brother—but a reflection of their mother, the same soft sorrow, the same quiet strength.

In the distance, the valley yawned wide. The forest whispered, a low susurration that pulled at the edges of the world.

Gideon closed the journal, pressing it to his chest. The leather was warm, its worn edges like the grip of a hand.

"The valley is not land. It keeps what it is given."

They had been given.

But they were not yet lost.

Not while they still drew breath.

Not while their mother's name still sat between them, a fragile hope, a tether in the dark.

Gideon rose, his shadow stretching long behind him, swallowed by the first touch of night.

"Come on," he murmured. "Lets figure out whether we can communicate back."

Ezra followed, the blue-silver gleaming beneath the twilight, a promise of what lay ahead—and what they might still save, if only they were not too late.

* * *

Rebecca stood near the northern cliffs of Empyrean as they cut sharp against the twilight sky -- staring down at her hands. The ink stained her skin, dark and unyielding, seeping into the fine lines of her palms. She had scrubbed until the skin split, raw and red beneath the smudges, but the words remained—a brand, a reminder.

Her fingers trembled, curling into fists. She could still feel the rhythm of the writing, the way her hand had moved in the night, guided by something not entirely her own. Each stroke of ink had felt both forced and inevitable, as if her body were a vessel for a will that ran beneath the earth, old and unsleeping.

The wind gusted, sharp and cold. It bit into her, the salt air mingling with the copper tang of blood where her nails had cut crescents into her palms. Below, the cliffs fell away into a tangle of rocks and shadow. The sea beyond was a silver line, distant and dreaming.

Footsteps behind her.

Rebecca did not turn, but her spine stiffened, a taut line from neck to heel. The sound of boots crunching over loose stone crept closer, each step deliberate, unhurried.

Then—silence.

Hiram stood just behind her, a dark silhouette against the bruised sky. He did not speak. His presence stretched into the space between them, filling it with something heavy and unspoken.

Rebecca swallowed, her pulse a drumbeat in her ears. The ink seemed to throb, a stain that pulsed with its own heartbeat.

"You saw something, didn't you?"

His voice was soft, lacking its usual bite. The absence of cruelty was unnerving. She turned sharply, her heart slamming against her ribs.

"What?"

Hiram's expression held none of his typical amusement. His features were drawn, the sharpness of his jaw more shadow than flesh. His eyes—usually bright with mischief or malice—were dull, ringed with exhaustion. He looked not at her, but through her, as if she were a window into something beyond.

The ground felt thin beneath her feet, the stone cold and unyielding. Her throat tightened, a noose of unspoken fears.

Hiram exhaled, the sound low and drawn. "You're thoughts are easy for me to see." He smiled gently.

Her breath caught. The words wound around her, pulling tight, binding.

The wind stirred, threading between them, and the world seemed to lean closer.

She searched his face for the lie, for the glint of mockery. But there was nothing. Only the raw edge of truth, stripped of its pretense.

"What do you mean?" Her voice was thin, barely more than a whisper.

Hiram's jaw tightened. His hands, usually loose and quick with gestures, were still. His fingers dug into his sides, knuckles white beneath the skin.

"I've been watching," he said, but there was no smugness in it, no arrogance. Only certainty.

"I'm a spy, remember? I observe."

He hesitated—just for a fraction of a second, barely enough to be noticed.

But Rebecca caught it. The same hesitation she had felt, that first moment of realizing the world was not what she thought. The same hesitation before you admit that you know something is real.

He smiled again.

The sky above darkened, clouds gathering at the edges of the horizon. The first stars bled through, cold and distant.

Rebecca's mind raced. She had thought herself alone—set apart by this strange communion, this silent language that wrote itself into her skin. But if Hiram, too, had felt it—if others had seen—

The weight of it pressed down on her, a stone on her chest. They were not mad. They were not alone.

And whatever truth threaded through them, Solomon did not see it.

Or perhaps—he did. And that was the greater danger.

Hiram took a step closer, his shadow swallowing hers. The cliffs loomed behind her, the drop a whisper away. But his voice was low, grounding.

"You can tell me, whatever it is you've seen. You can trust me..."

Rebecca nodded. She did not need him to finish.

It would change everything.

A tremor passed between them, a silent vow. For the first time, Rebecca saw Hiram not as a threat, but as an ally—however fragile, however fleeting.

The ink on her skin burned cold. Hiram watched her, waiting, unblinking. And beneath the cliffs, a sea of indigo blooms—one neither of them could ignore any longer.

<h1 style="text-align:center">22</h1>

CHAPTER 22 – THE FIRST FRACTURES
The valley obeys the will—but not without memory.

Rebecca woke to silence—not the natural hush of morning, but a stillness so deep it pressed against her ribs.

Not a tent. Not the open air of the valley.

A house.

She sat up slowly. The walls around her were seamless, as if the dwelling had not been built but placed. The air was cool, scented with damp stone. Light stretched across the floor from a single window carved into the rock.

She hadn't asked for this.

Wrapping her shawl tightly, Rebecca rose and stepped outside. The valley had changed.

Buildings had appeared, not constructed by hands, but formed.

Rebecca exhaled sharply. Something deep in her bones told her—this was not a gift.

And when she turned, McBride was watching her.

The woman stood at the edge of the firepit, cane in hand, expression unreadable.

"You don't like your house," McBride mused.

Rebecca swallowed. "It wasn't here yesterday."

McBride's lips curled slightly. "Neither was the temple. Neither was the Creation House."

Rebecca's stomach twisted.

"This isn't right," she whispered.

McBride tilted her head. "Then why does he keep growing it?"

Rebecca's breath caught.

Solomon stood before the orrery, its celestial rings shifting slowly in the dim torchlight.

It had changed.

The stars etched upon its spheres had moved overnight. A new alignment. A new command.

Beyond the temple, the royal manor had formed at the valley's edge—a vast structure of white stone, untouched by tools. This was the new home of Solomon and Virginia. Nathaniel and Hannah had been given a small home. The temple's corridors stretched further, its ceilings arching higher.

And then there was the Creation House.

Solomon's fingers rubbed over the edges of the orrery.

He had not spoken its existence.

He had not willed it into being.

Not consciously.

And yet—it stood, solid and waiting, as if the valley had pulled the thought from his mind before he had even formed it.

The valley had answered him.

It was listening.

Behind him, Nathaniel entered the chamber, his footfalls cautious on the temple's stone floor.

"Brother," Nathaniel greeted. His voice was careful.

Solomon turned. He gazed upon his brother, seeing him more than a brother now.

Nathaniel hesitated. "I...I don't know... ."

Solomon smiled. "what is it? what don't you know?"

Nathaniel's jaw tightened.

Solomon waited.

Then—Nathaniel bowed his head.

"We are the divine race."

Solomon placed a hand on his shoulder. "Good."

But even as he spoke the word, his fingers trembled slightly.

Virginia stood apart outside, watching.

Her long hair unbound, curling over her shoulders. But it wasn't her appearance that unsettled Rebecca.

It was the way Virginia appeared.

Nathaniel stepped from the temple, his movements slow, deliberate.

He passed Virginia without pause.

Not just failing to greet her—failing to register her.

His gaze was unfixed, empty, as though he were seeing something else entirely.

Rebecca's breath hitched. Virginia turned her head slightly, as if sensing Rebecca's gaze. Their eyes met, and a ripple of unease passed through Rebecca.

Virginia's lips parted in confusion.

She had just realized it too.

The temple had reshaped itself overnight. The valley responded to Solomon's unspoken will, its halls stretching into new corridors.

But within those walls, something else had changed.

Hannah ran her fingers along the smooth stone. The texture felt different beneath her touch, as though something unseen was woven into its foundation.

She exhaled, pressing her palm to the altar.

The pulse of resistance was subtle—faint, but present.

She had never questioned Solomon's authority before. But now, something in her own body felt—opposed.

She pulled back, breath catching in her throat.

The altar beneath her fingertips thrummed, an almost imperceptible vibration—like the valley itself was resisting.

A whisper of knowledge imbued her thoughts. She could undo this. The valley had told her so.

She just didn't know how yet.

* * *

The abandoned town of Hindostan had awakened.

Hammers struck wood. Stones were lifted into place. The skeletons of buildings once ruined now stood firm, repaired by hands both calloused and determined.

Gideon wiped sweat from his brow, watching as Ezra and a few others worked to reinforce the watchtower.

It was slow. It was difficult.

But it was real.

Ezra stepped back, inspecting their progress. His skin—touched with silver-blue undertones, veins shimmering in certain light—was still unfamiliar to them all.

"One more beam," Ezra muttered, voice edged with exhaustion.

Gideon nodded, gripping the splintered wood of the structure.

They had to finish.

Not just for protection.

Not just to survive.

But to prove they were different from the ones they had left behind.

The valley did not shape their world for them.

They built it themselves.

Lucy was sweeping out one of the old schoolhouses when she saw it.

At first, she thought it was just dust—dark streaks marking the wooden floors.

But then she stepped closer.

Her breath caught.

Letters.

Not written in ink. Not carved by hands.

But formed—etched into the grain of the wood.

She turned sharply, calling out: "Gideon!"

He arrived within moments, brow furrowed. "What is it?"

Lucy pointed.

Gideon knelt.

His pulse quickened.

"The valley is not land. It keeps what it is given."

Ezra entered next, staring down at the writing.

"Who did this?"

Lucy shook her head. "No one. I was the first in here this morning."

A chill settled over them.

Gideon touched the words.

They had not been written by hand.

They had appeared.

Something was trying to reach them.

Something unseen.

And then—

Ezra's breath hitched.

"Look."

Gideon followed his gaze.

There—beneath the writing.

A pause.

A hesitation before the truth fully settled.

Two small words.

A name.

Rebecca Whitmore.

The room seemed to shrink, the air thickening.

Gideon's breath came sharp, too loud in the quiet.

Ezra's pulse thundered against his throat.

23

CHAPTER 23 – MESSAGES THROUGH THE VEIL
To speak across worlds is to surrender control of your voice.

The wind murmured through the empty schoolhouse, slipping through the cracks in the warped wooden walls like an unseen presence. The torch outside flickered against the deepening dusk, its glow casting restless shadows that stretched and retreated against the timbers.

Gideon Whitmore stood at the front of the room, his fingers pressed against the worn, splintered surface of the teacher's desk. Beneath his hand, the words carved into the wood had not faded. If anything, they had deepened overnight, as if the message itself wished to be seen. "The valley is not land. It keeps what it is given."

He exhaled slowly, the weight of it pressing against his chest.

Lucy stepped closer, her hands folded neatly before her. "You don't have to believe it," she said softly. "But you can't deny it's there."

Ezra, standing just behind them, crossed his arms. The low light caught the unnatural gleam beneath his skin—his silver-threaded veins shifting beneath his flesh like liquid moonlight. His transformation was further along than the others. Perhaps that was why **he** felt the message more keenly than Gideon did.

"This ain't the first time it's happened," Ezra murmured, eyes never leaving the inscription. "It ain't the first time the valley's spoken."

Gideon's jaw tightened. He had spent his entire life resisting his father's talk of prophecy and divine lands, and yet here he was—witnessing something impossible.

Eleanor approached from the doorway, her soft footfalls stirring the dust along the floorboards. Her gaze flickered between the three of them, settling last on Ezra. "You feel it, don't you?" she asked. "Like somethin's waitin'."

Ezra was silent for a long moment, then gave a slow nod. "I do."

Gideon let out a sharp breath, rubbing a hand over his face.

"This is madness." His fingers tightened around the journal, the leather warm from his grip.

"Even if it is a message, even if it's from my mother—how in God's name are we supposed to answer it? You don't just write a letter in the dirt and expect an answer." Eliza stepped forward, her presence quieter but no less firm. "The journal."

Gideon turned to her. "What?"

She met his gaze evenly. "The old journal. The one from the people who lived here before. They wrote about things like this, didn't they? Messages. Signs. The one you carry around with you all the time—use it."

Gideon hesitated, then reached into his coat pocket, withdrawing the worn leather-bound book. The pages were brittle beneath his fingertips as he flipped through them, searching for anything—anything—that might bridge the impossible distance between them and Rebecca Whitmore.

The words blurred beneath his gaze, scrawled in a hand long since stilled. "Spirit-writing is the tongue of the unseen. It speaks in shadow, in sleep, in silvered hands."

Gideon frowned. "Spirit-writing ain't meant to reach the living. It's a language for the dead."

Lucy stepped forward, her voice quiet but insistent. "Maybe that's what your father told you. Maybe that's what he believed. But your mother ain't dead, Gideon. And neither are we."

Ezra ran a hand over the back of his neck. "We don't need to send a message to the dead. We just need to send a message through the veil."

Gideon met his brother's gaze, the realization settling between them like an unspoken agreement. "Then we find a way to do it."

Midnight had settled over Hindostan like a cloak. Inside the schoolhouse, the fire in the silver chalice burned low, casting strange shapes against the walls. The scent of myrrh and crushed quartz curled in the air, mingling with the metallic tang of the silver-infused oil spread across the wooden surface.

Ezra knelt before the makeshift altar, his breath hitching as the firelight caught his skin. The silver threads beneath the surface pulsed—not just reflecting the light, but moving with it, shifting in time with the air, as though sensing what was to come.

"We ain't writing this message like a letter," he murmured. He brought forward a knife and cut his fingertip, drawing blood. He then dipped finger into the fine silver dust. He gasped slightly as the silver salts burned his self-inflicted wound,

"We ain't speakin' it aloud. We're sending it the only way it can be sent. Through the thread that binds blood to blood."

Lucy stepped forward, the bowl of herbs cradled in her hands.

"You ready?"

Ezra nodded once. "Light the fire."

The flame flared as the herbs were thrown into the silver basin. Ezra inhaled deeply, letting the smoke settle into his lungs. His fingers trembled only slightly as he reached out, pressing the tip of his silver-coated finger against the wooden surface.

The moment the first mark was drawn, the air shifted.

A hum, low and resonant, vibrated through the floorboards. The symbols did not simply appear—they emerged, rising from the wood like breath against glass, like something surfacing after being buried for too long. Ezra's fingers burned, the message carving itself as much into him as it did the wood.

His breath came faster. The weight of the message pressed into his mind, into his hands, guiding him without words.

"Mother, we received your message. Gideon and Ezra."

The last mark burned as it was completed. A final exhale, a final whisper of breath over the inscription.

The fire flickered.

Then—

The words faded.

Not erased. Taken.

Ezra fell back on his heels, his chest rising and falling in shallow bursts. The silver shimmer along his skin had dimmed, but the heat of the ritual still lingered in his bones.

Gideon stepped forward, staring at the now-blank wooden surface. "Did it work?"

Lucy tilted her head. "If it did... she'll know soon enough."

The silence stretched between them, vast and waiting.

Then the wind stirred again—soft, whispering—

And somewhere, far beyond their reach, Rebecca Whitmore heard.

24

❧

CHAPTER 24 – UNLOCKING THE PASSAGE
There is no veil. Only vision, once it is returned to you.

Rebecca lay still in the flickering candlelight, her fingers trembling above the worn wooden floor. The symbols had appeared again—etched into the wood, the script neither hers nor entirely unfamiliar. She swallowed hard, her breath coming slow, measured.

It had worked. They had answered.

She traced the silvered letters with her fingertips, the words humming with unseen energy:

Mother. We received your message. Gideon and Ezra.

Her throat tightened. The words blurred, silvered letters wavering under her breath. They were alive. The boys she had left behind had broken through the veil, speaking to her across a distance that should have been impossible. And yet—their names burned in the air, humming with the weight of something real.

But how? And what did it mean for her now?

A voice broke the stillness.

"What did I tell you, child?"

Rebecca flinched, turning sharply. McBride. The woman stood near the doorway, her gloved hands resting on the silver head of her cane, her silhouette cutting a sharp figure against the dim lantern light.

McBride stepped forward, her dark eyes flickering over the symbols. "The silver road runs both ways."

Rebecca exhaled. "They heard me."

Temperance squinted at the glowing letters, her lips curling into a smirk.

"That's it? 'We received your message'? Lord have mercy." She tapped her cane against the floor, the sound sharp and impatient. "Did they run out of parchment halfway through, or are your sons just that charming?"

Rebecca's brow knitted.

"They're alive. That's all that matters."

"Sure, sure." Temperance waved a dismissive hand. "But a little poetry wouldn't have killed them. 'Dear Mother, we languish in the wilderness, but your voice is the silver thread that binds our weary souls.' Something! Anything! Instead, they've sent you a list."

She muttered under her breath, "Men."

Rebecca stared down at the message, her heart pounding against her ribs. The fire crackled in the silence. The weight of it settled over her. The path was open.

McBride tilted her head. "Sleep well. Tomorrow, we start the real work."

Rebecca lifted her gaze. "The waking dream."

McBride nodded. "You'll see them as you did before—but this time, you'll know it for what it is."

Rebecca swallowed, her pulse thrumming with a mixture of unease and anticipation. She would see her sons. Not just their words scrawled in silver light—but truly, fully see them.

McBride tapped her cane against the floor. "Now rest, child. You'll need your strength."

Rebecca hesitated before nodding, drawing the blanket around herself. As she closed her eyes, she could still feel the lingering pull of the message beneath her fingers.

She would see them again.

Tomorrow.

At midday, McBride led Rebecca deep into the forest—back to the place where they had first met.

Rebecca had expected secrecy—cloaked figures and whispered chants beneath the shroud of night. But instead, McBride had led her here: a clearing bathed in green, sunlight fracturing through the canopy, the wind alive with voices that only the leaves could translate. It was not the silence of darkness, but the silence of waiting. The silence of something about to begin.

"The Waking Dream can only take root in nature," McBride explained, gesturing to the space around them. "It is a thing of life. Of breath. Of motion. It must be performed under the sun."

Rebecca inhaled slowly, letting the warmth of the light settle into her skin. The moment felt strange, sacred.

McBride knelt, drawing a slow, deliberate symbol in the dirt. A spiral, twisting inward. A path that did not end.

"This is where we begin."

Rebecca swallowed. She was ready.

McBride guided her through the motions,

"Sit upon the earth. Let it hold you.

Breathe. Slow and deep.

Let the world blur."

Rebecca obeyed. She focused on her breath, on the feeling of sunlight filtering through her closed eyelids.

And then—something shifted.

For the briefest moment, the air folded inward, pressing against her like the weight of deep water. The world dimmed, the edges softening, slipping away. And then—

A voice. Not loud. Not clear. But there. A thread in the dark.

Rebecca's breath caught. Gideon.

She reached for it, straining to grasp the thread of his presence, to pull it toward her—but the moment she did, the connection snapped.

Rebecca gasped, jolting upright. The vision was gone.

McBride sighed, shaking her head. "You pulled too hard."

Rebecca clenched her jaw, frustration bubbling inside her. "I saw him. I heard him."

McBride sighed, shaking her head.

"You reached for him with your hands when you should have reached with your breath. That's why you lost him." She tilted her head, considering. Then, with absolute certainty, "Tomorrow, you will not."

Rebecca exhaled, nodding.

Tomorrow, she would succeed.

25

CHAPTER 25 – THE COST OF DOMINION
The kingdom built in silence always cracks in silence first.

The air inside the temple was thick—too thick. The scent of burning myrrh and frankincense oozed through the chamber, cloying and heavy, as if it had weight. As if it pressed down upon the lungs of those who breathed it.

Solomon stood at the center of the great hall, the dying candlelight flickering against the smooth, impossible walls of Empyrean. There was no escape from the weight of his words.

"Empyrean has been tested," he said, his voice steady—too steady. "But we have remained faithful. And now, we will be rewarded."

Rebecca stood among them, her spine straight, her fingers resting against the fabric of her skirts. The ceremonial robes Solomon had commanded them to wear hung from her shoulders like shackles. She had been quiet all day, watching, waiting. Solomon's grip was tightening.

Virginia and Hannah stood to her left, their faces half-hidden in the glow of the fire. They did not speak.

Nathaniel knelt before Solomon, his forehead nearly touching the smooth floor. The oil glistened on his skin, the scent thick, suffocating. Solomon's fingers brushed the back of his head—slow, deliberate. He traced the ridge of Nathaniel's spine with his thumb, pressing the oil into his flesh, tracing the spine to the small of his back. Not an anointing. A claim. Solomon reached down, brushing his fingers over the back of Nathaniel's head.

"You understand, don't you?"

Nathaniel's voice was soft—too soft. "Yes, Prophet."

Rebecca's breath hitched.

Something inside her twisted at the way Solomon touched her youngest son—not cruel, not tender, but possessive.

Solomon smiled, fingers tightening ever so slightly against the base of Nathaniel's neck before releasing him. "We are the foundation. We are the divine."

Rebecca clenched her jaw.

Virginia exhaled slowly beside her.

The weight of the moment was suffocating.

Solomon turned his gaze toward Virginia.

She stood, unmoving. Her golden hair loose, cascading over her shoulders. Her ceremonial robe—pure white, untouched by the oil that marked Nathaniel's skin—seemed to resist the light.

"Come forward, my wife" Solomon said.

Virginia did not move.

Rebecca felt it—the shift in the air, the way Solomon's authority should have pulled Virginia to him, but it didn't.

The others may not have noticed, but Rebecca did.

Solomon's jaw tensed. The silence stretched between them, longer than it should have. The air felt thick—wrong. He had felt it too. And for the first time, he knew what it was to be defied.

Finally, Virginia stepped forward, slow and deliberate, as if she had chosen to move—not because he had commanded it, but because she allowed it.

Solomon's expression flickered. Just for a moment.

Then he lifted his hand, fingers grazing her forehead. "You're next for the anointing," he murmured. "You belong to me."

Virginia's lips parted. Not in a gasp, not in protest—but in something unreadable.

Rebecca saw the way her eyes did not quite focus on him, as though she were standing just outside of his reach—not physically, but in some other way.

She was slipping from him.

And Solomon did not yet realize it.

Solomon stepped back, turning toward Hannah next.

She lowered her gaze before he could catch her eyes.

Rebecca knew why.

Hannah was the softest of them—the quiet, obedient one. But that did not mean she was blind.

Rebecca had seen it—the way Hannah's fingers sometimes hovered over the sacred symbols Solomon had carved into the temple walls, as though she could unmake them.

The Gift of Undoing.

She had it, even if she did not yet understand it.

And Rebecca wondered—had Solomon felt it? The way things seemed to decay under Hannah's touch?

Solomon pressed his palm against her forehead. "And I will anoint you last."

Hannah's breath trembled, just slightly.

Rebecca nearly stepped forward, nearly reached for her—

But she stopped herself.

Not yet.

Solomon turned at last to Rebecca.

She did not kneel. She did not bow.

She had followed Elias into Empyrean, believing in something.

She did not believe in Solomon.

"You are the Matriarch," Solomon said, voice smooth as silk. "You, above all, understand the sanctity of this place."

Rebecca met his gaze—unflinching.

Solomon smiled. "You will stand beside me in this."

Rebecca's heart pounded.

She saw the pieces shifting into place, the pattern forming before her like a snare closing around her throat. This was not about Virginia. Not about a single union. Solomon would take them all, as if he was the valley. He would weave them into the foundations of his kingdom, their bodies bound as tightly as the stone of the temple itself. And there would be no escape—not unless they shattered it from within." He would use Nathaniel, Virginia, and Hannah for his own purposes – for his own desires. Each of them a part of the divine race he sought to build.

Her stomach twisted.

"This is the will of Empyrean," Solomon murmured. "And none shall stand against it."

Nathaniel whispered, "Yes, Prophet."

Rebecca could not breathe.

She felt Virginia tense beside her.

Hannah clenched her hands.

And outside the temple walls, the valley did not move.

As if it were waiting.

They left the temple in silence.

Nathaniel followed Solomon without hesitation.

Hannah and Virginia walked beside Rebecca, their robes whispering against the ground.

Rebecca swallowed. *"We cannot stay."*

Virginia did not look at her. "Then we will wait."

Hannah exhaled, staring ahead at nothing. "And when the time comes—"

Rebecca nodded. "We will be ready."

Above them, the stars flickered.

Somewhere, deep in the valley, something stirred.

The cost of dominion was high.

But the cracks had begun to show.

And beyond the valley, something unseen turned its gaze toward Empyrean.

The kingdom would break.
It was only a matter of when.

26

CHAPTER 26 – THE WAKING DREAM
The dead don't always whisper from the grave. Sometimes, they knock from the other side of the veil.

The next morning, Rebecca would enter the forest once again to attempt the waking dream. She felt overwhelmed and drained from the experience she had in the temple just the day before. She reached the edge of the forest and there, standing, was Temperance. The light filtered through the canopy in green shafts, dappling the lime trees lining the path. Rebecca followed McBride deep into the forest, the same place where they had first met. The air was thick with the scent of damp earth and wildflowers, the hush of the valley pressing around them like a living thing.

McBride walked ahead, leading her with an easy confidence, as though she had always known the path.

Rebecca pressed a hand to her chest, feeling the nervous thrum of her heartbeat. She was ready. She had to be.

They stopped in a clearing where the sunlight pierced through the thick branches above, casting a pattern of shifting light on the forest floor. McBride turned to her, removing one glove with slow deliberation before pressing her bare palm to the earth.

"This is where it begins," she murmured.

Rebecca lowered herself onto her knees, mirroring McBride's gesture. The ground beneath her felt different—warmer, pulsing.

McBride reached into her coat, pulling out a small vial. Silver salts. She handed it to Rebecca. "Place a pinch on your tongue."

Rebecca hesitated only a moment before obeying. The metallic taste spread across her tongue, sharp and burning.

McBride leaned in, her voice a low murmur. "Breathe deep. Close your eyes. Let the valley carry you."

Rebecca exhaled slowly, pressing her fingers into the earth.

The world around her began to shift.

Rebecca knelt in the same place, sunlight filtering through the trees.

She did not ask McBride to repeat the instructions. She already knew.

This time, she did not rush.

She let the earth cradle her, let the light flicker across her skin, let the sound of wind and leaves lull her deeper. Her breathing slowed. The world softened.

And then—the veil parted.

At first, there was only darkness.

Then—a flicker.

A whisper of wind against her cheek. The sensation of movement, though she remained still.

Then light. Soft, silvery, unfurling like mist.

Rebecca opened her eyes—and she was there.

The schoolhouse. The city of Gideon. She stood in the doorway, the lantern light inside casting long shadows over the wooden floor.

She turned—and Gideon was there.

He saw her. His breath hitched, eyes widening in disbelief. "Mother?"

Rebecca's throat closed. She stepped forward, her fingers trembling at her sides. She could feel the warmth of the air. She could smell the faint scent of old books and candle wax. This was real.

Ezra's chair scraped against the floor as he stood, his silver-blue skin catching the light. "How?"

Rebecca swallowed hard. "The waking dream."

Gideon exhaled sharply, his hands clenching into fists. "Then listen, because we don't have much time."

Rebecca nodded, her pulse hammering.

Ezra pulled the old Hindostan journal from his vest pocket, flipping to a page marked with hurried ink. "We found something."

Rebecca leaned closer, her breath uneven. "Tell me."

Ezra hesitated only a second before reading aloud.

"The valley is not just land. It is a gate. And a gate must have a key."

Rebecca inhaled sharply, her heart hammering.

A key.

Ezra looked up, his silvered gaze burning into hers. "Mother. We know how to open the passage."

Rebecca pressed a hand to her chest, feeling the steady thrum of her own heartbeat.

She could feel them- the solidity of her sons—their presence. Gideon's furrowed brow, Ezra's silver-brushed hands tightening at his sides. The warm light of the Hindostan ruins felt more real than the cold stone she knew awaited her back in Empyrean.

She wanted to stay.

But something was shifting.

Rebecca opened her mouth, but her voice came apart like mist. Her fingers, once firm and present, had blurred at the edges. She reached for Gideon, desperate to hold on.

He felt solid. She did not.

Gideon noticed. His chest rose sharply, eyes widening in realization.

"No—stay!"

Rebecca's breath hitched as the world continued to pull away. The moment stretched long enough for her to think that maybe—maybe—she could hold on just a little longer.

But the light changed.

The filtered sunlight fractured. The warmth of the Gideonites' fire dimmed. A cold breath of air—Empyrean's air—wrapped around her ribs, stealing her from them.

Ezra lunged—his silver-stained hands ghosted through her as if he were trying to catch water slipping through his fingers.

"Mother!"

Rebecca exhaled as the last of the light peeled away. The ruins, her sons, the warmth—all of it dissolved.

And then—nothing.

The first thing she felt was the damp ground beneath her.

Cool beneath her palms. Unforgiving against her back.

Her breath was sharp- too sharp. Her lungs expanded too fast, her body reacting before her mind fully returned.

The air smelled sweet. The filtered light gleamed through the forest trees.

She was back. Rebecca gasped, bringing herself to stand and orient to reality. The dream—not a dream, no, it was real—had left an aftertaste in her mouth, something metallic, something unfinished. She reached for the feeling, but it was already slipping.

Gideon. Ezra. They had seen her. Had touched her.

She had touched them.

The loss hit her like drowning—like being pulled beneath black water, the last glimmers of firelight flickering above, unreachable.

Her hands pressed against the earth, nails digging into damp soil, as if she could hold on to something—anything—but there was nothing left to hold.

And then—McBride's voice.

Soft, steady, knowing.

"You did well."

Rebecca turned sharply.

McBride stood before her, her gloved hands resting atop her cane, eyes dark with something unreadable.

Rebecca exhaled slowly, something in her chest tightened.

"I don't belong here," McBride said in a low tone. Her figure beginning to return to what it once was when Rebecca first imagined her.

McBride tilted her head slightly, her gaze drifting past Rebecca, toward something unseen. "You'll need to make a choice soon, child."

Rebecca stiffened. "A choice?"

McBride smiled, but there was sadness in it. "Whether to leave this place or let it claim you."

A chill ran up Rebecca's spine.

"Empyrean has no door, Rebecca," McBride continued, voice as smooth as river stones. "Only walls. You and I both know that now."

Rebecca's throat tightened. "Then how do I open the passage?"

McBride studied her for a long moment.

Then—"Blood."

Rebecca flinched.

McBride gave a slow, deliberate nod. "Not just any blood." Her gaze flickered downward. "The sword pointing to the naked heart."

Rebecca exhaled sharply, pressing a hand against her chest, just above her heart.

McBride continued as if she had not noticed. "You know what you have to do, girl. Await the message from your sons. Ezra has the remainder of the ritual. They will send it to you through their silver writing ritual."

Rebecca breathed heavily. "Why are you speaking like this? Like you're leaving?"

McBride smiled again—smaller this time. Softer.

"Because I am."

Rebecca shook her head. "You don't have to."

McBride's eyes darkened, something ancient settling behind them.

"I was never meant to stay."

A breath of wind stirred the forest.

Rebecca took a slow step forward, the damp leaves whispering beneath her feet. "Where will you go?"

McBride chuckled, the sound dry and low. "Where do the things of Empyrean go when they are no longer needed?"

Rebecca hesitated. "Temperance—"

McBride lifted a hand, stopping her. Not harshly. Just final.

"You'll see me again when you don't need to."

Rebecca's chest tightened.

"I need you now."

Temperance McBride smiled, the lines around her eyes deepening, as though she had lived a thousand lifetimes before this moment.

"No, child," she whispered, already stepping back, her figure blurring into the dappled light. "You just think you do."

The filtered sunlight wove through the branches, casting moving shapes across the damp ground.

McBride's outline blurred—not like someone stepping away, but like something dissolving into the green light. The trees did not rustle, but the air shifted, charged with something unseen. A final breath, a ripple in the space she had occupied. And then—she was gone.

Her voice remained.

"It is yours to finish now."

And then—she was gone.

Not like someone who had walked away.

But like something that had never fully been there at all.

The leaves stirred. The wind carried the last breath of her presence through the branches.

Rebecca stared into the empty space where she had stood, the weight of silence pressing down.

Her hands trembled at her sides.

"It is mine to finish now."

Rebecca pressed the heel of her palm against her chest, exhaling shakily.

McBride had left her the truth.

And now she had to decide what to do with it.

Rebecca left the forest, inhaling slow and steady.

The weight of everything— of Temperance McBride and her bless-ing, of Elias's death, of Solomon's control, of Nathaniel's eerie devo-tion—pressed into her ribs, constricting, suffocating.

And then—Hiram was there.

He didn't speak. Just stood at the edge of the forest, his presence grounding, indigo blooms surrounding his feet.

For the first time in weeks, she felt herself breathe.

"You're shaking," he murmured.

She hadn't realized.

Hiram turned slightly, watching her in the half-light. His gaze was unreadable, sharp in a way that unsettled her.

She exhaled. *"I don't know what to do."*

He reached out, fingers skimming her wrist. A touch—barely there, but present.

"Yes, you do," he said quietly.

Rebecca swallowed.

"Did you see everything? In the forest?"

She turned to him, truly seeing him in that moment. Not as a man separate from all this madness, but as someone else who had been caught in it—trapped, just as she was.

Something unspoken shifted between them.

Hiram's moved his hand further around her waist, slow and hesi-tant.

Rebecca didn't pull away.

For once, she let herself lean in.

Just for a moment.

Just for a breath.

Just long enough to feel something real before it could be stolen from her.

His lips were warm—just the faintest brush against hers.

A breath. A pause.

Then—a shadow.

Rebecca felt it before she saw it. The air thickened, pressing against her skin like an unseen hand.

The warmth of Hiram's touch evaporated, replaced with something colder—something claiming.

A shadow. A voice.

A sentence already passed.

And then—Solomon's voice.

"Mother."

She went still.

Hiram tensed, his grip on her wrist tightening— but it was too late.

Slowly, Rebecca turned.

Solomon stood in the clearing not far from them, his expression unreadable.

Nathaniel hovered behind him, silent as a specter. Chained with a lead to Solomon.

Rebecca's heart thudded painfully against her ribs.

Solomon's eyes swept over the scene—the space between them, the shift in Rebecca's breath, the flush in her skin.

Then, finally—his lips curled.

"I see."

The words slid like oil across the silence.

Rebecca's breath caught.

Hiram shifted forward, subtly, a protective motion.

Solomon exhaled, slow. Measured.

"How fortunate that you have finally revealed yourself."

Rebecca's pulse roared in her ears.

She knew. In that instant, she knew.

This—this moment—was what would lead her to the temple.

To her trial.

To her judgment.

To her reckoning.

The night air pressed against her skin.

No more escape.

No more running.
Only the inevitable.
And then—Solomon smiled.

27

CHAPTER 27 – THE TRIAL
"A throne built on silence cannot stand."

The temple doors were thrown open.

Firelight from the torches cast a sickly golden glow over the stone walls, flickering against the towering columns. The air inside was thick with incense, suffocating with the weight of judgment. The valley had never felt more silent—watching. Listening. Waiting.

Rebecca was dragged into the hall, her wrists bound before her, ropes biting into her flesh. She did not resist. She did not cry out. She had known this moment was coming.

The Chosen—if they could still be called that—stood in rows along the temple's edge, faces half-lit by flame, eyes unreadable. Virginia stood among them, her expression carefully neutral. Hannah, beside her, was pale, shoulders rigid.

And at the center of it all, on the raised dais above them, Solomon sat upon his throne.

The seat had not been carved by their hands. It had risen from the valley itself, smooth and seamless, as if Empyrean had always intended him to sit there.

Hiram stood at the temple's threshold, arms crossed, his jaw clenched. His eyes followed Rebecca as she was brought forward.

Nathaniel was beside Solomon. Draped in gold ribbon, nothing else. He did not fidget. He did not speak. He only stared at the floor, vacant. Owned.

Rebecca's stomach twisted.

The silence stretched unbearably long. Then Solomon spoke.

"Rebecca Whitmore, you stand accused of betraying the Prophet Elias."

Solomon's voice rang through the temple, smooth and controlled, yet thick with righteous condemnation.

Rebecca's throat was dry.

"You have defiled his memory," he continued. "You have consorted with the faithless. You have embraced the ways of the lost. And you have disgraced your sacred calling as Matriarch of Empyrean."

Rebecca did not lower her eyes.

"What say you?"

Rebecca inhaled slowly.

"I say Elias was a man, not a god."

Solomon's lips pressed into a thin line.

"You would deny his divinity?"

"I would deny the lie you have woven in his place."

Nathaniel glared. Virginia's hands held at her sides. Hannah took a step back.

Solomon's eyes darkened.

"You have turned from the truth."

"Or perhaps I have found it."

The torches flared, as if stirred by an unseen breath.

Solomon leaned forward, his hands gripping around the armrests of the stone throne. "It is not only your blasphemy that condemns you," he said, voice now dripping with venom. "But your whoredom."

The word slashed through the space between them. Rebecca exhaled sharply, but she did not flinch. She had known he would say it. She had known, from the moment she stepped into this temple, that this would not be a trial of her faith—it would be a trial of her body, her womanhood, her defiance of him. He did not want repentance. He wanted humiliation.

Solomon stood, descending the dais with slow, deliberate steps. The gold embroidery on his robe caught the firelight as he moved.

"I have seen you in the arms of a man who is not your husband."

The murmurs swelled into hushed scandal.

Rebecca's heart pounded. Not for herself.

For Hiram.

Solomon turned to the gathered.

"I ask you all—what does the Scripture say of a woman who betrays her sacred bond?"

The Chosen remained silent.

Rebecca's pulse roared in her ears.

Solomon's gaze flickered to Hiram.

Hiram tilted his head, smirking despite himself.

"And what of the man?" Solomon asked.

Rebecca's stomach twisted.

Virginia and Hannah were silent.

Nathaniel did not lift his eyes.

Solomon turned slowly toward Hiram.

"The Lord's justice is absolute," Solomon said, voice soft, almost gentle. "The sinner must be purged from among us."

A beat of silence.

Then—

"Take him."

The moment Solomon spoke, Hiram surged forward.

Hiram was fast.

A sharp jab to the ribs.

The temple erupted.

Torches swayed. The Chosen hesitated, startled.

Solomon fell to the ground, holding his ribs.

Hiram turned toward Rebecca, ready to free her—

But Nathaniel moved.

Fast. Too fast.

A glint of silver—a ceremonial dagger, unsheathed.

Nathaniel lunged.

Hiram barely dodged, grabbing the boy's wrist mid-strike.

"Nathaniel—" Rebecca gasped.

Nathaniel snarled. A sound feral, raw, inhuman.

Solomon smiled.

Rebecca's stomach plummeted.

Hiram wrenched the dagger from Nathaniel's grip, but did not strike.

Nathaniel breathed hard, chest rising and falling.

And then, Solomon stepped forward.

"This is the loyalty of Empyrean," Solomon said, touching Nathaniel's hair like a pet.

"My brother does not hesitate. He does not question. He knows his place in the divine order."

Rebecca wanted to scream.

Solomon's hand did not leave Nathaniel's head.

"You, Hiram, however—" Solomon's eyes darkened—"have no place here."

Hiram wiped blood from his lip, grinning.

"You don't scare me, boy."

"No?" Solomon's tone was mocking.

Then—the air shifted. Heavy. Pressing.

The torches flickered, and the walls *breathed*.

The ground trembled, slow at first, then stronger.

A deep, resonant vibration moved through the temple. The stone columns groaned. Dust drifted from the ceiling in slow, deliberate spirals, like something exhaling.

Rebecca froze.

Not now.

Not yet.

Solomon's eyes gleamed.

"Empyrean rejects the faithless."

The crack spread.

The walls shuddered. The torches flickered.

Virginia grabbed Hannah's arm, pulling her back.

Hiram glanced up, expression shifting.

Solomon wasn't doing this.

The valley was.

Rebecca's breath came short and fast.

Hiram's jaw tightened.

Then—

A stone cracked loose from the ceiling.

The temple split.

The earth lurched, as if something massive had turned beneath it – tearing at the black and white checkered tiles. Rebecca lunged before she could think.

Solomon did not move—perhaps he could not.

But Hiram did.

He held the dagger he took from Nathaniel, swung—And buried it deep into Solomon's side.

The Prophet staggered. The valley shuddered. The torches snuffed out. And Empyrean itself began to fall.

The air thickened.

The torches snuffed out.

And then—the temple began to crumbling.

The valley had spoken.

Rebecca ran.

Hiram wrenched the dagger free, stepping back.

Nathaniel screamed.

The great stone columns cracked, toppling—

And the trial became an execution.

28

CHAPTER 28 – BREAKING THE CHAINS
"A gate is not opened. A gate is broken."

The temple shook.

Not with the tremors of an earthquake, but with something deeper, something struggling.

The stone groaned, *bending* before breaking, the walls buckling inward as if Empyrean itself was being ripped apart from within. The walls groaned like a thing in pain, the great orrery overhead twisting of its own accord, the celestial bodies no longer in harmony. A terrible fracture in Empyrean itself.

Rebecca stumbled back, her chest rising and falling with rapid breaths. Blood stained the temple floor, the echoes of violence still fresh in the air. Solomon had fallen—thrown by Hiram's rage, cast against the sacred stone.

But it was not over.

The valley was reacting.

The fire that had always burned pure and controlled within the temple now roared wildly, licking at the air with tendrils of heat, illuminating the spiraling inscriptions along the chamber's walls. Smoke curled into the sacred sigils, distorting them, unraveling them.

Something was fighting back.

Rebecca felt it—the unraveling of a power that had bound them for too long.

"Now," she whispered, her voice trembling but resolute. "We must open the passage. Now follow me!"

Virginia and Hannah followed Rebecca out of the temple, their hands tightening around each other's. Nathaniel followed in slow, uncertain steps, his wide eyes darting toward Solomon's collapsed form, toward the way his brother's fingers twitched against the stone.

The temple pulsed.

The valley was listening.

Rebecca's heart thundered as she moved quickly to her home.

"The silver message. We must read the final ritual from Ezra's message."

She had hoped it was there.

When she flung open the door and looked to the ground, there it was. Glistening in silver. Ezra's message containing the remainder of the opening ritual.

Hannah, Virginia and Nathaniel stepped into the house and saw Rebecca pulling the sacred blade she had taken the altar. The dagger was forged before Empyrean, a relic of the world before they had crossed through. Silver. Pure. A blade that could sever bindings.

Hannah met her gaze first, her lips pressed into a thin line. No hesitation. No fear.

Rebecca turned the blade in her hands, feeling its weight, then pressed the cold tip against Hannah's chest, just above the heart.

"The sword points to the naked heart."

Hannah did not flinch.

A single drop of blood beaded at the tip of the dagger as Rebecca pressed, then withdrew.

The first offering.

Virginia stepped forward next. Her breath was slow, controlled, but her eyes burned with something defiant. As the blade kissed her skin, Rebecca swore she saw the faintest flicker of power shimmer beneath her flesh, as if the valley itself resisted marking her.

The blood fell onto the floor atop the silver message, joining Hannah's.

Nathaniel stood and watched the three women circling the silver message sent by his brothers.

His lips trembled. His body was not yet a man's, but his eyes had long lost the innocence of a child.

The ground shuddered beneath them.

Rebecca's breath came unevenly. The valley was responding.

The passage was forming.

A deafening crack split the air.

The temple lurched violently, the firelight flaring, casting monstrous shadows across the walls. A wind, unnatural and howling, swept through the chamber, extinguishing every torch at once.

Then—Solomon's laughter.

Low at first. Weak.

But growing.

Solomon rose from where he had fallen, his face half-lit by the shifting firelight, his lip curled, blood trickling from the side of his mouth.

He found his way to Rebecca's house and entered.

"You think you can leave?"

His voice was not his own.

It was deeper. Layered. As if something spoke through him.

Rebecca's stomach twisted. The valley was not letting him go.

Solomon took a slow step forward, his movements unnatural, as if guided by unseen strings. His eyes—

Black.

Not dark. Not shadowed.

Pure, consuming black.

The valley had claimed him.

Nathaniel froze, his breathing shallow, his hands curled into fists. Something flickered in his gaze—recognition.

He saw it too.

Solomon was no longer Solomon.

Rebecca took a step back, positioning herself between him and the others.

Virginia grabbed Nathaniel's wrist, pulling him away from Solomon. Hannah reached for the silver dust, casting it over the ritual markings, completing the final step. The air hummed, the unseen barrier between this world and the next beginning to tear.

They were so close.

Solomon tilted his head, his lips twitching into something inhuman.

His voice was silk. "You are mine."

Rebecca did not hesitate.

She spoke aloud, her voice unnatural.

"Αφήστε τη μήτρα της να ανοίξει και να μας ελευθερώσει"

The final words of the ritual.

The temple erupted.

A sound unlike anything they had ever heard filled the space—a roar of wind, of breaking stone, of something ancient giving way.

A rift tore through the air.

Not a door. Not a gate.

A wound.

A rip through the very fabric of Empyrean.

Virginia moved first, pulling Nathaniel toward it, Hannah at her side. The force of the passage's opening dragged at them, pulling them toward the unknown.

Solomon lunged.

His fingers grasped at Nathaniel's metal wrist collar.

Nathaniel turned, mouth parted, eyes wide.

Solomon's voice, raw and layered, spoke—but the words did not feel like his.

They coiled, many voices speaking at once, as if the valley itself had filled his throat.

"You belong to me!"

Nathaniel gasped, his entire body jolting as if struck. He wrenched away, his neck burning hot—Solomon's grip tightening just for a second before—snap. He broke free. Rebecca seized his wrist, shoving him toward the opening.

"Go!" Nathaniel stumbled, wide-eyed, and vanished.

The moment his body vanished, the rift began to collapse.

Solomon screamed—

And Rebecca let go.

She did not cross.

She turned—

And faced him.

The temple was falling.

The fire had consumed the altar.

Solomon stood before her, the valley clinging to him, pulsing in the dark of his eyes.

Rebecca exhaled, the scent of burning stone in her lungs.

She had made her choice.

Standing behind Solomon was Hiram. His eyes fixed on Rebecca.

And the valley had made its own.

She would not leave.

Not yet. And not without Hiram.

She lifted the dagger—

And took a step forward.

The buildings all collapse around them.

29

CHAPTER 29 – THE PASSAGE THROUGH

The gate opens only in the ruin of what was.

The final sigil burned bright upon the ground, carved with the blood of The Chosen. Virginia and Hannah clung to Nathaniel, their faces lit with the glow as they stepped through the opening passage.

Around them, the temple convulsed.

The walls cracked, not all at once, but piece by piece, as if something within it was resisting its own undoing. Shards of black and white stone tumbled to the ground, splitting the sacred symbols Solomon had so carefully etched into them—breaking not just the temple, but the very foundation of his rule.

The firelight danced in erratic flashes, illuminating the destruction as pillars gave way, ancient carvings reduced to dust. The Creation House, the unholy place where the doctrine of Empyrean had been consummated, began to collapse inward.

Hiram, bloodied and breathless, turned toward Rebecca. "We have to go—now!"

She turned toward the passage. The threshold shimmered—a doorway where no doorway should exist, carved from nothing, alive with silver and light. The first to step through would test it. The first to step through would prove whether or not the ritual had worked.

She took a step forward.

Then—Solomon's voice.

"No."

Solomon Whitmore, broken but not yet gone. His once-immaculate robes were torn, dirt and blood staining the sacred fabric. His crown had fallen, his hair matted against his forehead, but his eyes... his eyes burned with something terrible.

He reached for Rebecca, his movements slow yet deliberate, a predator with nothing left to lose. "You cannot leave!"

Solomon lunged.

But Hiram was faster.

Hiram drove his fist into the prophet's ribs, sending him sprawling. Solomon hit the ground hard, coughing up sticky blood, but still he rose.

"You think you can take my mother, the whore!?" Solomon's voice cracked with something less than human. "I built this. I bled for this. I have spoken to the valley, and it has heard me."

He staggered forward. The buildings of the valley continued to shudder, the sigils that once pulsed with divine energy cracking, dying.

Rebecca gritted her teeth. "No, Solomon. It was never yours."

Rebecca turned to the passageway—it was still open, flickering, unstable. Hiram stood at its threshold, his breath heavy, waiting for her.

She should leave.

She had to leave.

Then—the voice.

"You must confront your son."

It was soft. Commanding. Temperance.

Rebecca froze. Her body tensed as though unseen hands pressed against her back. The valley was holding its breath.

She turned back.

Solomon was struggling to rise, his body hunched, golden robes streaked with blood and dust. He looked smaller now. Not the Prophet. Not the ruler of Empyrean. Just a man—just a boy, once hers, once whole.

Her breath caught.

The manuscript.

It was still clutched in his hands—tattered, pages smeared with blood. And across the cover, where once the symbols of Elias's doctrine had been, new words had appeared.

"The Lost Books of Solomon."

Rebecca's stomach twisted.

She reached for it. The moment her fingers touched the worn leather, the ink darkened, shifting, twisting as though the valley itself was still writing.

Her pulse pounded in her ears.

The passage behind her crackled, unstable. The way out was closing.

She turned toward Hiram. "Go."

Hiram hesitated, eyes flicking between her and Solomon, who had lifted his head now, his murky blue eyes gleaming.

The temple groaned, the walls crumbling. The valley was collapsing, but Empyrean had not yet let them go.

"Go!" Rebecca screamed.

Hiram clenched his jaw. His hesitation lasted a second too long—but then he ran.

He vanished into the passage.

Rebecca turned back.

She was alone with Solomon now.

He exhaled, a wet, rattling breath. Blood smeared his mouth, his fingers twitching against the stone.

"You can't leave," he whispered.

Rebecca tightened her grip on the manuscript. The Lost Books of Solomon. The valley had rewritten them, reshaped them, just as it had reshaped him.

She inhaled sharply.

Temperance was right. She could not leave.

She stepped toward him.

30

CHAPTER 30 – BLOOD MAGIC
Every kingdom built in blood will be unmade by it.

Rebecca knelt beside Solomon. His body was broken, bloodied, barely breathing. His golden robes, once pristine, were torn and soaked with dirt. His lips trembled, his breath uneven.

She hesitated.

This is my son.

This is the child I bore.

She cradled his face, her thumbs brushing against his bruised cheekbones. He was beautiful once. Pure. Innocent. Now he was nothing but ruin.

She whispered soft prayers, her voice a breath against his skin.

"You were never meant to suffer."

"You were never meant to become this."

Her tears fell—and they were not clear.

They were red.

Each drop landed upon him, streaking his skin with crimson. And the moment her blood touched him—the valley shuddered.

Empyrean reacted.

Solomon's wounds began to mend. The bruises faded. The cuts sealed. His broken ribs set themselves. His fingers twitched, his breath evened.

Rebecca gasped.

This was her gift, her priesthood.

Blood as life. Blood as healing.

For one fragile moment, she believed she had saved him.

Solomon's breath steadied. His hands flexed, fingers tightening. His body stilled.

Then—he smiled.

Rebecca's stomach twisted.

"I knew you would see," he murmured.

Solomon rose, fully healed, power thrumming beneath his skin. The air shifted—Empyrean obeyed him again. His tattered golden robes faded into shadows. The bloodstains vanished. The hems of his garments sharpened—no longer loose, no longer holy. His temple robes transformed into a black waistcoat, crisp and perfectly fitted.

Draped across his waistcoat, gleaming brightly, was a thick Double Albert gold chain. One side anchored a heavy pocket watch, its gold case polished to perfection—exactly like the one his father wore.

The other chain did not hold a watch. Instead, a smaller, delicate but intricate orrery hung at his side—resized to fit within the palm of his hand.

A stark white dress shirt pressed against his newly healed skin, pristine as untouched paper.

His hands emerged from the cascading fabric, revealing gold cufflinks that gleamed like relics of a forgotten god.

His shoes—polished, gleaming obsidian—tapped softly against the checkered tile.

A long, black frock coat materialized over his shoulders, its tails sweeping the broken ground.

Last of all—a top hat. It formed slowly, solidifying on his head as though the valley itself had crowned him.

Rebecca stared, unblinking.

The ground beneath them trembled, sending fine cracks spidering across the checkered tile floor. A low, resonant hum shuddered through the temple walls, the very air thickening like it was turning to liquid. Rebecca steadied her stance, her heart hammering in her chest.

The valley was responding to Solomon's power, amplifying it, feeding him.

Solomon lifted his gaze to her, eyes gleaming with eerie dirty blue within-white light. A smirk at the edge of his lips, even as blood still streaked his face. He was not afraid. He was waiting.

"You thought you could undo me with your pity?" he murmured. His voice was a slow, deliberate thing, curling into the air like smoke. He lifted his hand, fingers barely twitching. "I built this. I am Empyrean."

A deep, grinding sound filled the temple.

The ground split open as massive boulders wrenched themselves free from the earth.

They hovered, shuddering midair like beasts waiting to be unleashed.

Then they came hurtling toward her.

Rebecca threw up her arms, summoning a living shield—a barrier of crimson energy. The first boulder slammed against it, shattering into dust. Another followed—larger, faster. She staggered as it struck the shield, the force sending cracks through her defenses.

She exhaled sharply, gripping her hands into fists. The shield expanded—pushing outward with a pulse of raw blood magic.

The remaining boulders were flung aside, smashing into the crumbling temple walls.

Solomon's expression didn't change. If anything, his smirk deepened. He was testing her. Measuring her limits.

"You fight with flowers and blood," he said smoothly. "I fight with the bones of Empyrean itself."

He raised both hands.

The temple shook violently. Black monoliths tore from the ground, rising in a circle around Rebecca. The air darkened, pressing in.

He was caging her in.

Rebecca took a sharp breath and flung her hands outward.

A surge of power erupted from her skin—red roses burst from the cracks in the stone, their vines stretching upward like grasping fingers.

The thorns struck fast, impaling the black monoliths before they could close around her.

For the first time, Solomon faltered.

He gestured sharply—and the thorns turned to white ash.

A cold chill crawled down Rebecca's spine. He wasn't just breaking her magic—he was unmaking it.

Solomon's voice was softer this time. More intimate. More insidious.

"I will reshape you, too."

Rebecca's breath came faster. He wasn't just trying to defeat her.

He was trying to make her his.

Her grip tightened. She forced herself to stand taller, to meet his gaze without fear.

"You cannot own me," she said, voice steady. "I am not something you built."

Solomon tilted his head, considering. Then his eyes darkened.

"Then I will break you instead."

The stone beneath her feet exploded upward, knocking her off balance.

Rebecca gasped as she hit the ground, rolling onto her knees. She barely had time to react before Solomon was on her.

His hand clamped around her wrist—searing hot, filled with raw power.

* * *

Hiram struck the stone with the flat of his palm, the sharp crack of flesh against unyielding rock ringing through the silent valley. His breath came hard and fast, his chest rising and falling with frantic desperation. Rebecca should have come through by now.

He pounded again. Harder.

"Rebecca!" His voice was raw, breaking under the weight of her absence. "Rebecca, damn it! Come through!"

But the monolith did not stir. It did not so much as tremble beneath his fists.

Behind him, Virginia stood frozen, her arms wrapped around herself, lips pressed tight as she muttered a quiet, fevered prayer. Each whispered word was swallowed by the vastness of the valley, but the urgency in her voice only deepened the horror of the moment.

Hannah stood beside her, her fingers curled into the fabric of Virginia's sleeve, wide eyes darting between the monolith and Hiram.

Nathaniel was silent. Too silent.

Hiram turned, his vision blurred with frustration. "What the hell are you standing there for?" he snapped. "We have to—"

"I see something," Nathaniel interrupted, his voice quiet but firm.

Hiram paused, his own breath still ragged in his throat.

Nathaniel stood apart from the others, his gaze locked on the horizon. The glow of the temple's destruction still flickered in the distance, but past that—

A different fire burned.

Not the furious, consuming flames of Empyrean's collapse.

A controlled fire. A settlement's fire. A beacon.

Nathaniel lifted a trembling hand, pointing beyond the ruins of Empyrean. His voice barely above a whisper, he said, "There's something out there."

Hiram turned, following the boy's gaze. He narrowed his eyes, watching the way the firelight flickered against the trees in a way that wasn't natural to a wildfire.

Virginia sucked in a sharp breath. "A town?"

Hannah shook her head. "No one lives this far out."

Nathaniel squared his shoulders. "Yes, they do."

Hiram's stomach twisted.

It was impossible.

And yet, there it was.

Hannah's voice trembled. "What if it's—"

"Gideon!" Nathaniel finished, the certainty in his voice chilling.

A heavy silence settled between them.

Hiram clenched his jaw. His first instinct was to stay. To keep pounding, keep screaming, keep waiting for Rebecca to come through. But what if she couldn't? What if she was already gone?

His fingers moved into fists, his teeth gritted hard enough to hurt.

Virginia stepped closer to him, her voice quiet but insistent. "We have to go. If there's a chance for help…"

Hiram hesitated. His muscles tensed, every nerve in his body telling him no, wait, stay.

Then Nathaniel turned to him. His blue eyes—eyes still raw from everything they had been through—met Hiram's.

"If my brothers are there," Nathaniel said, "we have to go."

That was it.

Hiram exhaled sharply, his hands shaking as he stepped away from the monolith. He didn't look at it again.

Didn't let himself.

He squared his shoulders. "Let's move."

Virginia and Hannah exchanged glances, then followed. Nathaniel was already moving ahead, leading them toward the distant glow.

The last remnants of Empyrean smoldered behind them, fading into the night. And before them, Hindostan awaited.

* * *

The temple groaned around them, its walls bleeding white, its columns fractured and swaying. The air itself crackled—thick, charged, as if the valley was gasping for breath. The battle had not yet ended. The valley had not yet chosen a victor.

Rebecca stood amidst the wreckage, her body bruised, her breath shallow, her heart pounding like a war drum. Solomon had taken her blood, had used it to mend himself, and in return, he had tried to reshape her into something lesser.

But she was not lesser.

She was his mother.

Solomon towered over her, eyes glinting with divine arrogance, his form haloed in flickering black light. Now clothed in black and white – he was pristine, absolute, colder, sharper and more civilized. Empyrean stitched him together, bound to his will. The valley was still his to wield, still his to command.

And yet—he hesitated.

For the first time since this battle began, Solomon did not lunge. He observed. Studied her.

Because she had done something impossible.

She had hurt him.

Rebecca wiped the blood from her lips, her fingers trembling—but not with weakness. With something else. Something vast and unstoppable, aching in the marrow of her bones.

Her pulse slowed.

A beat.

A whisper.

"No."

Blood surged.

Her veins burned.

Her body convulsed.

She did not fight it. She let it take her.

Her hands flexed—and then, without warning—

The blood in her arms surged forward, spears of molten crimson ripping through her skin.

They struck fast—not from her hands, but from her very flesh, extending from her forearms like jagged, glistening blades, ripping her skin apart as they extend. Blood-spears, sharpened by raw power, forged from her very being.

She thrust them forward.

The first struck Solomon's shoulder—tearing fabric, puncturing flesh.

The second tore across his ribs—deep, cutting, burning.

Solomon staggered. His breath hitched.

For the first time, he looked truly injured.

For the first time, he was truly afraid.

Rebecca advanced.

The blood-spears extended further, crimson ribbons unraveling from her arms, the scent of copper thick in the air. Her body trembled, her breath ragged, but she did not falter.

Solomon's face twisted—not in pain, but in rage.

His chest rose and fell rapidly, his hands curling into fists. The deep wound across his ribs pulsed—black light flickered in the cut, as if the valley itself was trying to stitch him back together.

But it wasn't working fast enough.

Rebecca had broken something.

She had severed something.

She saw it in his eyes—the first flicker of doubt.

Solomon snarled, his fingers twitching. His wounds smoked, but he did not heal.

"You will submit."

He raised both hands.

The valley screamed.

The floor beneath her split apart. The broken altar behind her surged upward, stone twisting into jagged spires. The temple ceiling cracked, and the sky above Empyrean shifted, no longer black, no longer white—but something unnatural.

And then—

He struck.

Invisible force slammed into her, sending her flying.

She crashed against the altar.

Her skull struck stone, stars bursting behind her eyes.

The world tilted, twisted, darkened.

Rebecca gasped, her limbs weak, the breath ripped from her lungs. The blood-spears flickered—her power wavered.

Solomon loomed over her now.

His wounds, though deep, had not yet brought him to ruin.

He raised a hand over her.

The temple shuddered.

* * *

The journey from the ruined valley to Hindostan had been silent. Too silent.

The only sound was the crunch of their footsteps against brittle earth, the rustle of wind rustling through the dying trees. The firelight in the distance had become their anchor, a beacon in the darkness, but none of them spoke of what they might find.

Hiram led the way, his jaw set, his thoughts imperceptible. Virginia and Hannah trailed just behind, clinging to each other, their exhaustion palpable. But it was Nathaniel who seemed the most restless.

He kept glancing toward the distant glow, nearly naked with only a ritualistic golden ribbon wrapped around him. Something about the flickering lights called to him.

When they reached the outskirts of Hindostan, the first thing Hiram noticed was the strange blue hue reflecting off the torchlight.

Figures moved beyond the fire—human, yet other.

Nathaniel stopped dead in his tracks.

Hiram turned, his breath shallow. "What is it?"

Nathaniel didn't answer.

His fingers tightened around the loose ribbons of gold still tangled around his wrists. He took a step forward, then another.

And then—

Ezra emerged from the firelight.

The sight of him hit like a punch to the ribs.

His skin, once pale, now gleamed with an unnatural silver-blue sheen. His hair was longer than Nathaniel remembered, his features sharper, aged by something beyond time. His veins pulsed beneath his skin—faintly metallic, laced with the remnants of the silver ritual.

Nathaniel stared.

His mouth opened—but no sound came.

Ezra's gaze locked onto him, his own breath stalling in his chest.

"Nathaniel?"

The sound of his name broke something loose.

Nathaniel surged forward, feet slamming against the earth, his voice cracking as he ran.

"Ezra!"

The moment their bodies collided, everything fell away.

Ezra caught him, gripping him tight, his arms crushing, desperate. Nathaniel shook, gasping, his fingers clawing at his brother's back, gripping, anchoring himself in the reality that this was real.

Ezra's hands found the golden ribbons still wrapped around his brother's wrists.

"What did they do to you?" he breathed.

Nathaniel shook his head, unable to answer. His entire body trembled as he clung to Ezra, his older brother's warmth grounding him in a way he hadn't felt since before Empyrean.

Virginia and Hannah stood frozen, overwhelmed.

A sob tore from Hannah's throat.

The sound was enough.

Lucy stepped forward from the shadows, her skin the same eerie silver-blue, but her eyes unmistakably warm.

"My girls—"

Hannah and Virginia collapsed into her arms.

Tears, choking, trembling hands gripping at fabric.

Lucy held them, rocking slightly, pressing kisses to their hair. Her breath hitched as she pulled them closer, her voice breaking over them.

"You came back to me."

Eliza and Eleanor joined them, their hands pressing against their sisters' shoulders, their own tears slipping free. It was too much. Too long. Too impossible.

Hiram stood back, watching, absorbing the weight of it all.

This was what Empyrean tried to take.

This was what Solomon had tried to erase.

And yet—they had survived.

Then—another voice.

Deeper. Rougher. Older.

"Nathaniel."

The sound stopped him cold.

Nathaniel turned slowly.

At the edge of the firelight, Gideon stood.

The moment their eyes met, something in Nathaniel cracked.

Gideon.

The older brother he had once idolized. The brother who had fought with Elias, who had abandoned them, who had left.

The brother who had been right all along.

Nathaniel moved—but slower this time.

He took a single step forward. Then another.

Gideon didn't move.

His blue-stained hands hung at his sides, his shoulders rising and falling in slow, controlled breaths. But his face—

His face was unreadable.

Nathaniel swallowed. His hands curled into fists at his sides.

And then, without warning—

He lunged.

Gideon barely had time to react before Nathaniel slammed into him, arms wrapping around his torso, gripping him with desperate, violent force.

For a moment, Gideon didn't move.

Then—his arms came up.

He gripped Nathaniel's back, pulling him close, his jaw clenching as his body shook against his own will.

Nathaniel's fingers dug into Gideon's coat.

"I thought you were gone," Nathaniel choked, his voice broken, raw, almost childlike.

Gideon's breath caught.

Slowly, his hand lifted to the back of Nathaniel's head, cradling it the way he had when they were boys.

"I thought I'd never see you again."

The words cracked.

Nathaniel's body shuddered.

For the first time since Empyrean, he let himself feel safe.

For the first time in years, Gideon let himself feel anything at all.

Then—it happened.

Gideon's hand moved, noticing the golden ribbons wrapped around Nathaniel's arms.

He froze.

His stomach turned to ice.

The ribbons weren't just symbols of Solomon's rule.

They were proof.

Gideon stiffened. His body locked.

And then—he pulled back.

Nathaniel didn't let go. Didn't want to.

But Gideon's hands came to his shoulders, pushing him just far enough away so he could see his face.

His eyes scanned him.

The ribbons.

The bruises.

The vacant look in his baby brother's eyes.

Gideon's fingers trembled.

"What did he do to you?"

His voice broke.

Nathaniel froze.

The fire crackled, sending twisting shadows across Gideon's face. Memories surfaced—flashes of something buried deep. He had seen things before. Signs. Years ago.

Solomon had always been the favorite. The gifted one. The chosen. But Gideon had seen it—the way Solomon looked at Nathaniel when they were younger. The way Nathaniel had acted around him. The way their brotherhood had never quite been right.

And he had tried—God, he had tried—to protect Nathaniel.

Had Solomon done it again?

Had he finished what Gideon had once stopped?

His jaw was tight, his throat bobbing. His hands—once strong, once unshakable—were shaking.

Nathaniel didn't answer.

He didn't need to.

Gideon already knew.

His fingers dug into Nathaniel's arms, as if holding him together, as if keeping himself from falling apart.

Ezra watched in silence. Virginia and Hannah clung to their mother, unable to speak.

Gideon clenched his jaw.

"She's still in there," Nathaniel whispered.

Gideon inhaled sharply.

"What?"

"Mother. She stayed."

The warmth of reunion shattered.

The moment of stillness collapsed into urgency.

Lucy's fingers tightened in her daughters' hair.

Ezra's breath came sharp, fast.

"Why?" Gideon's voice was deeper now, edged with something darker. *"Why would she stay?"*

Nathaniel swallowed, his throat burning.

"She had to fight him."

Ezra's expression darkened.

He turned sharply, reaching into his coat, withdrawing a leather-bound book.

"Then we bring her back."

Nathaniel blinked at him. "How?"

Ezra held up the Shelmire Journal.

"We can reach her."

The words settled over them.

Hope. Determination. Fear.

The fires of Hindostan burned bright.

And in the distance—the valley still watched.

* * *

It did not hesitate now.

His voice changed.

Layered. Deeper. Resounding.

It was not just him speaking—it was the valley itself.

"Empyrean does not break. It does not fall."

Long gone were the beautiful bright blue eyes of her son. But now the corrupted blue eyes had begun to change into something else entirely.

His hand lifted.

The valley obeyed.

Black iron chains surged from the white stone, twisting toward her. The sigils of Empyrean reformed, pulsing along the temple walls. The monoliths shook as the valley reshaped itself.

"Kneel."

The chains cut deep into Rebecca's flesh, cold bands of black constricting her limbs. Bright white Symbols—Solomon's symbols—glowed across the temple floor, pulsing like the rhythm of a heartbeat. Her breath was steady, but her vision swam, blurred by the steady flow of blood that continued to drip from her eyes, streaking down her cheeks.

The temple restored itself.

The golden shrine. The Creation House. The altar of sacrifice.

It was all coming back.

She had not saved him.

She had made him stronger.

Solomon stepped toward her, triumphant. "You see now. You cannot fight it."

He reached for her.

Rebecca inhaled. Blood pouring from her eyes.

She lifted her gaze.

Solomon stood above her, golden ribbons of light and blood swirled around him, gleaming - breathing. The temple walls trembled, groaning under the weight of the valley's unrest, but he did not falter. He smiled.

"You will kneel before me," he said, voice thick with power. "You will be my Matriarch."

Rebecca did not speak.

The valley pulsed beneath her, the air shifting with unseen forces. She could feel it—something waking inside her, something ancient, something waiting.

Her breath slowed.

Her pulse pounded in her ears.

The priesthood was calling.

Solomon lifted a hand, ready to bind her fully—ready to seal her to him.

She knew what that meant. She had seen it before. She felt the weight of Solomon's prophetic powers. She kept her eyes closed.

She could see Elias, his life, his visions and his death. She envisioned Hiram, wreathed in indigo smoke, his skin glowing under unseen candlelight, the promise of something she had never been allowed to want. She could see the pain of childbearing. She could feel it again—the tearing, the gasping, the raw, unbearable weight of bringing something into the world. First Gideon, her oldest boy, crying bloody from birthing. She held him to her, bonding in ways words cannot describe, sacred. Then a burst of vision toward another baby being born. This time is was her second son, Ezra. He cried less than Gideon and seemed more content. And again, she held him to her, seeing his eyes, bonding. Then the envisioning scene moved to the time of Solomon's birth. A bright blue light filled the vision, she could hear his cry. She could see him. She held him, loved him, bonded with him. Her heart breaking as she realized her beautiful baby boy had become a monster. Then, last of all, she saw in her vision, Nathaniel. He was born under the same haze of bright blue light. His cry a whimper. Rebecca cuddled him. Held him close then gazed deeply into his eyes. A bond formed that only mothers understand. Her body trembled. Her lips parted. And the blood came.

Solomon leaned forward to begin a deadly ritual. But before the words could leave his lips, Rebecca exhaled.

And opened her eyes.

The world cracked open.

A burst of blood and iron exploded outward, a violent rupture of power. The chains holding her shattered like glass, shards of sigils and molten symbols scattering into the air. The force of it blasted Solomon backward—his body lifted from the ground, flung through the air like a discarded relic.

He slammed into the temple floor, gasping, stunned, his top hat smoldering from the impact. For the first time, he was not standing.

For the first time, he was lower than her.

Rebecca approached him.

Blood dripped down her chin, soaking her torn garments, pooling at her feet. Her hands trembled—not with weakness, but with something vast and uncontainable. Something bigger than her. Something divine.

Solomon coughed, struggling to rise, his fingers clawing at the stone floor. He looked up at her—

And for the first time, he was afraid.

"Mother—" he gasped, voice raw. "What are you?"

Rebecca stepped forward, her breath steady.

She placed her bloodied palm against his chest.

"I am your mother."

His body tensed beneath her touch.

She convulsed.

Her lips parted—her mouth stretched wide. A violent, guttural heave wracked her body as her priesthood surged forward, demanding release.

A stream of burning blood poured from her mouth.

It struck Solomon in the face, and forced itself inside his mouth, flowing like molten lava, seeping into his skin, into his veins.

The fire did not burn him from the outside.

It burned from within.

Solomon's screams curdled.

His spine arched violently, his fingers clawing at his own body as the prophecy—his prophecy—was ripped from him. The marks on his flesh, the symbols that had bound him to Empyrean, blackened and curled like parchment in flame.

His veins glowed, a sickly golden hue turning red, then black.

"No—" he gasped, voice cracking. "No, I am Empyrean—I AM—"

Rebecca exhaled one final time. Her body lurched forward, her face inches from his.

She whispered the final word of power, the last command of the Red Priesthood.

"Καθαρίστε το ψέμα."

(*Purge the lie.*)

The blood-fire inside him consumed him whole, at least the mad prophet within.

The temple walls trembled. The ground beneath them quaked. The air turned heavy, thick with the scent of smoke and something older, something raw and sacred.

Solomon gasped, his blackened fingers twitching against the stone. His blue eyes—once bright, once full of promise—flickered.

Dimmed.

Darkened.

His lips parted one last time, barely a whisper.

"Father... help me."

Then silence.

The temple groaned.

The altar cracked, splitting down the center, jagged like an open wound. The monoliths began to disintegrate, their sacred inscriptions fading as if they had never been carved. The golden shrine of Empyrean, the Creation House, the false city—all of it began to unravel.

The valley was rejecting its Prophet.

Empyrean was unmaking itself.

Rebecca turned away, staggering toward the threshold. Her body ached, the power still humming in her blood. She pressed a hand against her ribs—

And felt it.

A scar.

Deep, permanent, seared into her flesh just above her heart. The mark of what she had done. Of what she had become.

The price of power is written in blood.

She reached the passage. The air shimmered around her, the gateway flickering, the monolith shut tight and black. She turned back one last time.

The world behind her was no longer a temple, no longer a kingdom.

It was just a valley.

The grass stretched untouched, the river winding through the land as it had long before they arrived. The deep forest loomed in the distance, its shadows indifferent.

Empyrean was no more.

But something remained.

A flicker of blue.

A small bird, impossibly bright, perched upon the last standing stone.

It did not move.

It did not fly.

It only watched.

Rebecca exhaled. She did not know if she would ever return. Was she to remain in empyrean forever, and become a Sophia of the Forest?

But the bird remained.

She felt a peace about her. Not knowing if she was every going to escape Empyrean. She gazed upon the blue bird as he watched her.

"and what of my Solomon?" she whispered to the bird.

And at that very moment, the bird perched himself comfortably on Rebecca's shoulder.

Tears formed and dripped down her cheeks

31

C HAPTER 31 – BLACK CROW, WHITE DAEMON
There is no resurrection without blood. No passage without loss.

Ezra quickly thumbed through the Shelmire Journal.

"There it is, the Ritual of the Black Crow, and the White Daemon."

Ezra's gaze locked onto the title; a chill racked up his spine. It was the passageway. A way into the valley. A way back to Empyrean.

The inked illustrations sent a ripple of unease through his chest.

At the top of the page—two figures, stark in contrast. One shrouded in pale robes, faceless and looming. The White Daemon, a spirit of departure, of passage, of unmaking. Beside it, a black-winged figure, half-man, half-bird, its talons grasping at something unseen. The Black Crow, the gatekeeper, the force that determined who passed and who remained lost.

Ezra inhaled sharply, his pulse hammering as he read the passage aloud under his breath.

"To open the way, one must call upon the Daemon, but only under the eye of the Crow.

Blood must mark the crossing. A heart must open. And words must be spoken."

"Αφήστε τη μήτρα της να ανοίξει και να μας ελευθερώσει"

His mouth went dry.

Ezra's breath hitched. His fingers traced the inked sigils at the bottom of the page—complex spirals, symbols older than scripture, shapes that burned into his mind.

He could feel it.

The weight of the truth.

His grip on the journal tightened.

"We can open it," he whispered. "We can bring her back."

Behind him, the fire flickered violently.

The wind outside shifted.

Gideon yanked him by the arm, half-dragging him toward the door. It was happening.

They were going back to Empyrean.

The others were already in motion—Virginia, Hannah, Eleanor, and Nathaniel moving fast, their breath clouding in the cold air. Lucy Mercer, however, was doing something entirely different.

"Hold on now, hold on!" she huffed, arms full of supplies. She had shoved a quilt under one arm, a basin in the other, and a bottle of whiskey dangling from her fingers.

Nathaniel, Virginia, and Hannah stared at her.

"Lucy," Nathaniel said slowly, watching as she tossed a rope over her shoulder, "What—exactly—are you expecting to happen?"

Lucy, utterly unbothered by the confusion, adjusted the pile of absurd supplies in her arms and shot him a glare. "Boy, I do not know. But if somethin' is fallin' out of that portal, I intend to catch it."

Virginia blinked. "You think Rebecca's just... gonna come tumbling out?"

"Or a demon," Lucy said seriously. "Could be a demon. Either way, I'll be prepared."

Hannah pressed a hand to her mouth, stifling a laugh.

Ezra, already frantic, swore under his breath, slinging the Shelmore Journal under his arm. "We don't have time for this!"

"But we have time for this—" Lucy held up a wad of soft linens.

"What is that for?" Gideon groaned, exasperated.

Lucy huffed. "What if she needs wrappin' up? What if she's naked? You ever come through a divine portal, Gideon? Do you know how it works?"

"Yes," Virginia muttered, "you just... arrive."

Lucy pursed her lips. "Uh-huh. And if she arrives wriggling and screaming, I'll have a warm blanket and a catchin' basin. And a gun!"

Nathaniel exchanged one look with Virginia and Hannah.

Virginia tilted her head, considering. "Alright, let her be."

Eleanor was already running ahead, calling over her shoulder, "If y'all are done with the baby-catching supplies, we need to get moving!"

Ezra groaned, pinching the bridge of his nose. "Yes, please!"

Lucy stuffed the whiskey bottle into Nathaniel's coat pocket, just in case, and took off after the others.

* * *

Hindostan to the Monolith.

They ran through the fields, the night stretching wide and endless around them. The moon cast silver light over the hills, the wind howling through the trees as they rushed toward the stone monolith at the entrance of Empyrean.

Gideon led the way, his stride long and fast, Ezra gripping the Shelmore Journal like a lifeline.

Eliza and Eleanor ran close together, faces flushed, their breath coming in fast bursts.

Behind them, Lucy clutched her absurd collection of supplies, dodging roots and low-hanging branches.

Nathaniel, Virginia, and Hannah stayed close together, hearts hammering, knowing what was coming.

They could feel it.

The valley was waiting for them.

And when the monolith came into view, standing tall and ancient against the night sky, Ezra knew—

This was it.

The final moment before everything changed.

The air thickened the moment they stepped into the clearing.

The monolith loomed before them, carved with symbols older than time, its edges glowing faintly under the moon's cold light.

Ezra flipped open the Shelmore Journal, breathless. "This is it. This is where we do it."

Virginia stepped forward, her gaze locked onto the monolith, remembering. The sword points to the naked heart.

Hannah pressed a hand to her chest, fingers brushing the place where she had drawn her own blood before.

Ezra looked down at the final inscription, his heart hammering.

It was time.

Ezra stood before the looming monolith, his silver-threaded hands trembling over the Shelmore Journal. The final page lay open before him, the inked diagrams swirling with meaning he could almost grasp.

Almost.

But something was missing.

He had the instructions. He had the silver. But the ritual resisted him, like a door that would not open no matter how hard he pushed.

Virginia and Hannah stood on the either side of Ezra. Watching. Waiting.

Ezra exhaled sharply. "This should be working."

"It's not," Virginia murmured.

He shot her a look, frustration burning behind his silvered gaze. "I know it's not."

Hannah pressed her fingers to the old wooden altar, feeling the etchings beneath her touch. "Because you're missing the last key."

Ezra scowled. "What are you talking about?"

Virginia's eyes flickered to Hannah's. A silent agreement passed between them.

McBride had told them.

Ezra had given them the method. But only they knew the final step.

Virginia reached for the silver dagger, the same one she had carried through Empyrean, the blade still stained with the first blood she had given to escape.

Ezra's expression tightened. "What are you doing?"

Hannah spoke softly. *"The sword points to the naked heart."*

Ezra's blood ran cold.

"What?"

Virginia met his gaze, steady and unflinching. "The ritual isn't just about silver, Ezra." She lifted the dagger, pressing the cool metal against her chest—just above her heart. "It's about us. Our blood. The valley will not open for symbols and language alone. It needs what was taken."

Ezra stepped forward, alarm flashing across his face. "That's insane."

Hannah tilted her head. "Then why did it work when we did it before?"

Ezra's breath came short. He hadn't known. He had believed his instructions, the silver, the inscriptions—he had thought he was leading this ritual.

But Virginia and Hannah had already been through this.

They had been the ones to escape Empyrean.

And now, they were completing what he started.

Ezra exhaled, his frustration softening into realization. "You knew."

Virginia nodded once. "We always knew."

She took a steady breath, then pressed the dagger's tip into her skin, just above her heart.

The silver blade sliced clean, a thin line of crimson beading against the steel.

The air shuddered around them.

Ezra felt it immediately. The ground responding, the ritual acknowledging them for the first time.

Hannah followed next, mirroring Virginia, her hands steady as she offered her own blood to the monolithic stone.

A tremor ran through the wooden floorboards. The valley was watching.

With a final exhale, Ezra pressed the dagger against his own chest, piercing just enough to draw blood, letting it mix with Virginia and Hannah's on the stone.

The moment the third offering fell upon the silver markings, the wind shifted.

Hannah lifted her voice, clear and strong, speaking the words McBride had taught them—the words that Ezra had never known.

"Αφήστε τη μήτρα της να ανοίξει και να μας ελευθερώσει."

Virginia and Ezra echoed the final words together.

The air ripped apart—

The passage tore open before them—

And for the first time, the way back to Empyrean was fully revealed.

And neither would the scars of Empyrean.

* * *

The blue bird, perched on her shoulder, eyes dark and knowing, watched her. For a moment, she swore she felt something familiar in its gaze. Something too human.

Solomon?

The thought sent a chill down her spine. The part of him that had been good, the part of him that had been her son—was it still here? Had it escaped the destruction? Had he?

Or had she simply imagined it?

Rebecca exhaled slowly.

The valley keeps what it is given.

Her fingers twitched at her sides.

Should she reach for it? Should she take it with her?

The portal flared behind her, the shimmering veil of silver and purple vibrating in the air, unstable, waiting. She didn't have much time.

The bird it spread its wings.

It did not flee into the forest.

It flew into the mystic blue light.

Rebecca's breath left her in a sharp exhale.

For a single, breathless moment, she hesitated.

Then she ran through the opening portal.

The moment she crossed the threshold, the world welcomed her.

The air changed. The scent of pine and earth rushed into her lungs, thick and fresh. The weight of Empyrean vanished, and with it, the unnatural stillness that had pressed against her ribs. The night was real again. The stars stretched vast and endless above her, the ground beneath her feet firm and whole.

She was home.

A stunned silence as she gazed upon the group of friends of family gathered to rescue her.

The air shimmered in the center of the gathering, warping the space between them like the surface of a lake disturbed by an unseen ripple. The portal was not gold—not anymore.

Ezra stepped back, his silver-streaked fingers trembling from the exertion of the ritual. The deep green glow that had threaded through his veins during the incantation still pulsed faintly beneath his skin. Hannah and Virginia stood beside him, their lilac-colored auras weaving into the energy, their presence tangible, real. The edges of the portal swirled—silvery violet moonlight on water, deep green like untouched forests, lilac mist curling through like something fragile yet unbreakable.

It was nothing like Elias's golden gateway. This was something else. Something born of survival, not prophecy.

Nathaniel reached her first.

"Mother!" His voice cracked as he crashed into her, arms wrapping around her waist, gripping her as if she might disappear again. She gasped at the force of him, the way he clung to her, his breath hot and ragged against her shoulder.

He was trembling.

She gripped him just as tightly, pressing her cheek against his hair, feeling the reality of him—his warmth, his pulse, his life.

"Oh, my boy," she whispered, kissing the top of his head. "My sweet boy."

Then Gideon was there.

He didn't throw himself at her like Nathaniel had. He just stood there, staring. His eyes scanned her face, her torn dress, the blood staining her cheeks, her lips, her hands.

She turned toward him, a breath catching in her throat.

"Gideon."

His jaw clenched. His blue-stained hands curled into fists at his sides. He swallowed hard—then, with a sudden exhale, he closed the distance between them.

His arms wrapped around her shoulders, strong, solid. For a moment, he simply held her.

No words. Just breath. Just presence.

Her fingers threaded into the back of his coat, gripping him the way she had gripped him when he was a child. When she had carried him through storms, through sickness, through loss. When he had been hers to protect.

And now—he was protecting her.

"You're safe," he murmured, and it was unclear if he was telling her or telling himself.

She nodded against him. "I'm here."

Ezra hesitated.

His grip on the Shelmire journal was tight. He swallowed, glancing down at his hands, as if suddenly aware that his fingertips were no longer his own. The silver sheen had deepened, threading faintly beneath the skin. Rebecca saw it immediately.

She turned—and looking at all the others who were left behind – who never entered Empyrean.

Lucy. Eleanor. Ezra. Eliza. Gideon.

Her breath caught.

"Elias's curse," she whispered in terror and sadness. *"He really did mark them for their rebellion."*

The silver had claimed them—not fully, not yet, but enough. Enough for her to recognize the curse she had once feared.

Ezra shifted uncomfortably under her stare. He knew she had noticed.

"Remember Mother, he cursed us. Daddy cursed us. He made us sick. We was dyin'" he muttered, then looking at Lucy, "But Ms. Lucy saved us with Silver. We keep drinking it. It keeps us alive. But it doesn't stop."

Lucy, standing just behind him, scoffed lightly, but Rebecca saw the sadness in her expression.

"Don't look at us like that, darlin'," Lucy said, her voice softer than usual. "We made our choice."

Lucy—in an attempt to lighten the mood - let out a dramatic sigh, shaking her head.

"Well, hell," she muttered. "I suppose you ain't a ghost, after all."

The tension shattered.

Rebecca laughed—a real, breathless, exhausted laugh. It was too much. Too absurd. The horror, the loss, the impossible miracle of being alive.

Lucy marched forward, pulling Rebecca into a tight, crushing hug. "I ought to slap you," she then wrapped the warm quilt around Rebecca's shoulders. "Disappearing like that. Making me cry."

Rebecca squeezed her tighter.

Hiram cleared his throat.

"Well," he drawled, stepping forward, hands shoved into his pockets. "I suppose that means I don't need to go charging in to rescue ya after all."

Rebecca turned to him, eyes soft. For a moment, they just looked at each other.

Then she smiled, tired but real. "I rescued myself."

Hiram smirked. "Shoulda figured."

Nathaniel wiped at his eyes, sniffling. "We did the ritual," he said, voice thick with emotion. "We brought you back."

Rebecca cupped his face, stroking his cheek with blood-stained fingers. "You did, my love."

Ezra held up the Shelmire journal. "Did we get all of ya'll, where's Solomon?"

Rebecca hesitated.

For a moment, she thought of the bird.

She thought of the valley, the battle.

She thought of what she had left behind.

Then she exhaled. She paused longer than she meant to.

Then, Gideon finally spoke.

"Where is he?"

The fire crackled. The wind shifted.

"Where is Solomon?" Gideon repeated. His voice was steady. Too steady.

Rebecca looked up at him.

She could still see the boy he had been, the sharp, stubborn eyes of a child who had never trusted Elias's visions, who had never believed in Solomon's divine calling.

And she saw the man he had become. One who had survived despite it all.

Slowly, she exhaled, tears welled.

She saw Solomon's color—the beautiful, bright blue that had once filled his innocent eyes.

And she saw how that color had darkened, twisted, become something inhuman.

But then—she had seen the bird.

The color untainted. The blue unbroken.

Was he still alive?

Had she saved something?

Or had she only imagined it?

Rebecca met Gideon's gaze.

She should tell them.

She should tell them what she saw, what she *thought* she saw.

But instead—she reached for Nathaniel's hair again, smoothing it down as she whispered the only truth she could give.

"He is gone."

Ezra exhaled. Virginia closed her eyes. Nathaniel let out a breath that almost sounded like relief.

Gideon did not move.

He only watched her.

Watched her too closely.

But he did not press further.

Rebecca turned toward the others.

She reached out, brushing her hand against Lucy's arm, then Ezra's, then Eleanor's. Her touch lingered for just a moment on the strange, blue-tinged skin of her children.

They had all changed.

But they had survived.

32

CHAPTER 32 – THE LITTLE BOY BLUE
They thought they were writing history. But it's us doing the burying.

Rebecca woke to the scent of burning wood and damp earth.

For the first time in what felt like forever, she was in a real house. A real room. A real bed. She had not dreamed of Empyrean.

Not of Solomon.

Not of the valley.

Only the distant hush of water—the Hindostan Falls, roaring beyond the settlement.

She exhaled slowly, pulling herself upright. Her limbs ached, the weight of the last night's journey still pressing against her ribs. She traced her fingers over the fabric of the blanket, unfamiliar, yet real. Not woven by invisible hands, not conjured from the valley's will.

Just a blanket.

Just a home.

She was home.

The house was quiet—most of the settlement still slept. But a sound caught her attention.

A soft clink.

A whisper of movement outside the door.

She swung her legs over the bed, reaching for her shawl. The moment her fingers brushed the fabric, her eyes landed on the manuscript.

Elias's Manuscript.

The Lost Books of Solomon.

It lay on the bedside table, untouched yet unbearably heavy.

She had carried it out of the valley, out of Empyrean.

And yet—her fingers tingled as she reached for it, a cold whisper slithering through her palms.

Her mind swirled intrusive thoughts of the manuscript's impact on her family. She remembered when Elias first showed it to her. It seemed ancient. A grimoire of an Egyptian mystic named Abramelin. Once titled *Geheimnisbücher Moses* or The Secret Books of Moses, she recalls watching Elias etch his own subtitle, *"The City of the Divine."* He claimed a vision from this manuscript. A vision that would lead her family into certain death and despair. And now the manuscript lay before her, changed. Changed by her son Solomon. He, somehow, retitled the entire book to *"The Lost Books of Solomon."*

It does not belong in this world, she thought.

She swallowed hard, pressing the book against her chest. It had brought nothing but ruin. Nothing but pain.

Today, she would burn it.

She rose, stepping toward the door—

And almost collided with Hiram.

Hiram stood in the kitchen doorway, his hair tousled, his expression kind.

He held something in his hands.

Rebecca blinked.

It was a crimson priestly cap.

One of Solomon's.

No. Nathaniel's.

Hiram turned it over slowly, running his fingers along the fabric, his expression caught between disgust and something quieter. Something sadder.

"I found it on the ground, near where Nathaniel slept for the night. He must have dropped it." he murmured. "Didn't think I'd be seein' one of these again."

Rebecca exhaled softly.

She reached forward, plucking a thread from the cap, a single red string.

Hiram arched a brow as she stepped closer, threading the red strand into the collar of his coat.

Her hands were steady. Warm. Deliberate.

"I don't deserve that," Hiram muttered, glancing down at her fingers. "The Hero's of America must think me dead anyhow."

Rebecca smirked, tightening the knot.

"Well, you're my hero."

Hiram let out a quiet, breathy chuckle. He reached up, brushing a loose curl of hair from her face. His fingers lingered for a fraction too long, his eyes unreadable.

For a moment, she let herself feel it.

Then—she stepped back, gripping the manuscript tighter in her hands.

"I have to take care of something," she murmured.

Hiram hesitated, but nodded. "I'll walk you there."

The fire crackled, hungry and waiting. Rebecca knelt before it, the worn leather of the manuscript heavy in her hands.

She had built the fire herself, gathering dry kindling from the river's edge, striking the flint with steady hands. The flames caught quickly, licking up the brittle wood, feeding on the remnants of dead things.

This was where it would end.

Her thumb brushed over the embossed lettering on the cover, its edges softened with age and use. This was where Elias's madness had begun. This book had whispered to him in the dark, had shaped his delusions, had given birth to the chains they had all worn.

And now, it would be nothing but ash.

She lifted the manuscript over the flames.

Her breath hitched.

The lettering flickered.

For the briefest moment, it was not the fire's reflection but something else—something beneath the surface, something alive.

The words on the cover glowed.

Not gold, but blue.

The Lost Books of Solomon.

It was blue.

A soft, pulsing blue, flickering just beneath the leather, like the last traces of fire smoldering under embers. Almost a heartbeat. The same color that had once lingered in Solomon's eyes before the valley had devoured him. Before he had become something else.

Rebecca froze.

A scent—his scent.

Not the scent of burning parchment. Not the stale must of aged ink. But something warm, something familiar. The barest trace of cedarwood and pressed linen.

For a single, fleeting second, she felt him.

Not the Prophet. Not the monster.

Her son.

A shudder passed through her chest. Her grip loosened.

Was he still alive?

The fire snapped and spat, its heat licking toward her fingers, demanding its offering.

But she pulled the book back.

No.

Not this way.

She closed her eyes, steadying her breath. She had come here to destroy the last piece of Elias's madness. To make sure no one else could wield it. But this—this was not Elias's madness anymore.

It was Solomon's.

And perhaps, deep beneath the ruin and the horror, Solomon still was.

She turned away from the fire.

The night stretched quiet around her, the sound of the river steady and unchanging. She knew what she had to do.

Carefully, she moved toward a limestone shelf near the water's edge. The rock jutted out over the river, its surface smooth from years of erosion, its base half-buried in soft earth.

She could not bury the manuscript as it was. The damp would consume it.

Her eyes flickered toward the remnants of Gideon's settlement, known once as Hindostan.

She remembered a tin document case—a simple metal box, once used for storing deeds and important papers, tucked away in an old desk in the abandoned church. She had seen it when she first arrived, barely noticing it beneath the dust and decay.

Moving quickly, Rebecca retraced her steps toward the empty buildings, her breath uneven, her pulse quickened by urgency.

Inside the church, there was Lucy Mercer, tending to the morning breakfast and silver ritual. Lucy hadn't noticed Rebecca enter, so she quietly walked over to the desk where she saw the blackened tin box.

She opened it, brushing away flakes of rust. The interior was lined with oilcloth, the fabric still intact—protection against dampness and decay.

She turned, ready to leave—

And Lucy's voice cut through the hush with that same Southern warmth that had survived all the horror of Empyrean.

"Good to see ya this mornin'..."

Rebecca froze.

"... Now where you sneakin' off to without invitin' me?"

Rebecca turned slowly, her grip tightening around the tin box.

Lucy leaned lazily against the altar, wiping her damp fingers against her tattered skirts. There was humor in her voice, but her sharp eyes held something else—something knowing.

Rebecca exhaled through her nose, shaking her head. "You always know, don't you?"

Lucy gave her a smirk, tilting her head. "Don't take a prophet to see when someone's tryin' to slip out quiet."

Rebecca hesitated.

She could have made an excuse. Could have walked away.

But instead, she held out the tin box.

Lucy's smile faltered—just slightly.

She didn't ask what was inside.

She already knew.

"Well I'm comin' with ya's." Lucy followed.

The sky was painted in the soft hues of a rising dawn, the air cool against their skin as they stood together on the limestone shelf overlooking Hindostan Falls. Below, the river rushed on—indifferent, eternal.

The two women knelt side by side, the tin box resting between them.

Lucy's hands were steady as she helped Rebecca pry the lid open. Rebecca carefully lay the manuscript inside, its leather cover worn from years of handling, from the hands of men who had believed it held salvation.

Two husbands. Two prophets. Two graves.

And now—an ending.

Rebecca touched the edge of the book, her fingers brushing over the embossed letters.

Lucy exhaled. "Ain't it funny?" she murmured, her voice low but edged with something wry. "All them men thought they were writin' history. But it's us doin' the buryin'."

Rebecca huffed a quiet laugh, though there was no joy in it. Only truth.

The contrast between them was stark, even in the golden light of morning.

Rebecca—pale, veiled in deep crimson and faded ivory, the remnants of a matriarch's dignity clinging to her like old silk.

Lucy—tawny-skinned and plump, wrapped in what was once a fine dress of dark green line in silver, now torn at the hem, stained with earth and smoke.

Two colors that had once marked them as wives of powerful men.

Now, they stood alone.

Lucy dug the hollow, her fingers pressing into the damp earth just next to the limestone shelf, while Rebecca lifted the tin box.

She did not hesitate.

She placed it inside the ground.

The wind sighed through the trees as they covered it together—pressing the dirt firm, sealing away the last remnant of the faith that had consumed their lives.

And then—Rebecca reached for a stone. A heavy, smooth piece of limestone, pried from the river's edge. She placed it carefully over the burial site.

Lucy dusted off her hands and rose first, stretching.

"Hope to God none of them fools ever come diggin'."

Rebecca stood beside her, watching as the first rays of sunlight stretched long over the water.

She swallowed. "If they do..."

Lucy turned, expectant.

Rebecca glanced once more at the hidden grave beneath the stone.

"...They won't find prophets."

The wind danced around them, lifting the edges of their tattered skirts, catching in the loosened strands of their hair.

Rebecca exhaled.

Lucy smirked.

And together, silhouetted against the rising sun, they walked back, arm in arm as the great matriarchs to their families in Hindostan, The City of Gideon.

33

E PILOGUE
  Hindostan Falls, Present Day – Martin County, Indiana

The hiker adjusted his pack, wiping sweat from his brow.

The falls roared ahead of him, mist rising in thick, ghostly ribbons over the limestone formations. The place was isolated, untouched, save for the faint remnants of an old trail.

He had read about Hindostan, about the abandoned settlement, about the legends.

But that wasn't what had brought him here.

It was the carvings.

A few weeks prior, a researcher had mentioned strange etchings found near the falls—markings they could not identify.

He was here to see them.

And now—he had.

He knelt down, his fingers brushing over the smooth, time-worn stone.

The symbols were etched deep, defying the centuries of erosion.

A pyramid.

A radiant sun.

An open hand.

Beneath it—the words.

WITZ.

MA' KAB.

MO' KAB.

JOOL.

His breath came faster. He flipped through his field notes, his hands shaking as he translated:

The valley is not land. It keeps what it is given.

He muttered the words aloud.

The wind shifted.

The trees whispered.

For a moment—he thought he heard something.

A woman's voice. Soft. Just beyond the tree line.

He turned sharply.

There was nothing there.

Only the forest, still and watching.

About the Author

About the Author

Stone Eugene Clark is a writer of psychological and historical fiction exploring exile, identity, and the haunting weight of belief. Raised in the American West, he draws from buried archives, fractured faith, and ancestral memory to craft stories that bridge myth and blood.

The Road to Hindostan is his debut novel.

For updates and contact:

Email: stoneeugeneclark@gmail.com
Instagram: @stoneeugeneclark